FILLING SPACES

FILLING SPACES

Stan Hey

Hodder & Stoughton

Copyright © 1995 by Stan Hey

First published in Great Britain in 1995
by Hodder and Stoughton
A division of Hodder Headline PLC

The right of Stan Hey to be identified as the Author of
the Work has been asserted by him in accordance with the
Copyright, Designs and Patents Act 1988.

10 9 8 7 6 5 4 3 2 1

A CIP catalogue record for this title is available
from the British Library

ISBN 0 340 61829 9

Typeset by Avon Dataset Ltd, Bidford-on-Avon, B50 4JH

Printed and bound in Great Britain by
Mackays of Chatham, Chatham, Kent

Hodder and Stoughton
A division of Hodder Headline PLC
338 Euston Road
London NW1 3BH

'Journalism – an ability to meet the challenge of filling the space . . . '

Dame Rebecca West, *New York Herald Tribune*, 22 April 1956

CHAPTER ONE

It was just after eight in the morning when Frank Brennan took his first steps back into life. He'd been up at six, allowed a shower and a shave, and then given back his civilian clothes. They hung off him like a job-lot from an Oxfam shop. But then six months of prison food and, more crucially, six months without a pint of beer, had taken some of the fat off him as neatly as a bacon slicer. With work three days a week on a spread of the neighbouring farms, Brennan's body hadn't been in better shape since . . . well, since he was born probably. No wonder some of the lags called Erlestoke Prison 'The Hospital'.

Indeed, as he and a handful of other ex-prisoners filed quietly out of the main gate, up past the neat rows of border plants and the incongruous beauty of the Georgian gate-lodge, it crossed Brennan's mind that his wife Janet and son Lester might not recognise him at first. He needn't have worried – they weren't there. The cluster of expectant relatives and girlfriends moved past Brennan, and a Kiss-o-Gram girl in black underwear and suspenders jumped into the arms of 'Dodgy' Derek Smith, the finance wizard who'd done a bunk with his clients' money. Brennan buttoned up his coat against the spring chill and set off for one of the four taxis parked on the prison's slip road.

Then a car horn sounded urgently. He turned. An L-reg Scorpio with chauffeur was pulling in off the main road, and there was his editor Stuart Gill stepping out from the back, cashmere overcoat and silk scarf hanging loose. Frank took one look at Gill's freshly scrubbed face, and guessed that he must have come down in the small hours after putting the paper to bed. He'd probably treated himself to a night in the nearest country-manor hotel to break the journey from London.

'Frank!' Gill shouted unnecessarily, pumping a leather-gloved hand at him. 'I was terrified I was going to miss you!'

'*Three*-course breakfast, was it?' Brennan asked with a smile. Gill patted him on the shoulder.

'You're coming back with me right now to have just that, my son,' Gill said with the beaming smile that all the lads on the paper recognised as his pre-troughing trademark. 'Little place about four miles away. In *The Good Hotel Guide*!'

'I've eaten,' Brennan said sourly.

'It doesn't show, son. I've seen more meat on a butcher's apron,' Gill said, tapping Brennan's lean left cheek with his fingertips.

'See you around, Frankie baby!' Derek Smith said as he passed, carrying the Kiss-o-Gram girl on his hip towards a waiting Mercedes saloon, one which the receivers must have missed when they'd folded his company.

'Cheers, Derek!'

'I *did* think about bringing you a bird,' Gill offered plaintively.

'Bad taste,' muttered Brennan. 'I'll settle for a big lunch and my old job back.'

The jollity evaporated from Gill's face. He pulled at the end of his nose and peered distantly across to the ridge of Wiltshire hills which overlooked the prison. As body language went, this was a neon-lit redundancy notice.

'I noticed the "Free the Holborn One" campaign had petered out,' Brennan said, as accusatory as any of the smart-arse barristers who'd got him sent down. 'What's the problem?'

Gill shuffled, affecting a stamp to beat some warmth into his Gucci-clad feet. 'It's the Old Man.'

'*Lord* Old Man, as he now is,' corrected Brennan.

Gill nodded. 'I'm sorry, Frank. He just thinks the time has passed for your sort of thing.'

'My sort of thing? What's that exactly?'

'Well, you know,' Gill said with a shrug. 'Agitprop. Investigations. All that shit-kicking stuff. The readers are bored with it.'

'*Bored?* You sure they're not just beaten down by the awfulness of what passes for public life these days?'

'There you go, see!' Gill trumpeted. 'They want a nice jolly read in the mornings and what do they get? Some comfortably off, right-on git telling them how hopeless things are. Life's bad enough as it is for most people without you bringing them down!'

'Is that how you see it, then?'

Gill took his eyes off the ancient ridgeways and gave Brennan an utterly modern glare. '*My* interests have always been what sells, Frank. We've had a revamp while you've been away. Put on nearly two hundred thou' a day!'

'I noticed.' Brennan smiled. 'Fitness plans and prize draws! Not to mention the price cut. Wouldn't it be more profitable to sell the prize cars and *give* the paper away?'

'Don't be a pain, Frank. There's a different climate now. We've got to go where the money is. Come on – let's go and have a bit of nosebag . . .'

Brennan brushed past Gill, hunching his shoulders against the breeze. 'I told you, I've eaten.'

Gill scratched his right ear and stood his ground.

'Frank! I've got some things for you in the motor!'

Brennan turned. 'One of them being my P45?'

Gill scuttled back to the car and reached in, his great fat, well-fed arse offering a symbolic gesture of rejection. He straightened up, holding a satinwood box and a big buff envelope. He walked back across to Brennan.

'A little something from the lads,' he said, thrusting the box at Brennan. It was a humidor, packed with fifty Monte Cristo Number 1 cigars, a bunch of cedarwood spills, and a neat black and chrome cutter.

'And there's a card in there,' he said, handing over the envelope, 'together with all the doings.'

'The doings' embraced a £50,000 pay-off cheque, formal notice of termination of contract, and some of Brennan's dog-eared address and contact books. Most touchingly, there was also a bundle of unopened letters from readers of Brennan's page.

'That's about three and a half grand for every year's service, eh? A golden boot up the arse more than a handshake.'

'Frank, I had to fight tooth and nail for that! Some of the board thought you brought all this on yourself, you know. The cost of the trial was only a spit away from half a million quid!'

Brennan looked at the good luck card, dotted with familiar signatures and obscene messages of goodwill. In all the scrawls, he could read the shiftiness, the embarrassment and yes, maybe some jealousy at his escape from a once-great newspaper that was now in free-fall.

'You'll be all right, you know,' Gill sniffed. 'Once word gets out, the offers'll come flooding in!'

'I'm not interested, to be honest, Stuart. I've had six months to think, you see. Take stock. Everyone should do it at some time in their life.'

'Under different circumstances, I hope!'

'Well, maybe – but you can't hide in there,' Brennan said, gesturing

back over his shoulder to where the main gate had closed up again, sealing
off both prisoners and staff inside their drab treadmill. 'I've got a file of
cuttings, a few little victories, a damaged liver and an apology of a marriage
– not much to boast about after over twenty years in the game, is it?'

'Christ, Frank, it's not that bad! Sure we suffer for it – not that the
public would ever notice. But the knocks are worth it, son. Aren't they?'

Brennan picked out one of the cigars, prised the cap off the end with
his thumbnail and held it to his mouth. Gill took the hint and fished for
his gold-plated Zippo.

'So you wouldn't have come back to us anyway, is that what you're
saying?' Gill pressed as he held the flame to the cigar.

Brennan took several short puffs, igniting the cigar till the end was
glowing and the rich blue smoke billowed up into the breeze.

'I guess not,' he said, with the first genuine smile of his freedom, his
two freedoms to be precise. 'I've worked out that I'm no good being an
employee, you see. I reckon a lot of what you regard as my bolshie attitude
comes from plain old-fashioned resentment at having someone looking
over my shoulder. Even someone as enlightened as you used to be . . .'

'I don't know whether to be flattered or insulted,' Gill said with a
sarcastic smile. 'So what are you going to do, then? Join a hippy convoy?'

'I'm going to plough my own furrow, Stuart. I mean, I even did it one
day when we were working on a farm across the valley . . . there I was sat
up in a tractor, happy as Larry. Not that I know Larry, or how happy he
is!'

Gill scratched the back of his head. 'Look, I've got morning conference
at eleven. Do you want a lift back to London at least?'

Brennan pulled deeply on the cigar and exhaled a plume of fragrant
smoke. 'No thanks – better start as I mean to go on . . .'

Brennan patted Gill fraternally on the shoulder and moved off in the
direction of the last cab left on the gaol-bird run.

'See you around, Stuart,' he said without looking back at the man he'd
spent more time with than his own wife.

'I'll give you a month before you're back scuffling with the rest of us!
Journalism's your drug, Frank! You'll never kick the habit!' Gill shouted.

'Watch me!' said Brennan.

Gill slunk back to the Scorpio, offering one last image of apparent
hangdog regret for Brennan to dine on. Brennan knew it was bogus. Gill
would be on the car phone in an instant, crowing to the paper's managing
editor about how he'd been able to dump an award-winning columnist
without any fuss whatsoever. Well, Brennan didn't give a fuck about

letting them off the hook – not for now anyway.

Brennan installed himself in the back of the cab, grateful for the sight of a sticker on the window reading, 'Yes! You May Smoke in This Taxi!'

'Any chance you could run us over to Wincanton, my friend?' Brennan asked.

'Certainly, sir,' said the driver.

'I've got the money,' Brennan offered as reassurance.

'I'm sure you have, sir,' the driver burred. 'No point in going horse-racing if you hadn't.'

Brennan smiled serenely as the cab pulled away. Even the sight of the green Rover saloon, which had neither dropped anybody off nor picked anybody up, but which was now seemingly locked and framed in the taxi's wing mirror, couldn't disrupt his peace of mind.

The Rover tailed the taxi all the way across to Wincanton, never dropping more than thirty yards back. As inconspicuous as a barrow-load of horse shit, Brennan thought, but then the bullying obviousness of the move was the whole point of the exercise. It was a message from 'the chaps', as the security goons liked to refer to themselves, that though Brennan may have frustrated them last time – if six months inside could ever be described as a victory – they were still on his case, determined to make him pay for his crimes.

There was an additional subtext – Brennan's trial had centred around supposed offences against the Official Secrets Act, relating to a leaked Home Office study on the paid repatriation of West Indians and Bangladeshis from Britain as a means of reducing unemployment. While Brennan had been in the dock for publishing the details of the document, the real purpose of the case had been to intimidate him into shopping whoever had handed over the document. Nailing a lefty hack was a minor prize compared to rooting out a dissident civil servant working at the heart of government.

Backed by Stuart Gill and the paper's board in what turned out to be their last gesture of solidarity, Brennan had stoically refused to give up a name, provoking the trial judge, and the government front benches, into separate but virtually identical tirades about the irresponsibility of contemporary journalism. If he'd written a considered essay on the beauty of Princess Diana's tits, Brennan couldn't have come in for greater condemnation.

Brennan clambered out of the taxi as it parked outside the bank in the centre of Wincanton, and he gestured 'five minutes' across to the two

goons in the Rover which had pulled in behind. If they were just letting
Brennan know that a gaol sentence wouldn't wipe the slate clean, he
thought he should let them know they were wasting their time. Brennan
asked the taxi to wait and disappeared inside the branch.

Even in rich, Euro-subsidised farming country a fifty-grand cheque
didn't come in every day, and nor did customers asking if they could
borrow a phone to call their branch manager in London. Installed in the
deputy-manager's office, Brennan confirmed his return to society to Ed,
his main man at Lloyds in Highbury, and arranged for an immediate cash
advance of £500. Returning outside, he found his taxi-driver in angry
conversation with the two guys from the Rover. They were council officials,
cracking down on unlicensed drivers using licensed vehicles. Brennan
tipped the driver £20 in sympathy and wandered away, chiding himself
for the residual journalistic arrogance that had made him believe he was
still of interest to an overstretched security service.

The jump-racing at Wincanton that afternoon began to ease the
twitchiness and uncertainty Brennan had felt for the last few weeks in
gaol. He'd been lying to himself of course, trying to pass off the certain
knowledge of his dismissal as a constructive change of life. He'd pretended
that the new start he'd worked out – no more journalism, a move to the
country, a patch-up with Janet – was what he really wanted. Yet he knew
that had Stuart Gill welcomed him with open arms that morning, and
suggested a major piss-up with the lads on the paper he'd have probably
done handstands on the prison forecourt. So the rejection, the abandonment,
the ending of so many links, burned into his gut.

Once he got on to the racecourse, however, the pain and the turmoil
faded. It had always been his greatest source of escape, going to the track.
Brennan's dad had taken him round all the courses a train ride from
London, including the long since departed Alexandra Park. It was there
that he had backed his first winner – five shillings of hard-earned paper-
round money increased seven-fold in less than a minute by a four-year-
old sprinter called Selvedge. It wasn't just the profit though – it was the
sight of ordinary men and women transformed into vibrant characters and
uplifted from drudgery by the races, the drinks, and the chance to win a
few bob when life generally had given them nothing.

Stepping into the Stalbridge Bar at Wincanton, Brennan felt instantly
at home. Sure, the faces – flecked with red veins and framed by tight
bushes of hair and tweed caps – shouted 'country', but the spirit was the
same. The few London types who'd bombed down the A303 for a day out
were hunched in a corner conducting side-of-the-mouth conversations,

occasionally reaching inside their jackets as mobile phones warbled. Brennan sank his first pint easily – too easily. The sudden intrusion of alcohol into his body after six months' abstinence had both a giddying and an unsettling effect. For one thing, the taste was not how he remembered it, being sour and unpleasant. He was aware too that the swirling reactions in his head – which he used to associate with creativity and wit – seemed more like panic and confusion. Brennan declined the barmaid's offer of another drink. His body was resisting the old dependency and for the time being he would have to respect its wishes. Still, it had seemed to like the return of Havana tobacco so all was not lost.

Brennan lit up his second cigar of the day and padded across to the betting ring. The London 'faces' were scanning the boards for any fractions they could get over the odds before moving in like torpedoes. Brennan went in behind one of them and stuck fifty on their gamble before it could shorten too much. The race – a two-mile hurdle – started and Brennan took up a place in the stands where he could see both the final two hurdles and the expressionless faces of the London raiders. Their horse was beaten three furlongs out – hanging on grimly, tongue lolling. 'Cunt,' one of the faces muttered as they shuffled away. Brennan looked at his ticket – Loveless, the perfect name for a bookie – and shredded it on the spot.

The second race went no better, but by the third Brennan was beginning to see the lines of form again in the *Racing Post*. After six months away, it had seemed like a lost language, but now the phrases, the names began to cohere. He stuck two hundred on Panto Prince at 3-1 for the big steeplechase of the day, and crossed the course to stand by the last fence. Though Wincanton was oval-shaped and largely flat, it offered a pleasing panorama of rising hills and ancient copses, and with the sun now lowering in the south-west, the horses and riders were framed by an orange aura as they started out from the far side of the course.

Frank followed their progress as up above a skylark sang. Round they came, a noise like distant thunder, Panto tucked in third, jumping what would be the second last next time, and now pounding towards the fence where Brennan stood. There was a cacophony of grunts and shouts from the jockeys and a snap of whips as the four horses took off virtually in a line – Hope, Prosperity, Drink, Fellowship, an alternative view of the apocalypse. Panto stumbled on landing, pitching forward a little then twisting right to regain his footing. The movement torqued the jockey out of the saddle and off on to the tufted grass. He smacked the ground with his whip in annoyance – Brennan thought momentarily about running over to kick him up the arse; but let the disappointment evaporate with a rueful smile. It was time to call Janet.

'You're taking the piss, aren't you? Ringing up from the races!' Even from a hundred and fifty miles away, Brennan could feel the frost.

'Look, can we talk, Janet?'

'We are doing.'

'About things other than me being at the races . . .'

'What else is there in your life – apart from work and going on the piss with the lads?'

'That's what I want to talk about – I'm over all that.'

Brennan turned. Although the phone was tucked away in an alcove just outside the members' bar the regular wafts of laughter and drinking ambience didn't help in the sincerity stakes. Especially when a wild-eyed punter emerged with his folded scrap of a racing page, plainly anxious to get on the blower for a bet.

'Look, can I call you tonight? When Lester's home? Would that be better? I'd like to have a word with him.'

'He's got homework to do. Make it about nine if you must.'

'Right . . . did you get the letters I sent?'

The punter behind Brennan twitched and began to mutter under his breath. He wiped the glass of his watch with his thumb as if trying to arrest time.

'I didn't bother opening them, to be honest . . . didn't seem much point.'

'Look, got to go. Money's running out. I'll call from the hotel about nine.'

'What fucking hotel's this, Frank?' Janet said with a laugh of exasperation.

Brennan pressed the follow-on call button. There was still thirty pence left on the display. He offered the phone to the punter.

'Sorry, mate. There's some money left there.'

The punter looked at him with contempt. 'Try Claire fucking Rayner,' he snarled.

Brennan had a coffee and cake back in the Stalbridge, and finally won on the fifth – twenty at 5-1. Honour satisfied, he left the course and found a trio of taxis waiting at the crossroads overlooking the unsaddling enclosure. The first two were booked. He leaned in on the third driver, instantly aware that the cocktail of beer and cigar had rendered his breath foul.

'Any chance of going over to Bradford-on-Avon, mate?'

'Be about thirty quid, me old pal,' said the driver, hoping to put Brennan off. There was more dough to be made shuttling punters to Gillingham station.

Brennan showed him his wad from the fifth race.

'Call it fifty.'

The driver's tattooed forearm reached out and opened the rear door.

Brennan had first glimpsed Bradford-on-Avon from the prison van, *en route* to work on a pig farm north of the town. Even the gut-turning stench which poisoned the day couldn't disturb those first images of the town: a stone bridge over the River Avon; a tall, handsome mill-type building and behind it tiers of Georgian houses and terraced cottages, lit by the morning sun. On the hill up out of the town there were antique shops, a cosy-looking bar with large windows, an art gallery. Brennan knew that a motorway service station would probably have looked like the Taj Mahal after the drabness of prison, but there was definitely something about Bradford that stuck with him.

Now, as the taxi pulled over the same bridge five months later, and turned into the courtyard of the Swan Hotel, Brennan couldn't deny, as rational as he was, that although he had never spent more than a minute or two there, it felt like he was coming home. Brennan watched the taxi go and looked around the yard and the stone steps up to the hotel's bars. 'Ostler's Bell' read a hand-painted sign on the wall above a brass bell-pull. Sure it was a gimmick – if anyone actually turned up at the hotel on horseback now they would almost certainly be told to piss off. But the artefact, like the whole town, seemed to trigger a folk memory, of a simpler, rural life. As far as he knew, Brennan's family had never strayed from outside Islington once they'd settled from Ireland in the 1850s. But five or six generations back, there'd have been farm labourers, blacksmiths, maybe even a publican among the Brennans. If character traits, health defects and hair colourings could be passed down in the genetic code, then why not the imprints of earlier lives?

Brennan bollocked himself for these extended thoughts. He was just out of gaol. After a few days' peace, he'd probably be itching for the rough and tumble of London again. After all, the countryside was just for old people and losers. He climbed the steps, pressed the ostler's bell for a laugh and walked in to book his room.

After a shower, Brennan went down to the bar and found himself able to order a mineral water without self-consciousness, reassuring himself that his call to Janet later that evening would be best undertaken stone-cold sober. Rather like the emotional tug-of-war which had raged inside him over his career, Brennan had, during his time in goal, stripped down the failing marriage and tried to separate the parts that worked from those either burnt out or broken down.

It had been easy to fall prey to the inevitable weakness generated by the solitude of goal. He'd talked to a few of the older lags in there – too old to be sent to one of the hard-case joints – and they'd all said the same thing. 'Don't trust your judgement in here – wait till you get back in the real world.' Of course, these were what the social workers called recidivists, habitual offenders who knew no other life but one of crime interspersed with spells inside. They *had* to put on a brave face because to do otherwise challenged the legitimacy of the cycle they lived. 'I don't have to be afraid of indulging my emotions,' Brennan had told himself several times as the cell doors clanged shut at 8 p.m. each night.

So he'd given it the full works – self-pity, self-examination, self-loathing – and come up with easy answers. Sure he missed Janet, and it had largely been the fault of his work that the marriage had steamed into choppy waters. But if he filleted out the job, and all the excesses that it had entailed – travelling, late nights, drinking – that would get rid of the problem, wouldn't it? For a few weeks this notion had sustained him, until the thought of what else he might do if he had the bottle to resign from the paper had ambushed him. Maybe his life was just as fixed in its patterns as the old lags – he'd been on papers since he was sixteen, and barely knew any world other than the burden of deadlines, the hyper-ecstasy of meeting them, followed by the crashing darkness of worrying about what came next.

Even his elevation at thirty-one to a national newspaper with his own page of investigations and provocative questions had been part of the same habitual cycle. Only the landscape, and the dosh, had changed.

So as he sat on the bed in his room, lit only by the stark white night-light from the porch of the Catholic church opposite, Brennan felt more dread than exhilaration about talking to Janet. To say he'd missed her might be taken as a patronising reclamation rather than a gesture of affection; to say he wanted to get back together wouldn't be true because he wasn't even sure that that was what he wanted. It's what he *thought* he felt. 'Christ, what a mess,' he said quietly to himself, the optimism of that morning's release now just a faint memory. He reached for the phone parked under the brass and taffeta bedside lamp. The decision about going back to the paper had been taken for him. Maybe Janet would do the same for him now. Please.

They talked for about half an hour. It seemed she'd settled down with

Lester, their twelve-year-old son, at the house of Brennan's parents in Highbury. (Yes, *they* blamed him too!) The lease had expired on what was supposed to be the family home before he was sent down. Moving to the in-laws, dangling a grandson as bait, was a cinch.

'Why didn't you visit?' Brennan asked suddenly.

The silence down the phone seemed endless as he waited and listened.

'I guess because I don't love you any more, Frank. And I was damned if I was going to lay myself open to feeling sorry for you!'

'You could have brought Lester along once or twice.'

'To see his dad in goal!'

'Well, for the right reasons!' Brennan said plaintively.

'Bollocks, Frank, it's the biggest professional ego-trip any journo can get, short of getting killed on an assignment. A little noble sacrifice in the line of duty. You'd have been depressed as hell if they'd let you off with a fine or, even worse, found you not guilty!'

Brennan couldn't deny this. Janet's 'so fucking what' attitude to journalists had been one of the reasons he'd liked her instantly when they'd first met on the paper in 1981. Of course, as an unsung researcher she was always likely to have a down on the people who got the credit for much of the work she'd done. Not that Brennan had ever told her this.

'Yeah, probably right,' he offered defensively. 'Anyway, he doesn't have to look up to me now – Stuart Gill was waiting outside to give me the push.'

There was a pause. 'So that's what you meant when you said you were "over all that" this afternoon?'

'Yeah . . .'

'So how could you have been over with it when you only found out this morning? Branching out into horoscopes, are you?'

'It's what I wanted, I think. A break. A chance to start again . . .'

'As what?'

'Dunno. A writer. Proper one – books, you know.'

Janet laughed warmly, almost affectionately, cheering Brennan like a shot of whisky in the gut.

'You daft bastard, Frank! You're trained to write in five-line paragraphs with no words bigger than six letters!'

'Maybe I can learn!'

'And where's this fine writing to be done? Moving to Tuscany, are you?'

'I'm thinking of buying a place here actually.'

'Frank, I don't even know where you are!'

'Bradford-on-Avon. Near Bath. Will you come down and help me look?'

Another silence. 'Lester wants to have a word . . .'

There was some scuffling as the handset of the phone was transferred. 'Hello, Dad?'

The voice was different. Maybe it was just the phone.

'Hello, son. You got a cold or something?'

'My voice has broken . . .'

It was a good job they still hadn't got round to marketing video-phones, Brennan thought as tears welled in his eyes. All those years of shit-filled nappies, mixing milk powder at 2 a.m., trundling down Upper Street with a push-chair, and Sunday lunchtimes at Marine Ices in Kentish Town. His brain accelerated through the photo album. But the images were blurred. It had all happened so quickly, a child growing up, that he'd hardly had time to notice.

'Be nice to see you – maybe even buy you a pint now, eh!'

'Be a bit of a sore point, wouldn't it? You want to talk to Mum again?'

Brennan could sense the mouth and ear moving away from the phone. 'I missed you . . .' he blurted, too late.

He spent a few more minutes describing Bradford to Janet and gleaning just enough encouragement to suggest that he came down to London to see them this weekend. And then there was silence. Just the hotel room, the whirr of the occasional car outside.

Brennan watched TV for a while before slipping between the cool, white sheets and spreading himself into a star shape to fill every corner of the double bed. He drifted off with the set still on but woke up at six, his body still on prison time, to hear the first inanities of a morning television programme.

Mrs Aldridge moved reluctantly along the corridor as the creased faces peered out of the cracks of opened doors. They were just like silly kids, these old people, excited by the smallest event.

'Go back inside, please. It's not an emergency. We'll move you if there's any problem.'

Mrs Aldridge reached the oak-panelled door to the Dentons' room. She sniffed. There *was* a vague smell, she had to admit. Often, one of them only had to shit themselves to produce complaints or anxious witterings.

Mrs Aldridge knocked on the door. There was no answer. She tried the handle. The door was locked. She reached for the bunch of keys hanging from her belt and inserted the skeleton for Peachblossom Corridor. She gagged the instant the door eased open. She clamped a handkerchief over her mouth and dived into the room towards the fire. The pipe-clay grille was cold and white as the gas hissed wastefully out of it. She turned off the supply and crashed across to the windows, throwing them open as far as she could. There was no time for her routine, life-enhancing look out over Lyme Bay, because Mr and Mrs Denton lay dead and stiffening in their neat twin beds.

'Silly bastards,' Mrs Aldridge muttered through her handkerchief as she swatted the poisoned air with her right hand. 'Silly, silly bastards!'

CHAPTER TWO

Forty-fuckin'-two, Brennan thought to his twin in the bathroom mirror. 'Look at you. Three chins, cheeks like a pig's arse. Your tits shaking when you brush your teeth.'

The fair hair was greying too, spreading back from the temples behind the ears. He stood sideways on and let his stomach relax. The muscles sagged into a white paunch which made it look like he'd had a beach-ball implant. Despite the prison diet and the physical work, Brennan remained prone to flabbiness. One of the things he would try to do in this new life, this reprieve, this unexpected opportunity, would be to look after himself more. A few long walks a week, maybe even buy a bike. Cut down on the booze and cigars. Enjoy the fresh air after too many years on Planet Carbon – just a bit of will-power, that's all it needed.

Brennan went down for breakfast and, with the smells wafting from the kitchen, couldn't resist a full fry-up. 'Well, I deserve it,' he thought.

Brennan took one of the hotel's envelopes from the desk on his way out after breakfast, and in the shade of the arched doorway, filled it with five £10 notes before sealing it. The map in the foyer had suggested the house was a good fifteen minutes' walk back over the Avon bridge and out on the Trowbridge road. It would be a good chance to check out the less visible parts of the town.

Almost instinctively, Brennan found himself making a mental log of the pubs he passed rather than the shops. Old habits would die hard. By the time he'd reached the station roundabout where the roads for Trowbridge and Frome divided, he'd already got a wine bar, two pubs and the town's betting shop gazetteered. He began the stretch up the Trowbridge road, over the railway line (Portsmouth right through to Cardiff), past brooding, four-storey Victorian villas built in local stone, until gradually the houses became smaller terraced cottages, and then half a mile further on, it was all semi-detached 1960s developments. Like the rings of a tree trunk, each section of the town which he'd passed seemed to mark a stage in its outward growth and prosperity.

Established as a Saxon town, Bradford had made its money in the eighteenth and nineteenth centuries through the wool trade, processed in the large riverside mills which still stood, and then shipped down to Bristol. The mills had been later filled by a tyre and rubber company, but now that too had run its time, and the town faced a post-industrial future of tourism and heritage for which it seemed, at first glance anyway, handsomely equipped. As he walked, Brennan guessed that most of the people living in the houses around him either worked in small local services – shops, garages, pubs – or commuted into the bigger towns, Bath, Trowbridge or even Bristol. And then there was the prison officer's house.

There was nothing outside to distinguish it from any of the other semis, no blue lamp, or a varnished slice of oak bearing the name 'Dunriotin'. Brennan rang the bell and waited. All the houses looked in on one another – did architects secretly anticipate Neighbourhood Watch in the 1960s? – but the windows were free of faces, the front gardens empty of strimmers. A post-morning-rush-hour stupor hung over the estate. The men had gone to work, the kids to school, while the wives at home did . . . well, what? Mrs Hodges appeared with a nylon smock over a floral print shirt and maroon slacks, with her hands sealed inside a pair of pink rubber gloves.

'Mrs Hodges?'

'Yes. Sorry – I'm cleaning out the budgie's cage.'

'I er . . .' Brennan suddenly realised he had no idea how to conduct these transactions. 'I just got out yesterday . . . Erlestoke?'

'Oh, yes . . . ?'

He reached into his jacket for the envelope, and held it out.

'This is on behalf of Tommy Preston – I'm sure your husband will understand . . .'

'Thank you.'

She snatched the envelope and disappeared inside the house in an instant, closing the door firmly. Brennan hadn't anticipated any jolly chit-chat, but this was a bit abrupt, leaving him no time for the superior smile he'd been told must be used against all screws and their wives. 'Shit of the earth,' Tommy Preston had advised him early on as they'd lain in their cell. He'd brushed aside Brennan's attempt at 'well somebody's got to do the job' with an irreducible contempt.

Brennan had gradually realised that though Tommy was not right, he was not wrong either. It was because the screws had power – and knew it – that they could never be sifted on a basis of 'bad' or 'not so bad', or even 'quite good'. They were *all* bastards because they had it over you while you were inside. And coughing up fifty quid to their wives once you were out so that a cellmate could be provided with cigarettes, a bottle of brandy or even a bit of Bob Hope, was a last demonstration of that power. Brennan walked away wondering how much of the fifty quid would be converted into cuttlefish for Mrs Hodges' budgerigar.

Brennan headed back towards the town centre, brooding on the necessary corruptions of the prison system. If the prisoners didn't get their booze, or their smoke or their drugs, they'd probably riot, while the screws would almost certainly strike if they lost their chance to earn a bit of bunce. In the old days, he'd have written about this in his column. He'd have got Mrs Hodges, in her pink gloves, caught on a long lens pocketing the envelope. But these weren't the old days now.

He'd gradually got round to reading the papers again in the prison library about two weeks after sentence. Whatever they contained, it read like news from another planet, so contrary and different was prison life. So the latest shagging Tory scandal, or Quango backhander assumed a different quality to that which it might have achieved in his old life.

The prisoners would look at the pictures of the latest public mistress and loudly express their desire to give her one themselves. The Tory minister would be a 'jammy bastard'. The bent council official became a role model for easy money-making. And the investigative journalist became a spoil-sport or, even worse, a prick.

Brennan took a different route to the centre on the way back, joining up with the Frome road at an expanse of playing fields framed by rough stone walls. The playing fields – tennis courts, cricket square, football pitch, bowling green – gave way to a clutch of craft workshops, dwarfed by the huge sixteenth-century tithe barn to one side. Beyond these buildings the land opened out into a country park which ran alongside the river and out into the valley stretching back towards Bath.

From this aspect, Brennan thought the town took on new grandeur. He could see how the houses and terraced cottages followed the contours of the valley wall in a fashion which seemed both random and yet, on closer inspection, sympathetically organised. 'Harmony', that was the word the architectural wankers used. Brennan slowly panned his eyes across the town's skyline and felt the tug in his guts again. Call it a primeval instinct or whatever, but he knew that he wanted to live here now, to settle, to belong.

*   *   *

'It's all right. Give yourself a minute,' said Roger Hughes as Brennan
leant against the wall. The estate agent had not overexaggerated the climb
up from the town centre to the third tier of houses and cottages on the hill.
Even after the first gentle slopes, Brennan's calf muscles had begun to
tighten, and by the time he'd reached Tory – what giggles that would
create among his mates when he sent out the change-of-address cards –
he was heaving like a marathon runner at the end of a race.

'Best thing in future is to drive up on to the Winsley road then take the
first left and park. It's only a stroll down from there,' Hughes said with
practised ease.

Brennan, if he'd had the breath, might have countered that he'd actually
enjoyed the walk up. The secret paths through the walled gardens, the
wild flowers growing out of the stonework, and now this astonishing view
down over the town. My God, they were even a good fifty feet above the
spire of the church he had passed not five minutes ago.

'Quite a sight, isn't it?' Brennan managed, having sucked in a deep
breath of air.

'You get used to it eventually,' Hughes said. 'Watching the traffic clog
up as the ants go to work.'

Brennan took another look. The ancient pattern of the town could be
clearly seen now, spreading out from the bridge and the river – a 'ford-
on-the-Avon' made sense. In the distance, the same hills above Westbury
which the work-gangs from prison had tilled took on a new perspective –
it was like looking across from one Saxon fort to another.

'Almost makes you want to take up hang-gliding,' Brennan said jokily,
before offering his hand. 'Frank Brennan.'

Hughes shook it briefly before turning and going into the cottage's
narrow hall. 'Come and have a look round.'

The cottage was arranged on three floors, with a dining-room and open-
plan kitchen on the ground, a larger sitting-room with south-west facing
windows on the first, and two and a half bedrooms on the third floor.
Brennan did a quick projection here – the second bedroom would suit
Lester, with its views and its sense of privacy, while the half-room could
easily accommodate a desk and shelves for work, though quite what that
would involve Brennan couldn't envisage just yet.

'You're getting out of London, presumably,' Hughes said, opening a
Velux window to reveal the hillside still climbing behind the house.

'That's the idea.'

'Well, I hope you have better luck than me, that's all I can say,' Hughes said looking out of the window, studying the town. 'Out of sight, out of mind – that's what happens. You in business for yourself?'

'Sort of. You?'

'Management consultant.'

Brennan nodded, trying not to give a hint that he had no idea what this meant apart perhaps from long lunches and giving advice on sacking people.

'All this balls about the home-working, modem-linked society of the future – I fell for it.'

Brennan had heard better sales pitches. 'I'll just have another look downstairs if that's okay?' Brennan negotiated his way down the narrow staircase, leaning against the exposed stone wall. The cottage was perhaps two hundred years old. Built for weavers working in the mills below, it had retained, as the estate agents would put it, many of its original features, which had been given a late-twentieth-century gloss. There was a pewter wash-basin built into the alcove adjoining the large fireplace in the sitting-room. A small bread-oven door filled the other alcove. The floorboards had been stripped and varnished, and although there was central heating, the radiators looked like Italian versions of the gurgling monsters from Victorian English schoolrooms. Short of cutting off the electricity and water supply, Mr Hughes had done a reasonable job of re-creating the eighteenth century.

'Must be quite a closed little community up here,' Brennan probed, wondering about the neighbours on either side.

'Don't expect to find any locals,' Hughes said, laughing for the first time. 'Mostly the arty set, you know – writers, potters, painters, that sort of thing. They've got absolutely no conversation about business matters. World of their own most of them. I'll be selling some of the furniture if you're interested?'

'Maybe. I've got to let the wife have a look yet, if that's okay with you?'

Hughes shrugged. 'I can't hang around if another offer comes in.'

'I haven't offered yet,' Brennan said with a smile to diffuse the sharpness.

'No – right. Well. Let me know.'

Brennan left and took a slow walk along the rest of the terrace, trying to imagine himself up here, scribbling away at God knows what in a ten-foot by eight-foot room, exchanging daily pleasantries about geranium pots with the other residents of Tory. The terrace, for all its prettiness and period features, had the feel of a retreat about it. Was that what Brennan really wanted, to walk away from life? What if there was nothing there when he stopped? No talent for anything else, no taste for a slower pace of existence? He could be like one of those beagles that escapes from a laboratory only to die of confusion and madness, unable to adjust to a life without purpose and cruelty and all the other things that kept the heart pumping.

The 'Richard and Judy Show' blasted out from the wall-mounted television set in Chestnut Grange's communal lounge. Most of the residents had had their mid-morning tea from the trolley and had taken up their usual high-backed armchairs, either to stare at the telly, or to stare out at the sea. This morning, they had something different to look at, as three funereally dressed men carried the temporary coffins of Mr and Mrs Denton out on to the home's forecourt and carefully loaded them into a black transit van.

A couple of the female residents dabbed their eyes with Kleenex as they realised that more faces had disappeared from their daily routine. Sometimes they just went and nobody noticed for several weeks, but mostly the empty chair in the lounge signalled the ending of another life. To many of the residents, the everyday business of death was a form of comfort – it said, 'You have nothing to fear now, it's just like putting out the milk bottles'. To others, this aura of the commonplace robbed them of their last sense of adventure and dignity.

The men from the funeral parlour clambered into the front seat of the van, looking like crows on a telegraph wire, and then the black vehicle pulled away past the neatly trimmed lawns lined with the first spring showing of daffodils. Mr and Mrs Denton hadn't been that popular in the home. They'd kept themselves too much to themselves for that and, as a couple, they'd had an intimidatory presence to the greater majority of widows and widowers with their solitary lives and sad memories.

Mrs Aldridge came into the lounge, handing out the photocopied menus for lunch. She consoled one of the tearful women.

'Come on, now, Elsie – to go as a couple, side by side, that must be wonderful . . .'

Having looked at two more properties in Bradford, neither as practical nor as handsome as the one on Tory, Brennan returned to the Swan, paid his bill, and crossed the road to the Dandy Lion bar for lunch. An eccentric jumble of furniture – church pews pegged half-way up a wall to provide a drinking shelf – and a snorting Italian coffee machine made the first impressions as he walked in. And now a chubby-faced landlady was telling rude jokes at the far end of the bar, while a quartet of men, seated over coffees in one of the window alcoves, seemed to be swathed in blokeish laughter.

Normally Brennan might have wondered if he'd missed a sign reading 'private club' on the way in, but there was a distinct warmth and sense of anarchy in the atmosphere here. He'd lost all patience with those endless posturing waiters in the designer bars of Soho and Covent Garden which had been his normal beat. The once-over look to check on his (lack of) fashionability, the arched eyebrow as a cool substitute for 'What can I get you, sir?', the wilful inability to remember orders beyond two drinks and the all-too-frequent inanity 'Do you want a glass for that?' 'Of course I want a fucking glass, you berk! What am I expected to do, bring my own?' He'd thought that hundreds of times but never had the bottle – so to speak – to say it out loud.

'Mornin',' said the young barmaid with a smile. She was actually *looking* at Brennan, engaging in eye contact, waiting for his response. If she ever applied for a job in an American burger bar, she'd get turned down for being too human. Brennan smiled back, shyly.

'Morning . . . a Becks . . . no, er . . . yes, go on, I'll have one, please . . .' Brennan stuttered. His brain and body had been sending opposing messages, one saying 'impress the barmaid with your cosmopolitan taste in beer', the other reading 'stick to your guns, kid, and stay dry'. Brennan resolved that he could satisfy both impulses – he could buy, but he didn't have to drink.

Brennan watched as she bustled back to the glass-fronted cold-store and pulled out one of the all-too-familiar green bottles. Unquestioningly, she reached for a glass. First base. Now, instead of plonking both down in front of him, she poured the beer carefully into the precisely angled glass. Second base and running. She decanted the last drips into the meniscus of froth and brought the glass to him with a steady hand.'

'Can I order a fried fish platter as well?' Brennan asked, pointing to the blackboard menu behind the bar.

'Sure.'

Brennan reached for his wallet.

'S'all right, I'll put it all on a bill,' the barmaid said before he could extract a ten-pound note. Such *trust*, already? Third base was left behind.

'Be about ten minutes. I'll bring it over,' she said, scribbling down the order. Brennan retreated to the high-backed, richly upholstered sofa which looked out on to Market Street, registering the 'home run'. Courtesy, efficiency, hospitality – Brennan was in culture shock. And the food, when it arrived, was good too. Brennan settled into the sofa like a cat which had found its home. He risked a first sip of the beer. This time there was no recoil. A second confirmed the tingle of pleasure on his tongue. If he could stick to drinking for taste and not just to prove that he was one of the lads, Brennan was sure he could find a compromise. The immediate absence of any lads to be one of would be a profound help.

Brennan soon felt good enough to open the bundle of letters which Stuart Gill had kept for him. Most of them dated back six months to the time of the trial, and were – with two anonymous exceptions – wishing him well for his, let's paraphrase, 'courageous stand against an ever more authoritarian government and legal system'. The addresses were predominantly London NW3 and N1, although a Herefordshire vicar praised his 'Christlike sacrifice' in the face of barbarism. Brennan chuckled to himself, the more so when he read the purple-ink number anticipating with relish his 'nights of buggery in prison for being a stupid, interfering left-wing ponce'.

In the eleven and a half years in which he'd published his weekly column, Brennan had never been able to form a coherent picture of his readership through the letters they sent him. Some were plainly barmy from the outset – relatives possessed by aliens; assassination plots revealed in the back-spelt lyrics of rock songs; diabolic messages emitted in code from an unwitting daytime TV presenter. The majority of letters were based around fretful but minor complaints that could be better investigated and resolved by Citizens' Advice Bureaux or local councillors. But maybe seven or eight a week would be genuine cries for help and enlightenment from people too frightened to go to authority, too bamboozled to think straight, or too weak and powerless to believe they had a chance of justice.

It was this tremulous minority which formed the bulk of his work and, by and large, he had served them well. The falsely convicted killer, the ripped-off investor, the persecuted dissident, had all provided headline-grabbing triumphs for Brennan, for his paper and editor and for his researchers, the most persistent of whom had been Janet. There'd been awards, celebratory lunches, tributes from civil liberties groups.

Now, both the paper and editor had rejected him, and his wife and ex-researcher was a stranger. The clamour of celebration was like a distant echo, and the sense of a virile, arms-linked opposition had been dissipated by market forces and individual struggles against recession. 'Investigative journalism' was now dispensed as entertainment in garish five-minute reconstructed segments for television.

There was, indeed, no such thing as society now, just a nation of customers. As Brennan glanced through the last lamenting letter, he knew that Stuart Gill had been right to drop him. And he knew, equally, that he himself had been right to decide to give it all up. The new life started here. But, damn it, he now noticed that the barmaid with the smile was wearing an engagement ring . . .

The quiet dinner for two in the modest Italian trattoria on Blackstock Road had seemed like a good idea, especially as it had got Brennan and Janet out from under his parents' feet. No lasting truce was ever likely to be worked out under such crowded circumstances. But a table in a restaurant, flanked by socialising groups, was almost as bad. Brennan felt that they must have looked and sounded like two people who'd met up through a lonely hearts advert and who'd decided at first sight that they weren't going to go any further than the dinner. Brennan's decision to forgo wine added to the tension rather than reducing it. Janet's Mancunian bluntness had made it their first awkward topic of conversation – while she was pleased he wasn't back to boozing uncontrollably, the abstinence seemed a bit like an insult, a deliberate avoidance of a celebratory gesture. So they talked in jagged, inconsequential fragments, mostly about Lester, until they got back to Brennan's parents' house and found themselves forced to room together.

They each took care not to undress in front of the other, with Brennan retiring to the bathroom before returning in a T-shirt and shorts. Janet was already under the duvet, a picture of modesty in a white cotton nightshirt. Brennan squeezed in alongside her, making sure he didn't touch her, even accidentally. The restraints of prison life could be useful sometimes. But at least now they could talk, albeit in loud whispers.

'I haven't been with anybody else, you know.'

Brennan nodded. 'Neither have I – although it was touch and go in the prison showers on a couple of occasions . . .'

'Sounds like a new shampoo.' Janet deepened her voice. ' "Touch and Go" – for men on the move, but not very far . . .'

'What do you want to do, then?' Brennan asked, knowing he was pushing his luck.

'One day at a time, please, Frank. You owe me that at least. Sounds like you couldn't even be sure of your shoe size any more.'

'It's better than that. I can see some of the things that I should have disliked a lot earlier, if only I'd been sober and calmer.'

'Such as?'

'Well, the job for one. And not just mine. Newspapers are dying. They're being pushed right to the margins now by telly, satellites, computers. People don't want to know any more.'

'There's still plenty of stories breaking in the papers first, you know.'

'And they're all served up on a plate, every time. It's disinformation. Or propaganda. One party rat-fucking the other. One Royal putting the skids under another. Lobbyists paying for space. Proprietors with their own mad agendas. Papers are just a Punch and Judy show now . . . the real business is all out of sight.'

'Where's that leave *you*, then?'

'I dunno. I'm the string of sausages in the crocodile's mouth, I guess . . .'

'What else don't you like any more?'

'London,' Brennan said tersely.

'Bit late after forty-two years, isn't it?'

'No. I've served my time standing on my head in the great cesspit. From now on I get my nose in the fresh air. Get a look at the sky and a bit of greenery. I've had enough of traffic jams and breathing clouds of shite. I'm fed up being stopped by Iranians showing me the other side's torture albums. I've had enough of buskers on the tube singing "Here Comes the Sun" while you're stuck in a tunnel. I don't want to hear some cunt playing the bagpipes whenever the rain's pissing down in the West End. And I never want to smell another of those Magic Trees in the back of hackney cabs. No wonder so many people throw up . . .'

Janet looked at him. 'Let me just run that past the bullshit monitor. So – you won't be driving a car when you get your licence back, and you'll be giving up smoking, and not working for human rights any more. You'll be selling your Beatles albums and steering clear of shops and pubs. And you'll be walking instead of taking taxis?'

Frank rolled his eyes at her. 'I never said I was consistent!'

They laughed, and Janet lay her head on his chest, and for a few short moments it was like when they first went to bed and talked through the night.

'They came round here, you know?' Janet said, breaking the shared comfort of silence. 'About a week after you went down.'

'Who?'

'Well, the warrant cards said they were Special Branch, but I checked out the names later. Didn't exist at Scotland Yard. Nor City of London.'

'What did they do?'

'Just asked about your friends.'

'Any names in particular?'

'Mostly people at the paper . . . plus a few I could genuinely say I'd never heard of.'

'Did they search the house?'

Janet shook her head. 'I never left the room the whole time they were here. Your mum made them a cup of tea. After a quarter of an hour, they left. The car registration doesn't exist, either . . . well, it's not on the Swansea computer.'

'Did you check for listening devices?'

'Oh, come off it, Frank, what are they gonna get from your parents, me or Lester?'

Brennan looked at her accusingly.

'You tell me?' he snapped.

Janet felt the sting of tears in her eyes. She fumbled her way out of bed before Brennan could see them.

Brennan walked Lester to school the next morning, hoping to catch up on his son's news, or at least re-establish some dialogue between them. But something had changed in Lester apart from his voice. As they took on the steady descent of Highbury Grove, walking with the scuffling tide of rush-hour traffic, it became increasingly obvious that Lester was embarrassed that anyone might see him with his dad. After several monosyllabic answers to questions that wouldn't have taxed a seven-year-old, Brennan pulled him to a halt.

'What's the problem here?'

Lester shrugged, examining the cut of his training shoes. The Walkman's headphones still hissed despite the fact that Brennan had pulled them down on to Lester's shoulders as they'd left the house.

'Am I interrupting the Tony Blackburn show or something?'

'I don't listen to sad bastards,' Lester countered. Six words – progress at last.

'Look, I'm sorry. For everything that I may have done, and everything you think I should have done but didn't. I'm *sorry*. You won't understand how mad it gets being a man . . . of my age.'

'Right.'

'Tell me what you're angry about? A few clues will do. Money? Living back with Grandma and Grandad? Me being a cunt?'

There was a glimmer of a smile – it could just have been the *frisson* of intimacy produced by the swearing. Maybe he was smiling because Brennan had hit the nail on the head.

'I don't know, Dad. Or maybe that should be "I don't know Dad". Without the comma?'

Brennan nodded sympathetically.

'It's the same for me too, you know?' Brennan said softly. 'I can't remember the last time we went out together – a match, or what?'

'Arsenal v. Liverpool, 1993,' Lester said quickly.

If it had been a hunting knife it couldn't have wounded Brennan more.

'We'll make up for it. I've got time now. For once.'

'Maybe. Did you call me after Lester Piggott the jockey?'

The hunting knife, Brennan remembered, cuts on its way out of the body too. 'Your mum had just told me she was pregnant. I'd been to the Derby and won a lump on Teenoso. It was a joke. While we went to all the scans and stuff. But then when you came, it just stuck. It's not that bad, is it? There's Lester Bowie too, you know?'

They were back to shrugs again. 'Joke, eh? That's all I am to you two . . .'

'Lester—'

Frank reached for him, but he spun on his cushioned trainers and was several strides away in an instant. Brennan watched Lester ease across through the slow-moving line of cars and catch up with two schoolmates. Two kids who knew his own son better than he did – maybe ever could.

Brennan flagged down a taxi trying to squirt its way along the centre of the road.

'Holborn Circus, please.'

Brennan sat back in the seat and strapped on the belt. He tried to work out how he could have managed to do so much for other people, complete strangers whose only contact was often a scribbled note, while managing so little for that dense ball of helpless, plum-coloured flesh, hair matted with blood and bile-coloured fluid, whom he'd seen take his first breath.

The image faded as other stimulants muscled in on Brennan's privacy. First Tony Blackburn on the driver's radio, and then the sweet, sickly smell of a Magic Tree hanging in the window behind him.

'Fucking London,' Brennan mouthed, as a woman pushing a pram along the pavement overtook the taxi and left it for dead.

CHAPTER THREE

'Wait there – I'll be down,' barked Stuart Gill on the receptionist's phone. She took the receiver off Brennan and replaced it with a smile of victory. She had been right not to let him go up to the offices, despite the fact that she'd seen him come and go on a daily basis for the last four years of her working life. As the gap in the small row of photos of award-winning journalists around the lobby testified, Brennan had now become a non-person. He could almost see the difference in shading on the entrance hall's mock wood panelling where his portrait, with *What the Papers Say* trophy, had once hung.

Brennan circled the lobby trying not to catch the eye of anyone who might know him. But the familiar bustle of dispatch riders delivering envelopes and secretaries returning with pyramids of sandwiches continued without interruption. Then the door of the executive lift pinged open and Gill emerged in his ball-crushing uniform: Harvie & Hudson shirt with cuffs rolled back two turns; loosened silk tie; braces in the salmon and cucumber colours of the Garrick Club, of which he was not even a member; and a pair of half-moon spectacles balanced on the end of his red nose to make him look like a deep thinker.

'You don't half pick your moments,' Gill sighed.

'Flap on, is there?'

Gill looked around to make sure the dispatch riders all had their crash helmets on. He leant close to Brennan's ear, lips hardly moving.

'Bit of a bidding war for a bint who claims she's been shagging a member of the 1922 committee.'

'Nineteen twenty-two being their combined ages . . .'

Gill snorted a little laugh. 'May use that. So what is it?' he asked, looking at his watch to urge brevity.

'My contact books and notes—'

'I gave 'em back to you the other day . . .'

'I know – but did you have anyone asking for them?'

'Only when you were first pulled in – but I'd stuck them in the safe by then. And that's where they stayed.'

'Only Janet got a visit from two Special Branch officers who weren't. Anybody similar been sniffing round here?'

Gill hunched his shoulders and spread his hands. 'Not officially. Security's reported nothing funny. Besides, it's over now, isn't it. We won.'

'Exactly. But in the Big Lads' Game, the scores are aggregated.'

Gill acknowledged the expression immediately with a grave look. 'Big Lads' Rules, Big Lads' Game' – it was the self-regarding, intimidatory calling card of the intelligence services and secretive military groups with the power to do what they liked in the name of order.

'Christ, I thought this had been a clean fight!' Gill said with a deep frown.

'Not when they're after somebody on the inside who may leak again.'

'Well, you never even told *me* who it was, so I couldn't help them if they put the thumbscrews on me, could I?'

'But you can help them join up the dots, Stuart. Get them a picture. That's all they'd need. Did the Old Man ever ask you?'

Gill affected a rigorous act of memory which gradually dissolved into a slow shake of the head.

'He may have done . . . but like I said. What could I have told him which would have endangered your man?'

'I never said whether it was a man or a woman.'

Brennan reached and twanged the nearest of Gill's Garrick Club braces. 'Put you up for membership yet, has he?'

Gill scowled. 'I've played the white man with you, Frank! You could have ended up with fuck all out of this but for me!'

'I hope so, Stuart.'

'Don't hope – *believe*! If you get anything else on this line of things, or you find that these bastards are still getting heavy with you, come back to me. I may not be able to use your name, but I'll run the story. Promise.'

Brennan looked Gill in the eyes. He didn't blink. But then he never did.

'I'll send you a change-of-address card,' Brennan said offering a hand.

Gill shook it with both of his. 'There's a few more letters arrived since you came out. Somebody must be missing you. I'll forward them, shall I?'

'In your own time,' Brennan said, before turning towards the revolving door that once sparked so many jokes about job security. Now the joke was on Brennan, but he was still hoping to see the funny side.

They buried Mr and Mrs Denton in adjoining graves, with the minimum of ceremony in a plot on a hillside overlooking Bridport. Mrs Aldridge from Chestnut Grange attended, but only because it was her morning off. Nobody else came – there were no relatives, and the home's policy was not to encourage their guests into attending funerals for obvious reasons. If you were a special friend, you could ask permission. But Mr and Mrs Denton didn't have any friends, let alone special ones.

Mrs Aldridge winced as she caught the waft of whisky on the priest's breath – ten-thirty in the morning, she logged to herself for later gossip with the other nurses at the home, must be a new record, even for him!

The priest gargled his way through distantly familiar Latin phrases, made a sign of the cross, then invited the funeral operatives, as they now liked to be called, to lower the coffins into the yawning graves. Once completed he nodded to Mrs Aldridge to get her to take a handful of soil from the two piles which adjoined the graves.

Mrs Aldridge felt flushed with the responsibility. She took what she thought would be enough for both graves, but found the loose soil slipping from her fingers and powdering down on to just the one coffin. She reached for another handful.

'That'll do,' said the priest. 'We're not building a motorway here.'

Mrs Aldridge stood up, corrected. The priest made his final remarks and then turned and set off at a brusque pace. The funeral operatives each lit cigarettes and made their way back to the hearse without a look at Mrs Aldridge. The grave-digger, a young man with a collection of rings through both ears and nostrils, stepped up to begin his last work.

'You'll put that on top for me, will you?' she asked, pointing to the cellophane-wrapped flowers which Chestnut Grange had sent.

'Yes, ma'am,' the youth slurred, fresh spittle dribbling on to his chin. He speared his spade into the earth and began loading up with a grunt.

Mrs Aldridge walked away. Within an hour, the bouquet would be disassembled, and its contents flogged off around however many pubs it took to raise the price of a few pints of head-banging cider.

Brennan had thought that Willy Russell's *Blood Brothers* was the most appropriate ticket to send to his friend, and though there was a good chance he might have seen it already, it sounded like the sort of musical you could go back to and enjoy all over again. In any case, watching the play wasn't exactly the point of the exercise. Not this time.

Brennan walked up Shaftesbury Avenue from Piccadilly Circus tube. Early summer tourists were already apparent – looking the wrong way as they stepped in front of buses; wearing dayglo bum-bags as if to draw *increased* attention to where their money and travellers' cheques were stored; taking photographs of the face-painted mime artist who was enacting an obscure ritual with the traffic lights on the corner of Wardour Street; and yes, stopping to talk patiently to Iranians with their photo albums of torture victims.

Brennan moved deftly through these clumps of slow-moving human traffic, but not just because it made him feel good to be in command of the streets. If the visits made to Janet and Stuart Gill while he was in gaol were more than just token attempts at intimidation, he would have to be careful, especially tonight.

Brennan took one pass of the theatre's front entrance, paying no attention whatsoever to the groups of chattering tourists, or to the young men waiting for their dates to turn up. A hundred yards on, he paused to study the window of a kitchen equipment shop. If the Big Lads had a full file on him, and *were* following him tonight, they'd have known immediately that this was a bogus move – Brennan knew the relationship between an omelette and a frying pan, and that's about all.

Brennan angled his head so that the left eye could take in the upstream of people moving towards him. Nobody stood out immediately. Nobody flinched or made a sudden nervous deviation. Then a possible face emerged – a bloke in his late twenties, in jeans and a black bomber jacket, pausing to light a cigarette. Brennan had never gained access to the training manuals, but he knew a little about the double-cover system: if an operative felt even a twinge of suspicion that he'd been spotted, he'd signal and pull out, allowing a back-up – and there would be at least two or three – to take over. Brennan had often visualised this as similar to the observation methods used by a football referee and his two linesmen. Except that these guys didn't wave flags.

Brennan crossed Shaftesbury Avenue immediately taking the turn into the fringe of Chinatown. Here the early evening throng was dominated by a party of suited visitors from Hong Kong, probably checking out the business opportunities for their post-1997 future. Brennan paused to look at the rack of steamed ducks hanging in a restaurant window. 'Leather jacket' had crossed to the other side of the street and gone beyond him. Up ahead, on this side of the pavement, a shaven-haired man of about thirty-five, wearing a yellow and green Manchester United away shirt, leant against a bollard leafing through the *Evening Standard*.

Brennan moved down to the junction with Gerrard Street and turned right, heading into the pedestrianised, more blatantly themed zone of the Chinese quarter. He reckoned he'd got the two linesmen – but who was the referee?

'Leather jacket' strode on, left side, apparently oblivious, in reality regrouping for another pass. Brennan could sense 'Man U' behind – not overbearingly close, but hovering. Without warning, Brennan doubled back in an instant. He caught a momentary glimpse of a wild look in the eyes of 'Man U' – in football terms he'd been 'nutmegged', the ball pushed between his legs.

Brennan stepped up the pace. 'Man U' *was* out of the game. 'Leather jacket' had some ground to make up. The 'Referee', unless he was really clever, would be running now, to stay in touch. Brennan stopped at the junction again – teasing them with the possibility of three, maybe four routes. Down towards Leicester Square, or across towards Covent Garden. He decided to head back up to Shaftesbury Avenue, as memories of a particular Soho bar flashed up just as required – if it took years to train a surveillance operative, Brennan had every right to fall back on his own specialist knowledge.

He weaved his way between the home-bound cars and the show-bound taxis across to Dean Street. A hundred yards up was the French Pub, starting-off point for many a wasted night in his life. The bar, small and quite shallow, nevertheless had two doors – one south, one north – to accommodate the constant flow of art students, poseurs and hardened boozers who formed the bulk of its clientele.

Brennan ducked in through the south door. Familiar faces nodded and smiled in the throng. He heard a few 'wotcher, Franks', as if he'd never been away. Feigning a 'meet', he craned his head around, moving to position himself by the north door. He turned. The south door was being opened by a slightly breathless blonde woman, too well dressed for the bar, too unsure of her surroundings to be a regular, too alone to be meeting somebody.

MI5 is an equal opportunities employer, eh? Frank thought to himself, as he burst out of the north door and trotted into Old Compton Street. He criss-crossed the road several times before turning back down to Shaftesbury Avenue and diving into the side entrance of the theatre's foyer. Climbing the stairs to the bar, he glimpsed the 'Referee' giving 'Man U' her verbal equivalent of the red card, as the final whistle went on this particular game in the series.

Brennan bought a programme, slugged back a large glass of Perrier water in the bar, and made his way through to the dress circle to find his seat. The row gradually filled up – except for the seat on his right. Brennan prepared himself for the bum-numbing torture of seeing the show for the third time, all to no avail.

But as the house lights came down and a small band in the orchestra pit struck up the musical's opening chords, there was an irritated flurry as a single late-comer made his way along Brennan's row, and claimed the empty seat next to him. Brennan kept his eyes on the stage, listening as the late-comer recovered his breath. When the panting quietened, Brennan took a quick look across. Mark Fraser-Williams seemed to have greyed considerably in the eight months since they'd last seen each other at *Five Guys Named Moe* – or 'Five Guys Named MoD' as Mark had joked archly on the night.

Fraser-Williams was not an earnest, principled leaker of documents in the manner of some who had gone before him. In fact, Brennan had gained the impression over the years of oblique contact with him that Mark regarded his actions as a bit of a wheeze – rather like getting a sneak preview of school exam papers the night before. His additional cover, as a cheerful bon vivant, would have almost certainly earned him vital credibility when the Home Office had begun its internal investigations after the repatriation leak to Brennan. Besides which, his Etonian and Cambridge background still held good for being regarded as 'one of us' when the sniffer dogs came round. It was the bloody social-climbing grammar-school boys from the fifties and sixties who couldn't be trusted.

Fraser-Williams gave Brennan a reassuring wink during a scene change. He'd been quite willing to turn himself in when the furore over the repatriation story had broken, but Brennan had urged him to stay put, not because of any 'protecting my sources' code of honour, but from a purely practical and yes, selfish point of view.

Establishing contact with a closet renegade inside such a glowering monolith as the Home Office was a rare prize for a campaigning journalist. Worth going to gaol for, certainly. Besides, Brennan had come to like the man's languid unpredictability.

At the interval, Brennan went to the aisle to buy a tub of ice-cream, while Fraser-Williams stayed in his seat and read the programme notes. Brennan returned, glad to see that the theatre-goers around them had cleared off to the bars.

'How did you get on in "jug", dear chap?' Fraser-Williams asked without looking up.

'It was survivable,' Brennan said through a wooden spoonful of ice-cream. 'Though I wouldn't recommend it.'

'Terribly noble of you. And now I read that you've lost your job. I feel ashamed.'

'Forget it. You been okay?'

'Not too bad. Hauled me in a few times for a grilling, but I gather they thought it must have been someone higher up than me.'

'Nobody's been fingered though?'

'No, no. The fuss has died down now. The repatriation study's been abandoned. For the life of this government anyway.'

'Well, I've a suspicion that some element in Security still thinks it can get a result: even now. I'm pretty sure a little firm tried to follow me here tonight.'

Fraser-Williams chortled. 'Can't see them having an expenses claim for theatre tickets accepted!'

'It's you they'll be after, Mark. I'm out of the frame now – except as the cheese in the mousetrap. So be careful, right?'

Fraser-Williams looked anything but perturbed.

'Frank, for every little snippet I've passed on, there are *ten times* as many that have come from ministers or secretaries of state! I *know* – and I won't be afraid to name names if the bastards get silly with me. It's just a game, really, and what they hate most is other people being allowed to join in!'

The five-minute bell for the end of the interval buzzed in the background. Brennan moved to stand up.

'Not staying?'

'Seen it twice. Besides, I've got a train to catch.'

'Well-deserved hols, I hope?'

'A move actually. West Country . . .'

'Send me the address, won't you?'

'Like hell! I'm taking a risk sending theatre tickets to your home! It's a quieter life for me now.'

For a moment, Brennan thought he saw a glimmer of envy behind Mark's expressionless eyes.'

'What if I get something that might interest you?'

Brennan shook his head.

'Dunno. Doesn't seem to matter any more, does it?'

'Maybe I should try *The Spectator*? They seem keener on bringing down this government than anyone else!'

'Take care, Mark.'

'We'll have lunch one day, shall we? Somewhere very public. Get well pissed, hey?'

Brennan smiled and nodded, but couldn't imagine it somehow. The patrician games player and the bolshie proletarian hack could probably generate little beyond the making and throwing of mud pies. Besides which it would probably need an amnesty, or a change of government, to allow either of them to have the confidence to make open contact with the other. Mark would enjoy the musical at least, particularly the piquant ending, where two men from different social backgrounds face each other in a gun-fight, only to find out in death that they are really brothers.

Brennan took a cab across to Paddington to catch the 22.30 train to Chippenham. He bought a bagful of burger, chips and hot chocolate on the station concourse, narrowly avoiding a fight with a rolling drunk who was intent on jumping the queue. As he walked over to Platform Five, Brennan saw two transport policemen rugby tackle the drunk and handcuff him, before bundling him off to a detention room. Boarding the train, a huge sense of escape washed over him, and after eating, he lit one more of his Monte Cristos to enhance the feeling.

But as the darkness of the countryside enveloped the train more sober thoughts descended. Fellow-passengers drifted off at Reading and Didcot, climbing into cars to take them home to their families. These men looked secure in the routine nature of their lives. And here was Brennan, trying to start again, not really knowing what to do, risking all.

What the recruitment agencies would call his 'life skills' were few – he could write, albeit in journalistic left-jabs. He'd learned a bit of French. He liked his soul music and his modern jazz but neither of these would bring him work. He was passionate about horse-racing and betting, but this was more likely, on all known history, to lose him money rather than win it. The multiplicity of fantasies which had once sustained a sense of ambition in his early twenties had all been closed off now. He was never likely to become an ace saxophone player, or a leading racehorse owner, or a silver-suited soul singer filling Wembley Arena. So many little private hopes had dropped away. He couldn't even take consolation in sharing his passions with his son.

By the time he took a taxi from Chippenham just after midnight, Brennan was thoroughly depressed. Fortunately the driver, a burly Sikh with a huge bush of a beard, had the car radio turned up too loud for conversation. As the little Skoda saloon bucked and swerved down unknown lanes with dark walls of hedges, with Whitney Houston screeching her way through a terrible film theme, Frank had one of those instances that not even gaol had provoked. It seemed that he'd played virtually all his hands of cards, and wasted them all. So the simple question occurred to him – What the fuck am I doing here?

Brennan stayed at the Swan in Bradford-on-Avon for just over a week while the conveyancing on the house up on Tory went through. He rebuilt his morale by walking all over the town, discovering more and more hidden pathways, steps and passages that made him think of Venice – well, the Venice he'd seen in the movies anyway. He'd worked out that he should now think of his mind as a blank canvas – a blank cheque would be pushing it. So the first stage was to paint in the local landscape to get a sense of who he was, by getting a sense of *where* he was.

In other times, an inspection of Bradford's various pubs would have provided an ideal vehicle for such an enterprise, but being more circumspect about his drinking meant that he looked on each pub he visited more critically. In one, out on the high fringe of the town, he wrestled with that familiar town-and-country paradox – how come he could only get little plastic cartons of UHT milk for his coffee when less than two hundred yards away there was a field full of cows? Taking a new route down to the town centre, an attractive-looking pub turned out to be the haunt of the All-Time Lowest Scorers of a Mensa test, complete with their heavy-metal tattoos. In another, close to his home, the landlord had looked baffled by a request for food, eventually returning from an upstairs kitchen with a stale roll from which lolled a thin slice of ham glistening with a one-inch border of fat.

So he returned to the Dandy Lion one evening, and though the welcome was just as friendly as the first time, the youth of the people leaning on the long mahogany bar, or clustered round the juke-box, made him feel his age. The 1990s cover versions of Brennan's favourite sixties soul songs added to the melancholy.

And then, late on the second Friday afternoon, the keys to his new home were finally handed over and he was left all alone in his Tory retreat, surrounded by the furniture he'd bought from Roger Hughes. Brennan was finally ambushed by a surge of joy at the purposeful anonymity this move had granted him. The estate agent knew his name but not his business. A few people at the Swan had gleaned that he'd done the odd bit of journalism without guessing exactly what it was he'd written. The barmaids and staff of various pubs probably had him down as a cheerful loner, just passing through. No neighbours had poked their heads out to say hello yet. He had no phone, and nobody he knew had his address!

Brennan had bought a bottle of champagne at the off-licence, almost without realising that he would have nobody to share it with. As he trudged up to the first-floor sitting-room, and kicked off his shoes, he couldn't resist the urge to celebrate. He eased out the cork with his thumbs and then drank straight from the bottle, in a parody of the victorious Grand Prix driver on the podium. He took in the panoramic view of the town from the window. *His* window, *his* town!

Several hours later when he woke from a stupor to see that night had fallen, he groped for the lights. The first thing he noticed as they came on was that Roger Hughes, management consultant to God knows what piddling little company, had fucked off with the rather nice, fully lined curtains that were supposed to be included in the sale.

The next morning, a driver arrived from London with a small van full of boxes of books, files, magazines and reference material which Brennan had placed into storage before the trial, together with the majority of his clothes. He would have to get through quite a few more lunches and bottles of wine before he began to fill most of his suits again, although they were scarcely needed now. He hung them in the wardrobe, looking at them as though they were skins shed over the years by various versions of the same self. The baggy Hugo Boss number had been a big mistake – even in 1988.

The boxes of files proved more problematical. They were, strictly speaking, irrelevant to the undefined future towards which Brennan was groping. Yet each one contained many thousands of hours' work – reading, note-taking, transcribed interviews – on cases he'd taken up for the paper. It was too soon to burn them. More pertinently, as he casually sifted through the most recent collection, he became aware that not all was as it should have been.

A file of letters – correspondence between himself, a civil rights lawyer and a Home Office sub-division about a certain detention centre – was no longer in date order. Brennan was an untidy man around a house or garden, but his office, books and files were usually immaculately kept. Brennan checked the security tape which had sealed the box. He found where it had been razor-cut on one side, just under the lid of the box, then carefully repaired with a replacement section of tape to cover the cut. He desperately tried to recall if Mark Fraser-Williams's name had appeared – albeit innocently – in any of the other correspondence he'd kept, but couldn't summon a precise memory. Assuming the Big Lads had been through every box, they'd have found it if it was there, although processing and checking all the names would take many 'person-hours'. But to judge from the night at the theatre, Mark clearly hadn't been implicated so far.

Brennan stored the boxes of files in what would be his workroom on the top floor, with the single window looking out across the town and the Avon valley floor beyond. As he climbed and descended the stairs ferrying the boxes, the realisation that perhaps a dozen or so goons would have been laboriously sifting through these boxes while he was in gaol made working on a pig farm a happy memory.

More seriously, the realisation that his former line of work had provoked such deranged levels of scrutiny frightened him somewhat. At times, he'd found some of the precautions he'd taken equally deranged – using dead-letter boxes for notes to Mark Fraser-Williams; calling contacts on an ever-changing number of outside phones; never trusting messengers or dispatch riders to deliver something for him – but now they all seemed justified.

It was possible that soon word would get through to the Big Lads' committee – if indeed that was their structure – that Brennan was no longer a threat, no longer a player. If they persisted beyond that, there could only be malice and revenge in mind. If that proved the case he would need more than retreat as a strategy.

'Coo-eee!' Brennan heard this wafting up from below. Then again. 'Coo-eee!' A female voice. Definitely not Janet's – she'd promised a pre-arranged visit once he was settled – but posher, more confident.

Brennan edged down the narrow stairs. As he reached the first-floor landing he could see that the flap of the letter-box was up. 'Hell-low-oh!' said the voice, trying a more formal approach. Brennan bent to look through the letter-box – a pair of big blue eyes, framed by gold-winged spectacles, stared back at him.

'Oh, hello! Sorry to disturb. But your bell's not working.'

Brennan opened the door and was able to put the rest of the body to the eyes and the voice – a late middle-aged woman in a floral top and light blue skirt and sandals stood as close to the door as possible. She beamed, sending out fault-lines across the heavily foundationed cheeks.

'Mr Brennan?'

'Yes,' he said, as pleasantly as caution would allow.

'I'm Moira Backhouse. Number fifty-two, that way—' She pointed along the line of cottages.

Brennan offered a hand. She took it with a slight flutter of deference.

'I just wanted to welcome you to Tory!' she trilled.

'That's very kind of you,' Brennan said, trying to hide the dying fall in his voice – he had been neighbour free for less than twelve hours.

'If there's any help you need, or anything you want to know, do drop by for a cuppa!'

'Thank you.'

'Oh, and one more thing – I know this is a bit early perhaps, but I'm Chair of the town's Arts Festival Committee. If you'd consider giving a talk about your work during the festival, we'd be absolutely thrilled!'

'My work?' Brennan queried with a frown, trying to imagine how a copy of his old paper might ever have passed through her hands.

'Yes, you know – campaigning journalist. And now a writer to boot, I understand . . . we'd all love to hear about it.'

Mrs Backhouse – Brennan had logged the cluster of gold and sapphire rings on her left hand – bared her dazzlingly white teeth in another smile of triumphant capture.

The equivalent of the Thames Flood Barrier began to rise in Brennan's mind as the alarm bells sounded. He thought he'd been barely noticed in the town. Now he began to realise that the slightest of remarks – to the estate agent, to the outgoing owner, to the barmaid, to the man selling newspapers in the town-centre shop – had been pieced together as ruthlessly as any collation undertaken by the intelligence agencies.

'Perhaps I could let you know next week. I've only just moved in, you see.'

'Yes, I know. I saw the man with the boxes this morning!' Moira said, plainly relishing her own powers of observation.

'I'll drop by,' Brennan said with as much of a smile as he could muster, closing the door. He leant against it. 'I'd have been better off moving next door to Stella Rimington,' he muttered to himself.

CHAPTER FOUR

The first week of Brennan's new life in Bradford-on-Avon was dogged by interruptions which made Moira Backhouse look discreet. On the Monday, he was greeted by the sight on his doorstep of a lady of a certain age – she looked like a forty-year-old, but dressed like a teenager in a tight red leather skirt, black stockings and a tight, canary-yellow top.

'I hear you just moved in, so you'll be wanting a cleaner, won't you? I'm very good. Got effrences an' all that. Two mornings a week, four pounds 'n hour do you?' This was all said in a single breath, accompanied by a step inside the door.

'Er, hang on, love, I haven't got—'

'S'all right, I'll bring my own vacuum cleaner next week.'

'What I meant was . . . I don't think I need a cleaner. I can do it myself.'

At this the woman promptly burst into tears and lay her head on Brennan's shoulder. Aware that neighbours would almost certainly be watching, he levered her into the hall and closed the door.

'Look, would you like a cup of tea?'

The woman's eyes were smeared by moistened mascara.

'You're ever so kind. I'll do you proud, honest. Be able to eat your meals off floors affa I've done 'em!'

'What's your name?'

'Sandra.'

'I'm Frank. You took me a bit by surprise.'

'If there's any work going, I'm always first in the queue, me. Bloke in the Mason's mentioned you moving in last night so I thought I'd pop up soon as I could.'

'The Mason's?' Frank asked with a frown.

'Mason's Arms – down below here, on Newtown!'

The torrent of words had bludgeoned Brennan into the dumbest of images. He laughed at the picture he'd created – Sandra in her red leather skirt, kneeling down before the Grand Master of the Lodge to get a tip-off about a job.

'You laughing at me?' Sandra asked sharply.

'No, no! It was just something that came into my head!'

Brennan made a pot of tea while Sandra attempted a comically professional assessment of the house's cleaning requirements, before sitting down and offering him a cigarette.

'Thanks, but I'm cigars only, I'm afraid . . .'

'You don't mind if I do smoke then?'

Brennan shook his head. He looked her over again. She was well past forty, probably nearer fifty, which made the outfit more bizarre, especially married to a broad Wiltshire accent.

'Mondays and Fridays be all right?'

Brennan did the sums in his head. Four hours a week – sixteen quid. What the hell?

'Yeah, fine. Okay.'

'Want me to do some now?' Sandra asked, exhaling smoke at the teacup.

'No. Friday will be fine. Besides, you're not exactly dressed for it . . .'

This was a mistake. Sandra smiled like a dog that had just been given a pat on the head.

'I call he my interview suit. Never fails!'

A further ten minutes of fairly mindless bunny followed before Sandra made a move to leave. And then, in a manoeuvre that wouldn't have been out of place in an amateur dramatics production of *Entertaining Mrs Sloane*, she fluttered a folded sheet of paper out of her handbag and bent over, tits straining to escape from the canary cage.

'Mustn't lose him! I'll have to do something today or there'll be no job and probably no Sandra!'

She brandished the letter at Brennan. It was a summons bearing the crest of West Wiltshire Magistrates' Court. The gist of it was a claim by a credit company on non-payments for a microwave oven.

'Thirty-four pounds, I gotta find. That's nearly two weeks' wages!' Sandra widened her eyes at Brennan, making sure he got the point. She may have had the brain of a domestic pet, but this meant that Sandra was at least blessed with its survivalist cunning.

By now Brennan would have gladly paid thirty-four pounds just to get Sandra out of the house.

'Leave it with me,' he said.

'Ah,' Sandra mewed. 'You're awful kind. I'll be a good worker for you, Frank, promise . . .'

With that, Sandra scuttled off on her high heels down the slope of Tory towards the town centre, leaning backwards like a shod horse trying to get a grip on a metalled road.

The blitzkrieg of opportunism didn't end there for Brennan. The following day he had a prospective gardener call round *and* a window-cleaner, ready for action with a full bucket of water and a ladder on his shoulder. Toughened by the experience of Sandra, he was better equipped to repel their advances with non-committal platitudes. The garden, for example, was a walled patch just across the path in front of his house, and couldn't have been more than ten feet by eight – even Brennan could look after that. He asked the window-cleaner to come back in a month.

Added to these understandable intrusions – there was barely any regular employment within the town now, so *any* new source of money would provoke a minor feeding frenzy – were the early misapprehensions to which Brennan was also susceptible. Shop assistants gave out effusive good mornings and he found himself wondering what they were after, or suspecting that they were taking the piss out of him. Neighbours dropped round to introduce themselves or invite him over for a drink, and he automatically felt the shutters inside him closing up at what he sensed was their undisguised inquisitiveness.

But gradually, through daily contact, Brennan began to understand the rhythms and structures which underpinned the town's life. What his cynical metropolitan antennae had interpreted as prurience was nothing more than old-fashioned concern for another member of a community.

And the eagerness to know him, to speak to him, to welcome him, sprang not from curiosity – few of the people reacted at all to his name, or seemed to know what he'd done in the past – but from the sort of open-door courtesy he'd once found on a tour of small towns in Midwest America. Like there, it seemed that Bradford was a community which trusted strangers before it judged them.

All of which was fine but for the fact that Brennan had yet to trust the stranger within himself, this born-again creature who'd dragged him off to the country to discover a new life. Brennan had gone through the motions of setting up his study in the third-floor front bedroom, positioning a desk underneath the window and organising the files and books on shelving units around the three remaining walls. He'd bought a stack of A4 yellow pads on which, in the past, he'd done most of his work in longhand before passing it on to a copy-taker in the paper's office – they had tried over and over again to get Brennan to use the paper's direct-input computer system, but he'd never trusted its privacy, nor grasped the scope of its technology.

So here he sat, scribbling lists on the lined yellow paper which seemed to glow as the morning sun moved into position on the left of the window frame. Brennan listed his money-making ideas – a book of memoirs, a collection of the most celebrated cases he'd worked on for the paper, a novel? None of these prospects excited him. He wasn't important enough to produce an autobiography, and there were several periods, erased by drink and unhappiness, which he couldn't possibly recall. A case-book was probably more marketable, but would be a major chore. Besides, the results of his best investigations were already history, the wrongs had been righted – he'd need a new live issue to make that sort of book work.

And then there was the novel – he shrank even from using the word on his list, such was his self-consciousness about this elevated form of expression. Glimmers of ideas swam into the furthest corners of his mind but took fright as soon as he tried to reel them in. Apart from the self-consciousness, he knew he had another reason for such immobility. He'd witnessed too many real-life horrors and misery to ever escape their grip in fiction. He knew he'd be borrowing real faces, real pain, and couldn't escape the thought that this would be not far short of looting the dead. So Brennan decided to give himself a month, to see whether the darkness would recede enough to free him from his past.

He spent hours just browsing around in the second-hand 'barn' at the back of the neat little bookshop in The Shambles, the Dickensian-looking stone-flagged passage which lay at the heart of Bradford. Here in the silence, with great galaxies of dust particles circling slowly in the shafts of afternoon sunlight, Brennan drew both comfort and despair from the shelves stacked with fading, abandoned, half-read, never-read books.

He felt a kind of kinship with the authors who must have laboured for so long in solitude to so little apparent purpose. Had each of them hoped to become rich and famous? Had they been gratified just to see their names on the spine of a book? Had they been pressed by debt into drudgery, or flattered into vainglorious display? Brennan could almost sense the varied emotions still sending out mute signals as they lay trapped within their board and paper tombs. Would his own be laid to rest in similar fashion?

'Sorry. But you're Frank Brennan, aren't you?' asked the man sitting behind the till in the main bookshop as Brennan handed over his purchases – a collection of H. L. Mencken's letters, and a three-year-old pub guide to the West Country. After the silence and solitude of the barn, Brennan's lips could barely form a word.

'Er . . . yeah . . . yes. Right.'

'I used to like your stuff. Sorry to read you're giving it up.'

'Well, everything has its time, I suppose. Managed to outlast Thatcher at least.'

The bookseller carefully wrapped Brennan's five pounds' worth of sales as though they'd just been knocked down at an expensive Sotheby's antiques auction.

'I like the book barn,' Brennan offered as tribute.

'Well, it serves a purpose, I suppose. People always seem to find something of interest in there. It's quite a bookish town, you know.'

Brennan smiled, feeling a little easier about his own fragile ideas.

'I hear you'll be speaking at the festival?' the bookseller said, without a hint of doubt.

'*You* tell me!'

'Moira Backhouse always gets her man!'

'Thanks,' Brennan said as he took his parcel and headed for the door. 'I'll be back.'

Brennan closed the door but paused to look at the collection of postcards and notices in the window. There were various items for sale – violin, computer, mountain bike – and adverts for language and piano tuition, and a card which looked like the unmistakable handiwork of Sandra. 'Cleaner for Hire, Top Worker, Good Rates', it read, before inviting prospective employers to ring a phone box number between '8.55 a.m. and 9 a.m. only'. Brennan could picture her hanging around outside the phone box on Newtown each morning, waiting for it to ring, before going off to one of her 'customers', as she insisted on calling them. Sandra wouldn't know it, but she was a prime example of Europe's deregulated labour market in action.

Down in the bottom corner of the window however was evidence of the more ethereal job forms which the late twentieth century was throwing up. Reflexology – foot massage; tarot readings; psychotherapy (registered); hypnotherapy; and lastly, on a card bordered by hand-drawn figures of spouting whales, was 'the opportunity to get in touch with your body through aromatherapy with Alice'.

Brennan, conditioned to making calls in London phone boxes which were an Aladdin's cave of sex-service ads, made a discreet note of the number. He pushed the door to the bookshop open again. The bookseller looked up at him.

'Find anything interesting?'

'This aromatherapy – straight up, is it?'

'How do you mean?'

'Well, I'm presuming it's, well, you know, not a euphemism for anything a bit weird. But is it quack stuff?'

'No, no – not at all. She's fully trained, diploma and all that. It's fantastically relaxing. Do try it!'

'You've had a go yourself, then?'

'Oh, yes – I have a session every weekend. Alice is my wife, see.'

Brennan tried not to look too embarrassed.

'Sorry – I didn't mean to . . .'

The bookseller smiled. 'I'll tell her to expect your call . . .'

Mrs Aldridge had returned to work at Chestnut Grange expecting to be called into Mr Furnival's office for a chat about the Denton affair. She'd seen Bob, the maintenance man the home always used, come round after the bodies were removed, presumably to check for faults. But there'd been no sign of police or anything. Dr Simmons, the GP whose area covered Chestnut Grange, had been seen briefly on the fateful morning, but that was about it. The rest of the staff had shared a few thoughts in the tea-room and concluded that somebody was bound to get a telling off somewhere along the line. But nothing had been said so far. Life, and death, went on at the home as though nothing untoward had happened.

The residents certainly didn't seem to care too much. With the exception of Mr Green, who had asked several times about Mr and Mrs Denton's joint demise. He would often badger Mrs Aldridge when she came round the lounge with the trolley of morning coffee and biscuits.

'Any more news?' he'd ask, always leaning forward in his chair.

'I don't know what you expect, Mr Green. I hope you ain't thinking you'll be getting something in their will!' She'd have to shout this so that Mr Green, who was deaf in one ear, could hear above the noise of the television.

'They'll be here soon!' Mr Green said, raising a finger for emphasis.

'Who will? Didn't have any relatives, you know?'

Mr Green would exhale sharply in annoyance at this.

'To interview me!' His thin, quivering forefinger pointed up to the television screen.

Mrs Aldridge couldn't help but giggle. He was in a world of his own at the best of times was Mr Green, but imagining that 'Anne and Nick' or

'Richard and Judy' were on their way down to West Bay in Dorset to talk to him quite took the biscuit.

'Right, if you'd like to take your clothes off down to your shorts, now please,' Alice said as she put the finishing touches to her questionnaire.

Across the cool, white-painted room, Brennan began to unbutton his shirt with as much calm as he could muster. Alice was checking her notes, showing no interest in his progress to near nudity.

'What mood would you say you were in now?' she asked, an intense frown knitting her eyebrows together.

'Well, a bit uneasy to be honest. Not every day you get undressed in front of a complete stranger.'

Alice smiled. She was about forty, with short fair hair, and dressed in white top and slacks that hinted at a surgical uniform.

'I meant your mood cosmically – are you optimistic? Pessimistic? Worried? Stressed? Anxious? Happy?'

'Er, confused would be the best word, I think,' Brennan said, exposing the white ball of flesh which passed as his stomach. Alice didn't flinch.

'I'm between jobs, as it were – only I don't know what the new one is.'

'What do you want it to be?' Alice asked, with a tone that said 'life is simple'. Brennan took off his trousers and folded them over the armchair near him. He caught a glimpse of himself in the mirror of the dressing-table where Alice's bottles of oils were neatly stacked.

'Obviously not something that depends too much on my body,' he offered with a shy smile.

'The life of the mind, eh? Get on the table – face down.'

Brennan clambered on to the padded table, which had an oval-shaped hole at its head to accommodate his face. On the floor below, Alice had placed a photograph of an African elephant emerging from the bush. The uncertainty Brennan felt about lying down in front of a strange woman wearing only his underpants now doubled. He lifted his head from the oval.

'What's that for?'

'It's an image for you to focus on. To give you strength.'

Brennan nodded blankly. Alice was pouring assorted amounts of oils into a mortar and mixing them up. The smells began to fill the room.

'Smells like a vinaigrette,' he said, placing his face back in the hole and staring at the elephant.

'Not far out,' Alice said, walking across and placing the mortar on a side table. She stood at the base of the massage table. She reached out and

pressed the play button on a portable cassette-recorder and slowly sounds
– not music – but sounds, like that of a breeze and a river flowing, and
now bird-song, began to cohere into a pattern. Brennan was on the verge
of doing a runner. New Age stuff had always galvanised deep-rooted
suspicions in him. The sounds swelled so that he could almost have been
in a forest. The charging elephant remained frozen below. And then
suddenly he felt the warm puddle of oil caress the gap between his
shoulders and Alice's hands smoothing it out so deftly and quickly that it
felt like she had more than two of them at work.

The hypnotic effect of the oils seeping into his skin was remarkably
sudden. A sensation of ease came over him. Alice's hands smoothed out
his shoulder-blades as though they were ruffles in an unmade bed, pushing
them gently down and away from the spine. He could feel great knots of
tension, trapped like bubbles, rise to the surface and evaporate. After ten
minutes, with the oils, Alice's hands, the music and the image of the
elephant, Brennan was in a divine stupor. As she picked her way down
his spine, pressing her thumb on to each vertebra, shoals of long-locked
soreness and pain were released. By the time she'd kneaded his leg and
calf muscles, he was very nearly asleep.

Alice spoke only if Brennan spoke to her. For the rest of the time her
concentration couldn't have been more intense and intimate if she'd been
a heart surgeon. Only when she tried great circular sweeps of her hands
on his solar plexus, did he flinch from her touch.

'Sorry. Bit tense, there . . .' he said in apology.

'It's your chakra. The centre of your being. You're protecting it. Breathe
out as I press down.'

Alice lay her right palm on his stomach and slowly pushed down, while
Frank exhaled. He drew in air deeply, feeling her hand rise again on his
stomach before pushing down again. The tension, the knots, the defensive
reflex began to ease away as a swirl of nerve-endings tingled in his belly.

Half an hour later, Alice finished with a delicate fingertip massage of
his face, forehead and neck. She sealed him in warm towels like a Pharaoh
and whispered for him to relax. The music began to fade. Brennan's eyelids
drooped and he fell into a profound sleep.

When he woke, he thought he must have been out for hours. Alice told
him he'd slept for just ten minutes.

'Feel any better?' she asked.

'I feel incredible. As though every bit of my body's had a holiday.'

'I used a mixture of oils to put you in a more positive frame of mind –
basil, bergamot, elderflower.'

'I bet I get followed home now,' he said, cheaply, regretting the remark in an instant. But Alice laughed.

Brennan dressed, had a cup of fruit tea with Alice in the book-lined lounge downstairs.

'Have you always done this?' he asked as he wrote out the cheque in payment.

'No. Robert and I—'

'The bookseller?'

'Yes . . . we left London about six years ago. Gave up our jobs in advertising . . .'

'Must have been you who started the great media retreat, then!'

Alice didn't smile at the quip.

'Our daughter was knocked down and killed by a stolen car.'

'Jesus, I'm sorry.'

'We had no taste for life after that. Not life in the city anyhow. But we've been able to rebuild a bit now. The issues seem much clearer once you get out – health, happiness, sharing the earth, caring for others. Sounds soppy to you, I suppose?'

'No. Sounds just right,' Brennan said quietly.

'The trick is to deal with the unhappiness rather than let it fester . . . letting the light in on darkness.'

Alice looked at him directly. She'd sensed his own pain deep in those walled-up areas of his stomach. Brennan drained his cup and rose.

'When I get settled, would you and Robert come over for dinner perhaps?'

'That'd be nice, yes.'

Brennan sauntered back up the hill to Tory, feeling as light as a bird. He was filled not only with the sense of well-being which the aromatherapy had given him, but also with the fact that he'd been prepared to lay aside some of his old, encrusted prejudices and try something new. This gave him heart for the immediate challenge of writing for a living without the support of a newspaper. Maybe the novel wasn't such a daunting prospect after all.

'Coo-eee!'

It was Moira Backhouse, springing the ambush from her doorway.

'I hope this isn't presumptuous, Mr Brennan . . .'

Brennan smiled – he knew that it would be.

'. . . but I've booked you for Thursday the 8th, at seven-thirty in the Priory Barn. The Festival Committee will be very grateful!'

'I'm sure that will be fine,' Brennan said, without a trace of irony.

Moira disappeared into her doorway again, raising her voice to compensate for her temporary disappearance.

'Oh, and I've got your envelope here! I saw the dispatch man and knew you were out, so I told him I'd take it for you!'

Moira reappeared with a plastic courier wallet inside which was sealed an A4 envelope.

'There!' she said, handing it over ceremonially.

'Thank you, Mrs Backhouse . . .'

'*Moira*, please!'

'Thank you, Moira.'

Brennan moved away towards his house, feeling the weight of the envelope. He could see that the sender's name was Stuart Gill, so it was a fair guess that these were the readers' letters that had arrived since the news of his departure from the paper.

Brennan stepped into his kitchen and filled the kettle. He stripped away the plastic wallet which sealed the envelope, and then opened that in turn. Inside were four letters bound by an elastic band, with a printed compliments slip from Gill attached. No message was written upon it.

The envelopes were effectively the last rites of his career. Just four letters of commiseration – he presumed that's what they were – out of a readership of over two and a half million people. Brennan looked at the envelopes – all addressed by hand. His readers didn't have access to portable computers and laser printers, let alone typewriters. The uplifting effect of the massage ebbed away quickly. Brennan piled the envelopes into the china letter-rack that Roger Hughes had included in the sale – he simply couldn't face opening them yet.

'What do you think is the role of the investigative journalist in the 1990s?'

The questioner, a middle-aged lecturer type in jeans and cotton jacket, sat down and looked at Brennan expectantly.

Brennan smiled vacantly while he tried to pull his thoughts together. There were about twenty people in the room – a beamed hall with leaded windows and ancient stone walls – which made it look a desultory, one-third full. Brennan could see the faces peering up at him as he stood behind the table, his scraps of notes in front of him. Moira Backhouse sat at his side, sympathetically pouring a glass of water in case he needed additional time to think.

'Well, as I hinted in my speech – I feel that the time of the investigative reporter is almost certainly over. I mean, mine certainly is!'

This drew a brief ripple of laughter.

'Perhaps I should qualify that – the *newspaper* version has very nearly had his, or her, day. The thousands of us who were inspired or excited, for better or worse, by the Watergate investigation, and its stupendous consequences, are all middle-aged and toothless now. The job belongs to younger people – and they're more likely to see television, or probably the law, as the most promising vehicle for that sort of enterprise. Newspapers are the publicity arms of corporate individuals now – that's not happened by accident, obviously. It's a calculated move, in order both to exert power and to neutralise criticism. The same will happen, is happening *already*, with television. So the first role for the investigative journalist is simply one of survival . . .'

Brennan saw a few appreciative nods and took the opportunity to sip from the glass of water.

'Beyond that – well. I feel as though various alliances will have to be struck up, between lawyers, journalists, specialist campaigners, elected officials, because no one group or individual has the power, or indeed the credibility any more. You are looking at a dying species . . . *drying* certainly!'

Brennan took another drink and glanced at his notes.

'But although I believe that people like me are becoming obsolete, there is, perversely, a greater need now than ever before. We probably have less say in how our lives are run now than at any time since the 1832 Reform Act!'

A young man near the front, half-raised his hand in a reflex act of permission seeking, but spoke out before either Brennan or Moira could react.

'I think that's just ridiculous. The market has liberated millions of people in this country in the way that no socialist project could ever have done!'

There was an immediate chorus of 'hear, hears' on top of this from roughly half the audience. Brennan felt himself flushing – not with embarrassment, more like confusion. He'd encountered this on two occasions before – once on a late-night arts show, once on an edition of (Robin Day's) *Question Time* – but it still left him disabled and impotent for several moments, because he knew its source was genuine.

He was afraid to admit it, but he had known in his heart that metropolitan life – especially as led by North London journalists – had arrived at such an overwhelmingly 'soft-left' consensus that it was rare to encounter any dissenting voices at all. Brennan and his friends could all agree – as they munched on their grilled aubergines with pesto sauce – that something *had* to be done: about the under-class; about the corruption of democracy;

about the need to abolish the monarchy. And their views were rarely challenged, because they mostly never moved outside the consensus circles to hear what those they sought to help really wanted. While the wealthy and the powerful actively *conspired* to stifle opposition voices, the left were equally culpable via this conspiracy of neglect.

'You may have a point as far as a small majority of the population goes,' Brennan conceded, as he rediscovered the switch to autopilot, 'but there is a large minority who wouldn't agree. And I think it's the role – to answer this gentleman's original question – of the investigative journalist, whether in papers, TV, radio or books, to serve that minority, by whatever means possible.'

This brought a counter-attack of applause from the other half of the audience, which included Robert the bookseller and Alice, who both cheered him loudly. Moira Backhouse, sensing an appropriate climax, stood up and held a hand aloft for silence.

'We're running out of time, ladies and gentlemen, but I did want to leave space to thank Mr Brennan for coming and talking to us tonight. Some of you may disagree with what he said, but I'm sure we've had a most stimulating evening, in the tradition of the town festival! Thank you, Mr Brennan.'

Brennan bowed modestly as the audience applauded with various degrees of enthusiasm. He could feel his face burning with the heat of sustained public exposure. He was just dying for a pint and a cigar to calm himself.

Some of the audience wanted private chats – what did he think of *their* views? – before freeing him a good thirty minutes after the session had finished. Robert and Alice pulled him away and walked him down from Priory Barn into Market Street, and then to the Dandy Lion, where he thought about an attempt on the local record for consuming bottles of Becks, but settled for a modest two instead.

One incoherent hour later, after declining an invitation for coffee and brandy back at Robert and Alice's – the last thing he needed was people *agreeing* with him – Brennan made laboured progress back past the gift and clothes shops on Market Street, turned left past the now darkened Priory Barn, and began his ascent up Conigre Hill to Tory. Opposite the Middle Rank car-park, a cluster of teenagers sat on a bench sharing a couple of cans of Special Brew and what smelt like a joint. They sniggered at Brennan as he heaved breathlessly past them.

The light of the lamp-post at the entrance to Tory flickered as Brennan paused to regain his breath. Down below, the lights of the town formed twinkling geometric lines like those of a cruise liner on a night sea. The mid-May air had acquired a distinct element of warmth and on the breeze he could detect the scent of various flowers to which he could put a picture but no name.

Brennan smiled with relief – one ordeal was over at any rate, and he began to make his way along the terrace's path, making sure he didn't stumble into anyone's empty milk bottles or, worse, their geranium pots.

At the door to his cottage, he found one of the hollow terracotta dogs he'd inherited from Roger Hughes, with its display of gentian violets, lying on its side. The soil and the plants spilled forward on to the path. Brennan lifted it, and replaced the plants, as best he could. Such vandalism would normally make the front page of the local edition of the *Wiltshire Times*, so it was best to let this particular dog go back to sleep.

Brennan fumbled for the light switch inside the front door. In the instant of illumination he could see that virtually every item in the kitchen cupboards had been emptied out on to the floor. Crockery and cutlery littered the room like chip papers after a football match. Brennan's head began to thump. He sprinted up the narrow stairs, slipping several times. The lounge had received similar treatment – cushions tossed everywhere, linings of chairs slashed. Upstairs, he could barely get into his office, such was the chaos of paper and files.

Brennan retreated to the kitchen, sat on the table and began to cry. He knew in his guts who'd done this – the Big Lads. The bastards wouldn't leave him alone, wouldn't let him get away with his little victory. The only consolation to be had among the debris, was that the fuckers would have had a completely fruitless search for Mark Fraser-Williams's name. Brennan's tears stopped instantly at this thought, and as he wiped his nose with the back of his hand, he could feel a smile breaking in retaliation.

He moved round the kitchen collecting up any intact plates or cups, and placing them on the table. He caught sight of the china letter-rack – they'd even opened the four envelopes! What perfectionists! Brennan gathered the sheets of paper and torn envelopes. He could see that one letter – in the same handwriting and ink as previously used by the correspondent anticipating his prison buggery – was spectacularly abusive. He crumpled it and tossed it towards the pedal bin.

The second contained a £5 book token as a mark of respect from a former member of the Spanish Republican volunteers. The third featured a well-meant but terrible poem in the form of a eulogy – 'Who will protect us now/Who will slay the sacred cow?' – which Brennan left to one side for framing and an after-life on the toilet wall.

The final letter was on a single sheet of headed notepaper bearing the address of 'Chestnut Grange Retirement Home, West Bay, Dorset'. A thin, spidery, handwritten scrawl in black biro read: 'Mr and Mrs Denton – BOTH DEAD! How, Mr Brennan? HOW?' The 'HOW' was double-underlined, but the note was unsigned.

CHAPTER FIVE

'It's a bit on the small side, isn't it?' After a good five minutes of silent assessment, this was Janet's best effort at an encouraging reaction to Brennan's choice of home.

'I want a divorce – now,' he said, deadpan. 'You've never liked *anything* I chose on my own initiative!'

'That's because your taste is crap, Frank. I think people your shape must have trouble with visual projection, or something. You could never buy a suit to fit you. Your shirts never matched your ties. When you bought a car it was always a funny shape—'

'Alfa Romeos, a funny shape!'

'What you see and the real world are two different things, I'm sure. Now this is a great help when it comes to nosing your way round on a story, but it buggers up how you dress and where you live!'

'Go upstairs and have a look out of that window again! If there's a finer view this side of Rome, I defy you to find it!'

'You'll soon get bored with the view, Frank. It's the space that counts . . . and this place hasn't got any!'

Brennan wondered about telling Janet how little space there'd been the previous week after the 'visit' which had left all his belongings spread over three floors of the house. Sandra, to give her credit, had come in to do a few extra hours, and though he'd had to suffer her almost incessant ramblings, it had halved the time taken to restore the house to order.

'Must be very difficult to keep tidy,' Janet said, unerringly finding the exposed nerve.

'Stories I could tell you!' Brennan responded sullenly.

'What?'

'You wouldn't be interested.'

'Don't piss around playing games, Frank. What?'

Brennan walked Janet down to the Dandy Lion, taking the more scenic of the two routes, hoping the beauty would have some effect on Janet's hostile attitude. Some chance – the wild flowers growing from the stone walls of the walkway down to Newtown passed unnoticed, as did the gushing well in between Barton Orchard's rows of slate-roofed cottages, all hung with dreadlock-heavy flower baskets. The fifteenth-century Chantry House aroused no comment, nor did the row of old cottages which ran in a line to the town's oldest monument, a Saxon church, built in great golden-brown blocks of the local stone. The woman must have been hewn from the same quarry.

'Did the bastards take anything?' Janet asked, as they moved along Church Street, past the now empty and echoing riverside mill.

'Few quid in cash. Few compact discs. Just enough to take the mickey.'

'How do you mean?'

'Well, they have to nick *something* in case I report it as a burglary. So they take the sort of stuff kids would, stuff that'd turn up in a boot sale the next day. The police log it as a minor incident and do nothing about it.'

'So you *have* reported it?'

'Don't be daft! It'd have been a total waste of time! Mine and the police's.'

'But if it's not on file, there's nothing to show that it ever happened. And you'll need all the little things to stack up if you're going to build a case against them!'

Brennan paused at the zebra crossing on Market Street. 'I don't want a case against them. I want the fuckers to leave me alone. I'm out of the game – I don't want to be kicked any more, *that's* what I want them to realise!'

A car horn sounded in irritation. The car had stopped to let them cross only for the driver to see his courtesy ignored. He leant out of the window.

'Want a written invitation, do you?'

Brennan took Janet's arm and scurried across, waving his apologies. They turned into the Dandy Lion, and installed themselves in one of the window seats. Brennan went to the bar and came back moments later with two cups of cappuccino, two pastries and two glasses of Calvados.

'No wonder you're putting weight back on,' Janet said with a triumphant grin.

Brennan bit into his chocolate-filled croissant, catching the crumbs in his spare hand. 'Thing about living here is that people take you as you are. You don't have to posture. You don't have to spray on the old metropolitan varnish every day to make you shiny and hard. I can just be a bloke who likes his grub, his pint and his cigar and doesn't worry about what people think.'

'Because they *aren't* thinking?'

'No – because they couldn't give a toss what you look like or what you do, provided it doesn't disrupt the community!'

'Have you been tripping out on Mark Twain, or what?'

'God, you're a hard woman to please, Janet!'

Janet looked about her airily, feigning confusion. 'Pleasure – what's that?'

'All I'm saying is, I think you'll like it here. Once you get used to it.'

Janet's face gave nothing away. Brennan realised instantly that he shouldn't have phrased the key question so obliquely. Janet liked things out front – simple, direct, such as:

'So what are you going to do for a living, Frank?'

Brennan took a deep draft of the coffee, leaving a moustache of milk foam and cocoa powder on his upper lip.

'Well, I think I'm going to try and write a novel.'

' "Think", "try"? You don't sound too sure?'

'How could I be? But I'm getting there.'

'What's it about?'

'Don't know yet.' He shrugged apologetically. 'Life?'

'And is this masterpiece commissioned?'

'Christ, no! I wouldn't dare approach a publisher yet. I'll write it on spec, then see what happens!'

'Which means no dough coming in for, what, six months?'

'I've got a few bob left in the bank. Plus an overdraft facility from Ed.'

'So if I moved down here, giving up what bits of freelance work I can still get, we'd both be potless! Some future, Frank!'

'I can get other work . . .' he said defensively.

'What, lollipop man on that zebra crossing? That sort of thing?'

'I knew this was a mistake . . .' he muttered, throwing back the Calvados in one.

'Absolutely right! You can take the boy out of the city, but you can't take the city out of the boy! You'd be a fish out of water here, Frank. It's a bloody retirement town!'

'I meant, inviting you down for this weekend. It's too soon. Before I've settled properly. Before I've built up enough happiness and confidence to convince you that it could work for us here! That we deserve to be surrounded by some beauty and tranquillity before it's too late. My mistake. Sorry.'

Brennan's sudden vulnerability – or at least his ability to acknowledge it – had always been a factor in Janet's attraction to him. Most men, certainly most of the male journalists she'd met or worked with, kept the hard shell on all the time. The self-regard was armour-plated. But Brennan, when he was sober and thoughtful, wasn't afraid to let the professional mask drop. The night she'd fallen for him, at the dinner where he received his first national award, still lived with her, particularly his acceptance speech. 'Journalists giving each other prizes is like sex amongst dogs,' he'd said, to table-thumping laughter.

'I don't get what's in this for me, Frank, that's the problem,' Janet said quietly. 'Seems like you just want me around to complete some sort of rural fantasy while you work out what you want to do. But say the idea of a book doesn't come off? You'll find something to do on one of the rags, be out on the piss all the time, and I'll be left in the lurch like before, only I'll be another hundred miles from the escape hatch!'

'Janet, this isn't a fantasy. It's a practical proposition. If I do a case-book, you can be my researcher, just like the old days. And if I get a specific job to do, the same again. But I won't be in London. I won't be in the office. I'll be working from here – *home*.'

'Okay, then, Frank – show me around if that's what you want . . .'

It was possible to 'do' the best bits of the town within an hour at a steady walk – although the sheer variety of the passageways opened up all kinds of alternative routes. Janet gave little hint of appreciation, she just asked practical questions: 'How old must that be? Where did the money come from for all this? What do people do for jobs round here?' She'd thought like a researcher even before she'd become one.

Then Brennan took her for lunch at the Georgian Lodge, which overlooked the bridge and the river, making sure she got the right seat to register the view. The cool, oak-panelled room seemed to impress her more.

'Nice carpets,' she said nodding down. They both had the chicken with a tarragon sauce as their main course – food was one of the few areas where their tastes cohabited. Wine was another – and they effortlessly saw off two bottles of Chablis in the two hours.

'Fancy a walk?' Brennan asked as they left down the Lodge's stone steps.

'I don't think I could face any more hills just yet.'

'No, I meant on the flat, not National Hunt . . .'

Janet grimaced at this reminder of another element in the skeleton of contention between them – horse-racing. Brennan led her out past the station and down into the country park which filled one side of the Avon valley.

'We can go out this way, along the riverbank, have tea at Avoncliff.'

'Where's Avoncliff?' Janet asked suspiciously.

'About two miles along. There's a wonderful old aqueduct, carries the canal across the valley.'

'A *canal*? Here? Bit industrial for the countryside, isn't it?'

'The Kennet and Avon. Carried all kinds, right down from Newbury to Bristol. It's all longboats and pleasure craft now. We can come back on the tow-path.'

Janet took a deep breath then exhaled. 'While I'm here, then.'

Brennan led her out on to the well-trodden path besides the river. After five minutes all signs of the town were left behind as the path led into lushly grassed water-meadows. The river current seemed almost too slow to be detected, except here and there where clumps of rushes broke the flow, creating a permanent bubble of tiny waves. A single sculler swished past heading back to the boathouse by the railway bridge, the early summer sunlight glistening in the sweat on his shoulders.

Brennan and Janet walked in silence. He knew that she knew he'd be watching her for a reaction. And his expectation was neutralised by her caution. They eyed each other obliquely. Janet noticed his head carriage – it had been a long time since Frank had been so upright. The hunch-shouldered, 'just one last pint' scuffle had almost been his trademark. Now his head was up, taking in the sights and the air.

In contrast, Janet's posture was defensive, almost shy. She was on alien territory and there was a lot at stake. Brennan sensed she was ill at ease. Her walk was one of short, quick strides, as though she wanted to get this over with and go home. She was still elegant though – the long legs disappeared up into a plain, creamy cotton skirt. The outline of her bum was still kept trim by her exercise classes which he so despised in essence, but for which he was fulsomely grateful whenever he'd got his hands on her body. Brennan felt a first tingle of lust.

He pulled up to point out the little niches cut into the grass and the riverbank, where the local anglers could take their places in privacy. Janet looked at him curiously – recognising the familiar, first-date signals of the brain being intercepted by an organ whose primary concern was not compelling speech.

'I've seen guys pull out all kinds down here – er, perch. Trout. There's supposed to be a big pike living down this section . . .'

'Frank, do you want a fuck or what?'

Brennan's face broke into a boyish smile. 'What – *here*?'

Janet looked around. The meadows were deserted, and with the first serious heat of summer muffling the valley, there was no sound of anyone or anything around. Janet walked up to him and pulled him into a deep kiss. Her right hand gently cupped his balls.

'What if . . . ?'

'Shut up, Frank.'

Janet undressed him where he stood, tossing his clothes into the long grass to create a makeshift blanket on the ground. Janet shuffled off her skirt, and lifted her blouse over her head without undoing the buttons.

'Lie down,' she whispered. Brennan lay on his back among the tangle of grass and clothes as Janet stood over him, stretching her arms back to unhook her bra. Brennan reached up and peeled off the last of her underwear, before they fell into a sweet tangle of limbs. Then wordlessly, noiselessly, Janet mounted him, her eyes closed in rapture, and worked slowly but lovingly to bring them to an intensely hushed mutual climax.

They lay clinging to one another for about ten minutes, staring up at the cloudless blue sky, silently guessing at each other's thoughts. Then Janet slid into the river and stroked her way out of sight before returning, shivering to the bank.

Brennan looked at her with a wry smile as he helped her up out of the water and held her close to warm her.

'You could have had a stroke swimming after a meal!'

'It's so beautiful here,' she whispered as her head rested on his shoulder, cascading it with droplets of cold water from her hair. 'I feel as though I'm setting off on a long journey to somewhere I don't know, with someone I used to . . .'

'It only has to be one day at a time,' Frank said, stroking the nape of her neck. 'Nothing's for ever.'

They clung to one another, like new-born twins, sure only of each other's touch, as an afternoon breeze cut through the grass and rushes.

'What's this?' Janet asked, holding up one of Frank's most recent letters. She was sitting at the dining-table in his towelling dressing-gown, drinking coffee from a handless mug, courtesy of the intruders.

Brennan padded across from the grill where four rashers of rindless Wiltshire back were spitting a morning chorus. He looked over her shoulder, recognising the scratchy lines and deranged emphases.

'S'one of the letters Stuart Gill forwarded.'

'What's it about?'

Brennan shrugged as he returned to the grill to turn the bacon over. 'Old people's home. A death. Real or imagined, I suppose.'

'*Two* deaths. Mr and Mrs.' Janet looked down at the letter again. 'Denton.'

'It comes with the territory, I'd have thought – death.'

'This is an old person's handwriting . . .'

'Well, yes – I'd worked that out. Not too coherent though, is it? No "Dear Mr Brennan, Forgive me writing to you, but I just thought you'd like to know about the deaths of two of my fellow patients . . ." '

'They're not "patients", Frank. They're guests!'

Janet studied the letter again. 'It's private not state registered. Lot of money in those places. Take on a load of unwanted grannies, sit them in front of the telly all day, drain their pensions and savings dry. Pocket the rest when they die.'

Brennan was laying the bacon on to plates where he'd already assembled fried eggs, slices of fried bread and chunky pieces of black pudding.

'I think that's an unnecessarily bleak view, Janet.'

'It's one of the biggest growth industries in this country. Especially now a lot of the regulations have been legislated away.'

Brennan brought the plates to the table. Janet looked at the fry-up with a curled lip.

'Heart attack on a plate, eh?'

'Do you good, a bit of animal fat . . .'

They began to eat, with Brennan picking up the fried bread and forking some of the egg yolk and black pudding on to the slice. 'Dublin open sandwich,' he said with a grin.

'He must have spotted something desperate to make him write to you. Especially as you haven't been in the paper for nearly a year.'

'Exactly – who writes to a redundant journalist except the mad and the lonely?'

'Is that it then – you're not going to follow it up?'

Brennan spread his hands. 'How? Why?'

'Well, the "how" shouldn't be a problem – The Graun or The Indy would take a piece from you, wouldn't they?'

Brennan shook his head. 'I'm not highbrow enough for them.'

'What about *Today* then? It's vaguely left under Stott.'

'It's also owned by Murdoch – so even if I found Elvis Presley on my doorstep, he'd get nothing off me!'

'You precious twat, Frank! You've got a living to earn!'

'Right – a living. Not prostitution – it only takes one trick to make you a whore!'

'Easy with the misogynist rhetoric, eh?'

'Sorry.'

'I think you should go down to where is it . . . ?' Janet scrambled for the letter again. 'West Bay. Dorset. Not too far, is it?'

'And say what – "I've got this letter, could you explain what it's about, please?" '

'That's a fair start. I mean, it must be a little unusual for a married couple to die at the same time in the same home?'

Brennan looked at her with a smile of victory. 'It doesn't say that – you're slipping!'

'And *you're* being a pedantic git!'

'I'll think about it, okay?'

Brennan drew up the *Racing Post* to forestall further discussion.

'But only if the novel doesn't get off the ground?' Janet probed. Brennan stayed silent behind the paper.

The first thing to put a spoke in Brennan's creative wheel when he sat down at his desk was the view from the window in front of him. The panorama of the town and the Westbury hills in the distance was meant to inspire and soothe. What he hadn't realised until now was that it was almost precisely a reverse angle of the view he had enjoyed from the window of his cell at Erlestoke Prison. Indeed, for the first hour of the first morning on the novel, Brennan tried to work out if he could actually *see* the prison complex, using the White Horse of Westbury as a guide point. He decided that he couldn't quite, but this didn't stop him imagining fellow-inmates going about their daily chores under the punishing stare of the screws. This hour of non-writing also included a fruitless fifteen-minute search for his pair of binoculars, which he eventually realised he'd lent to a former colleague at the last race meeting he'd attended before being sent down.

Brennan made a note on the blank yellow pad which lay next to his electric typewriter which he had yet to switch on, firstly about giving Kevin Briggs a ring to get his bins back, and then about the idea that had struck him. It seemed as though there might be something in the image of a man imprisoned with thoughts of freedom, and a man free but burdened with thoughts of prison. He wasn't sure he could use it yet, but at least it was a start. Well, it would be when he switched the typewriter on.

Brennan swirled the idea round his brain for ten minutes or so and then a cold chill spread across his back. Wasn't all that stuff in *The Man in the Iron Mask*? Or was it *A Tale of Two Cities*? Brennan scratched a diagonal line through the note, put the cap on the pen, pushed back his chair and rose. It was coffee time.

On the walk down to the Dandy Lion, Brennan's thoughts turned to the letter from the nursing home. Maybe he should just pass it on to one of the lads at the old paper, let them take care of it. But then, whoever had written it had specifically sent it to Brennan, expecting him, and him alone, to do something about it. Brennan felt the black dog of obligation, not so much padding behind him, but already rogering his leg.

Brennan installed himself in his usual seat in the window of the bar, with his usual elevenses in front of him – cappuccino, chocolate croissant, Calvados. Janet had gone back to London, expressing no definite commitment to life in the country – well, life in a small town. There was Lester to think about before anything could happen.

It was all very well for adults to make a conscious break from familiar surroundings, they had a sense of self-direction and security. But expecting a twelve-year-old boy to uproot himself from the small area that had nurtured him was asking a good deal, especially when Brennan's relationship with his son seemed to have more than enough distance in it already.

'Hi, Frank!'

Brennan looked up – it was Robert from the bookshop.

'Mind if I join you?'

'No, go ahead.'

Robert installed himself opposite Brennan and sipped at his coffee. Brennan waited for the inevitable question.

'How's the book going?'

'Early days,' Brennan said with a grim smile. 'I'm still at the blank-page stage, I'm afraid. Least I had an idea this morning.'

'Would it help to talk?'

'I'm sorry?'

'You know – tell me the story. I go to quite a few of these Waterstone's readings, and some of the authors say it often helps them if they try and change internal thoughts into external words. Articulation, I suppose it's called.'

'I think anything I say would sound so flimsy at the moment. This cake probably has more substance.'

'Are you emotionally blocked, do you think?'

Brennan tried to smile – what the fuck was this, *The South Bank Show* with Melvyn Bragg? Or in the chair with Anthony Clare?

'There's a friend of ours who's a Jungian analyst. Lives on a longboat on the canal.'

'Sounds like a set-up for a new TV series – "The Floating Therapist"!'

'Just mentioning it in case you needed professional help, that's all.'

'Thanks, but I think I'll need Doris Stokes or someone to get an idea of what this book's about.'

'I hear your wife's been down to stay?'

Brennan felt uneasy – was *nothing* secret in this town? He could suddenly see how all the courtesies and good mornings and daily encounters with familiar faces might become oppressive and wearisome. How every weeping wound could be processed into microscopic gossip among the small circle of artists and therapists within the community.

'She was just getting a feel for the place,' Brennan said in the same non-committal tone that Janet had used as she boarded the train back to London.

Brennan slipped away from the bar without his usual second cup, the prospect of talking when he didn't want to talk proving too irritating to bear. He crossed the bridge and saw that the stalls and vans were laid out in the car-park in front of the library – Thursday was market day.

Brennan studied the display on the plastic 'slabs' of the mobile fish shop. He thought he'd treat himself and buy a Dover sole – a double treat in fact, because he knew that, unless he managed to get pissed out of his skull, he could cook the fish without ruining it.

'Just the one?' the fishmonger confirmed, a little too loudly. Brennan nodded tersely. He could almost imagine the ladies in the queue behind him muttering 'sad bastard'. Brennan trooped round the corner to the bookies – it was the fallow week before Royal Ascot when the crappiest tracks and the lowest grade horses jostle for the public's money. Brennan wouldn't risk more than a pound win 'Lucky 15' on such undistinguished animals, though if his four selections won of course, they'd be right up there with Silver, Trigger, Arkle, Desert Orchid and any other equine hero you'd care to name! When he was single, Brennan used to buy household items with his winnings, and leave a little tag or label on the object, bearing the name of the horse whose efforts had financed its purchase.

Brennan spent the afternoon in his study, tracking the horses' progress on the Radio 5 Live bulletins, in between trying to work. It was a slow death, with the results only being given every hour. The fragile assembly of ideas was kicked down each time like a sand-castle by the news of these distant failures – third, unplaced, second and 'withdrawn, not under starters orders', was the day's roll-call. The non-runner meant he would get £1.10 back, but he couldn't see himself summoning the will to collect it. He screwed up the betting slip and left it on the desk alongside the yellow paper balls containing the day's other little defeats.

Brennan opened a bottle of chilled white Rioja at six, piped an Art Farmer CD down to the kitchen from the lounge and tried to pretend this was the good life. After three glasses he believed himself. He managed to overcook the Dover sole, singeing the tail to a caramelised mush, but enough flesh survived the blaze to merit the title dinner. Brennan retreated to the lounge to watch the darkness fall across the valley. With the windows open, he could hear bursts of laughter and banter and music bubbling up from the town's pubs, and from all those gardens where dinner parties and barbecues were taking place. Even a cigar couldn't lift his mood. The day had come full circle – the prison cell had crossed the valley from Erlestoke and settled here, high up on Tory.

The sleep that might have refreshed Brennan was denied him by the noise from an army exercise on Salisbury Plain. The dull thump of artillery punctuated the night, accompanied by the rush of disturbed air which rattled the windows every so often. Brennan almost longed for the shrieking car alarms, police sirens and booming loudspeakers which he knew would be blighting Janet and Lester's night in Islington. God, how he wished he could be with them.

Brennan was woken from the sour remnants of sleep by a giggling scream from Sandra the cleaner. Probably unwisely, he'd been persuaded to give her a key to the house, although, to be fair, this had proved no problem until now. Brennan slipped on his dressing-gown and went down to the kitchen. Sandra was standing at the door of the small cloakroom, brandishing a bottle of bleach in her hand.

'Mornin', Frank, I think this'll get rid of he!'

'What's the matter, Sandra?'

She giggled again, trying to control herself by putting her blotchy, raw-skinned hand across her mouth.

'I tried two or three times, but he just won't go down!'

'What?'

'In the toilet! Somebody's parked a real gassy floater in it!'

Janet and Lester arrived just after nine that night on the direct train service from Waterloo. Brennan was encouraged to see Janet react with a smile to the view of the town from the station. In contrast, Lester's face registered only the sullen expression of a put-upon youth who plainly wanted to be elsewhere. Brennan led them down towards the town bridge and into the Georgian Lodge where he'd booked a table for three.

The first Bloody Mary had Janet sighing with relief.

'It's so nice to get out of London on a Friday night!'

'Did you enjoy the train, Lester?' Brennan asked.

'Was okay.'

'Did you see that stretch between Salisbury and Warminster – the Wylye Valley, bloody beautiful, isn't it?'

'I fell asleep after Basingstoke.'

Lester stared at the melting ice-cubes in his Diet-Coke. Brennan couldn't get angry with him. He felt his hurt and his dislocation. Boys should be cryogenically frozen between the ages of twelve and fifteen to spare them the agony of adolescence.

'I've booked us tickets for a jazz concert tomorrow night. It's in the gardens of a manor house about three miles down the road. We can take a picnic . . .'

Janet looked at Lester with a smile of encouragement but got nothing in return. Lester picked his way through a tagliatelle carbonara for an hour while Brennan and Janet tried not to show too much enjoyment, a task that became easier as the night went on.

They talked quietly in the kitchen with glasses of Armagnac after Lester had gone to bed, both sensing how much he was hating being here.

'Is it me that's stopping him liking the idea of the move, do you think?' Brennan asked.

'He doesn't want to move, full stop. You don't come into the discussions, I'm afraid.'

Brennan's face looked like the drink had just burst an ulcer for him.

'It's too much to ask of him, Frank. He's settled at school. He's got his friends and his social routines . . .'

'The school here's really good. He'd soon make new friends! He'd be well settled by Christmas!'

'He doesn't like the country, Frank!'

'He doesn't *know* the fucking country yet! His idea of a stroll in the woods is crossing Highbury Fields to the Arsenal ground! This is better for him down here! I know! The air's cleaner. There's less chance of him getting stabbed outside a chip shop, and there's not so many people pushing drugs at the school-gates!'

'Maybe so. But you can't make that decision for him!'

'I'm his dad, Janet! That's what I'm supposed to do in life! If my great-grandfather hadn't decided to come to England for the family's sake, neither

Lester nor I would have existed! You can't stay in one place simply because the prospect of disrupting your kid intimidates you! It's only six years till he's eighteen, for God's sake – it'd be nice to have at least had some proper time as a family!'

Janet glared at him. Brennan could read the subtitles before she could even speak.

'All right – I know it was all my fault for not being around. But this is a chance to make it better. Isn't it? I mean, you do like it here, don't you?'

'I do. But I can't if Lester doesn't. This is your selfish whim, Frank, don't expect us all to share it. What if Lester and I wanted you to come back to Highbury? You wouldn't do it, would you?'

Brennan remained silent, staring into his glass for an answer.

The following day was spent with the rancour suspended by wishful thinking. Brennan, Janet and Lester walked round the town, had lunch, took a boat-trip on the canal, had afternoon tea – all the sort of things that weekenders did to convince themselves the journey out of London was worthwhile.

Back at the house, Janet prepared a decent-sized picnic for the evening's jazz concert and at six they took a taxi down to Iford Manor, which was hidden in a small, but densely lush valley through which the River Frome ran. The manor looked astonishing in the early evening sun, the yellowing Bath stone reflecting and intensifying the natural light. The taxi parked by a small stone bridge decorated with Romanesque statues, a theme which was taken up with charm and precision in the gardens themselves. Among the sloping lawns, where the picnickers grazed from their rugs, were pillared cloisters and walkways.

By eight, when the music started, the air was thick with the scent from the rosemary bushes. Janet walked between Lester and Frank as they took their seats in front of the jazz group. The young players were immaculate, the altoist reminiscent in his lyrical tone of Art Pepper. As their melodies wafted up and across the valley in the warm night air, a team of stewards moved noiselessly around the gardens planting burning torches to light the paths for the interval. In a paddock beyond, a white horse moved slowly towards the house, the light fading on its shiny coat, like a cinema screen going dead.

Even if he hadn't had a drink, Brennan would have been intoxicated by now, but the four or five glasses of New Zealand Sauvignon Blanc meant that the resonant beauty of the music and the gardens threatened to overwhelm him. He put his arms around both Janet and Lester, as if to form a dam against the vortex of emotions swirling inside him. He tried to make the gesture seem carefree – inviting the three of them to sway with the music – and to his surprise, there was a response. Lester gave him a smile as the long-lost feeling of togetherness was recaptured, albeit for just a few hours, on just one night.

After breakfast the following morning, Brennan walked Janet and Lester down to the station for the mid-morning train back to London, where Lester had a friend's birthday party to attend. They passed wholesome families on their way to church, chapel or swimming-pool. Brennan wondered by how much they stood out from these paragons of normality.

At the station, Lester went off for a discreet pee. He hated seeing his mum and dad kissing almost as much as he hated them arguing.

'Let me work on him,' Janet offered as encouragement to Brennan. 'There's the school holidays coming up. Maybe the two of us can stay for a while – make a go of it?'

Brennan smiled humbly. 'I'd like that . . .' He kissed her on the forehead and they held each other.

'Marry me,' he said.

'I am already.'

'Then let's do it all over again!'

Janet let go as Lester reappeared. They heard the whistle of the train as it came down the line from Bath. Time took on a new intensity as both Brennan and Janet searched for words. Brennan pulled Lester to him and ruffled his hair.

'See you soon, yeah?'

Brennan thought he felt a distinct nod in his hands. He opened his arms and held them round Lester's shoulders, while Lester buried his face into Brennan's shirt. The train pulled up and the doors swished open.

'Bye, Dad,' said Lester as he turned to jump on board quickly. Janet took an envelope from her bag and thrust it at Brennan.

'In case you change your mind,' she said, turning to enter the train. Brennan watched Janet and Lester claim their seats, before the train surged away. Only then did he notice that his shirt was wet with Lester's tears.

Brennan opened the envelope on the move – inside was a colour brochure extolling the virtues of Chestnut Grange retirement home, and a photocopy of a Companies House document listing the names of directors owning the company which ran the home. Janet had been busy.

Brennan examined the anonymous letter again later that night, looking for subtexts. If the writer was obsessed with the 'how' of the deaths of Mr and Mrs Denton, maybe he or she already knew enough about the 'why'?

Brennan checked his AA book and local train timetable. He could get from Bradford-on-Avon down to Dorchester West in less than an hour and a half, and it would only be a ten- or twelve-mile taxi ride from there to West Bay. He rolled the blank page out of the typewriter and placed it back in the drawer.

CHAPTER SIX

'Hello, Mr Furnival? My name's Francis Dunlop. My wife contacted you a week or so ago for a brochure regarding Chestnut Grange, and as I find myself on business in the West Country, I wondered if I could pop over to have a look around?'

Brennan listened to the voice at the other end of the line, trying to form a picture of the man – middle-aged? Middle-class certainly. Warm? Maybe. Businesslike?

'Let me just check my diary,' Mr Furnival said.

Pompous git, thought Brennan. He's running an old people's home not a multinational corporation! Brennan pictured the diary pages with their entries for Rotary Club lunches and rounds of golf.

'Would tomorrow afternoon suit you, Mr Dunlop?'

'That would be perfect – say three?'

'Fine. You'll find us on the left, as you take the old road out of Bridport, a couple of hundred yards down from the bypass.'

'Thank you . . . see you tomorrow.'

Brennan put the phone down. He felt a tingle running through him. He had taken the fact that Janet had made her enquiry in her maiden name as a sign of her everlasting diligence, rather than as a pointer to their future. She'd always been an essential part of his team in the early days, knowing instinctively what details he might need before he went 'on the road'. This sense of a working unit being revived, and the undeniable thrill of a call to action, had his mind alert and buzzing even before the morning coffee at the Dandy Lion.

Brennan scoured his most recent copies of *The Good Food Guide* and *Good Pub Guide*, looking for suitable eating and accommodation in the Bridport and West Bay area. In the good old days, he'd always been offered the best by the paper, no questions asked, and he'd taken it, unless the nature of the investigation had required a local haunt. There hadn't been much point, for example, in staying in a five-star hotel on cases such as the murder in Herefordshire, for which a seventeen-year-old boy, with a mental age of eight, had conveniently been fitted up.

In fact, the key element in Brennan's successful attempt to have the conviction quashed had been his regular stays at the pub in the boy's village. Here, he'd been able to get beyond the television news images of vengeful locals – 'van-bangers' was the trade term – who'd daily attacked the prison truck taking the boy to and from court. He'd heard quieter voices, uncovered people too frightened to go against the mob rule, and, crucially, persuaded a local policeman to say what he knew had happened in the frenzy for 'justice' after the murder.

Chestnut Grange would almost certainly require a similar approach, with, initially at any rate, nothing too aggressive or probing. He would watch and listen, and not make himself too busy. Brennan had always found that smaller communities curled up into the tightest balls when they were poked by strangers. He was in luck with the guidebooks – among the listings were an unpretentious seafood restaurant in West Bay itself, and a highly rated pub with rooms, just up the road in Bridport. If he'd wanted to, he couldn't have designed a better case.

Brennan took the first Weymouth train the next morning. Although the schools hadn't broken up yet, there were still a number of families with younger children lugging cases on board. One or two retired couples sat closely together, a shopping bag between their legs with a Thermos flask poking out, sure signs of a day's outing to the seaside.

As the train trundled south, Brennan tried to clear his mind of any preconceptions about what may or may not have happened at Chestnut Grange. It would be too easy to assume a case of maltreatment or neglect, and then be blinded to other possibilities, the most obvious being that one of the inmates – sorry, 'guests' – deluded by a daily cocktail of pacifying drugs, had simply imagined something that hadn't happened at all.

So as the other travellers settled down to solve the crosswords in their 'Puzzler' books, Brennan simply took in the views of the countryside as the two-carriage train scuttled through it. The great patchwork of the English summer landscape began to unfold as he watched – fields of yellow rape; an enclosure of bluebells; several swathes of golden wheat awaiting harvest; and the terracotta scars where the earth had been ploughed up and left to rest. Each section marked a stage of growth and decay, and

Brennan wondered, as he drifted off into sleep, why it was that he should feel such a magnetic pull from the bare, exhausted soil.

'Train will shortly be arriving at Dorchester West,' announced the guard, triggering Brennan awake. The right side of his face was red and swollen where it had lain pressed against the window of the carriage. He had a few moments to gather his thoughts and look around to ensure that he hadn't said or done anything embarrassing in his sleep, but the other passengers were each in their own little worlds. Brennan took his holdall down from the baggage rack and stepped into the Dorset air. The smell of the sea was instant. Brennan heard the station clock clicking remorselessly. It was just after half-past ten. Plenty of time to get over to Bridport and dump his bag at the pub at which he'd booked a room.

The taxi took him along the A35 from which he could occasionally gain a glimpse of the sea to his left. But a stifling heat haze was beginning to rise over the coastal valleys, suggesting imminent storms. Brennan wound down the taxi's window and felt the rush of warm air.

Within half an hour, they were careening down the steepling hill into Bridport, ignoring the bypass which now sucked most of the traffic away from the town, and poodling along the main street, lined with simple, Georgian frontages. The taxi turned left by the clock tower, and pulled in. Across the street was The George Hotel, a handsome double-fronted, greystone pub.

The George opened at ten most mornings for fresh orange juice, coffees and breakfasts, so there was already quite a crowd as Brennan wandered in. Holiday-makers, idling locals, a fisherman, a couple of traveller types formed a kaleidoscopic backdrop to the pub's plain but comforting interior. A big-band jazz tape – Basie? – played through hidden speakers, while in the open-plan kitchen at the far end of the room a young cook with ginger dreadlocks was preparing the day's lunch ingredients, hunched over her chopping-board as if it were a spinning-wheel.

Brennan perched on a stool at the bar and ordered a pint of Palmer's, the local beer. He mentioned his booking – real name – and the barmaid nodded casually, promising a key for his room in a half-hour. Brennan let his shoulders drop and moved across to a window seat where he could stretch his legs. It would have been so easy just to get pissed for the rest of the day, to sit back, listen to the music, have a big lunch, and forget any burdens of obligation.

But he found his stomach knotting with unaccustomed tension at the thought of going to this home, to lie and to invade its fragile privacy. The time off during the trial and the months in prison had softened the protective crust which had enabled him in the past to walk into the most delicate and sensitive situations without a single worry about other people's feelings. He took a long slug of beer to douse the uncertainties.

'Just the one night?' asked the barmaid, dangling the key with her sunbronzed but finely tattooed hand.

'For now,' Brennan said with a smile.

Upstairs, he changed into a more persuasive business outfit, and took great trouble to cleanse the beer from his breath. He looped the striped tie, one of several he'd once bought in a jumble sale, under the shirt collar and began to knot it in front of the heavy Georgian mirror which the room boasted as one of its features. What could he be? Not a travelling salesman, because he had no car. He also lacked the breathless, time-is-money urgency. Serious professions – accountancy, the law – were out too. How about management consultant? Brennan suddenly summoned the image of Roger Hughes, the former occupier of his house, and various strands for his temporary identity began to gel together.

The storm broke just as he was about to leave The George, but fortunately there was a taxi-rank across the road. He dived into the back seat.

'Could you just run me down to Chestnut Grange, on the road into West Bay?'

'Look too young to be goin' there, me old mate!'

'Just preparing the ground!' Brennan said with a smile of interest.

'S'expensive, so they tell me,' said the driver, seeking and catching Brennan's eyes in his mirror.

'Well, nothing but the best for the old folk – that's what I say. Spent enough on us in their lifetime, eh?'

'Not mine, my friend. Buggered off when I was ten!'

'Well, you're spared the cost now then, I suppose?'

The taxi hit the fringes of the town – the brewery shop, the supermarket, the first new roundabout to accommodate the bypass. If the Romans had been *that* clever, Brennan had always thought, they'd have built their towns with bypasses included. The roadside landscape was changing now as the sea approached – large, post-war detached houses, some private, some hotels or bed-and-breakfast joints. On a ridge to the right, the first signs of holiday homes and bungalows could be glimpsed, clinging to the shallow slopes.

The taxi slowed and pulled in through a stone-pillared gateway on to a short, flower-lined drive. Chestnut Grange was a looming, three-storey, late Victorian house, with wide bay windows either side of a large entrance hall.

'Want me to wait?' asked the driver.

Brennan searched for change. 'Better not. Don't know how long I'll be.'

The driver offered a card. 'Give me a ring and I'll come down and fetch you.'

'Thanks – I may just do that.' Brennan offered a fiver, and took two quid change from the two quid fare. The driver gave him a big smile.

'Thanks – hope I'm not taking Granny's money though.'

'Granny doesn't need it where she's going,' said Brennan, clambering out and splashing his way across to the glass-panelled door.

He rang the brass-mounted bell to the side of the door, noting that the entrance was securely locked. Through the panel, he could see a nurse in her mid-forties, helping an old lady across the hall. The nurse gestured for Brennan to wait a minute. He nodded his understanding.

To his right, he could see high-backed chairs ranged side by side in the bay window. The one to the left contained the end of what was obviously a large, formica-topped dining-table, surrounded by stiff-backed dining chairs, padded with red leatherette.

The nurse reappeared, turning the Chubb key and unhooking a door-chain. She opened the door a few inches. Brennan could see a badge on her tunic reading 'Cathy Aldridge'.

'Sorry, can I help you?'

'Mr Francis Dunlop – to see Mr Furnival. I have an appointment at three . . .'

Mrs Aldridge opened the door wide to let Brennan through.

'Sorry about the palaver . . .'

'No problem. Can't be too careful, I suppose.'

'That's right. Anywhere that's got drugs and stuff on the premises is a sitting target these days. I'll just let Mr Furnival know you're here.'

'Thank you.'

Mrs Aldridge moved off to her left and turned down a corridor leading towards the rear of the house. Brennan guessed that admin and kitchens must all be down there. In front of him the wide staircase with chunky banister was flanked by a small but modern lift. From the lounge on the right, the jagged tinkling of an untuned piano started up. Brennan eased his way across and peered through the gap between door and architrave. A plump woman in a hand-knitted cardigan was sitting on a piano stool, trying to read the sheet music in front of her. After some effort, a few recognisable chords could finally be heard.

'Right, now – I'm sure you all remember this one. Singalong with me.

And if you don't know the words, just hum along, so we can have a nice, jolly noise.'

The woman took a breath and readjusted her posture before striking out into a staccato version of 'You Made Me Love You'. Brennan edged further round. He could see a line of old people in chairs mouthing the words as best they could. One or two of them slept on despite the racket.

'Mr Dunlop?'

It took Brennan just a few hundredths of a second longer than he'd hoped to recall his alias, so he made a point of turning away from the door deliberately.

'They're having a wonderful time in there,' he approached Furnival with an outstretched hand. He had been mostly right with his guessing about the voice down the phone. Furnival was late forties, but looked a good ten years older, thanks to his balding head and thin grey moustache. He wore a dark, three-piece business suit, and across the waistcoat hung the chain of a fob-watch.

'Francis Dunlop.'

The handshake was firm but short-lived. Brennan wondered at what point the fob-watch would be produced to punctuate, or more likely terminate, their conversation.

'Shall I give you a guided tour while you tell me about who you have in mind for us?'

'Fine. You're a man after my own heart, Mr Furnival – never do one thing when you can manage two. That's my motto!'

Furnival led him away from the lounge, back towards the dining-room. Metal tips on the heels of his shoes clacked against the polished wooden floor. Brennan guessed that Furnival liked this noise – perhaps it was a reminder of military life?

'This is our communal dining-room, although guests are entirely at liberty to take meals in their rooms if they wish.'

The panelled room was dominated by the refectory-style table, which, apart from its wipe-friendly surface, was also positioned over a large square of clear, padded plastic.

'So whom are you thinking of bringing to us – mother, father, aunt?'

'Father.'

'Widower, I presume?'

'Of about three years. He'd been fine until the last winter, but some of the simple tasks around the house are just beginning to get beyond him.'

Furnival nodded knowingly. 'I often think it's a kind of weariness that sets in. They gradually just give up on the little things which make the difference between being in control of one's life and letting it slip away. But that's what we're here for, of course.'

'Of course. How many . . . "guests" can you accommodate?'

'Up to thirty. They all have individual rooms. There's ten upstairs for those who don't mind using the lift or the staircase. But the majority are along here in our extension – it's all fairly recent. The two corridors fan out, you see, with six rooms on each side. That's "Peachblossom" and that's "Appleblossom".'

Brennan followed Furnival. The Victorian wooden floor gave way to a twentieth-century sea-grass floor covering as the modern extension began. Skylights made the corridors bright, and there were cheerful, floral still-life prints on the walls.

'It's quite feminine, this section . . .'

'Well, the majority of our guests are women. I'm afraid the stats prove it – they have the edge over us on longevity. We don't segregate as a matter of policy, but any particular needs for privacy can usually be accommodated.'

Furnival took a bunch of keys from his pocket and opened one of the doors to the modern rooms. To the side of the entrance was a modern toilet and bathroom, complete with support rails for both lavatory and bath. Beyond was the bedroom-cum-lounge, containing wardrobe and dressing-table and a large armchair in the window. Brennan moved across. From the window he could see a line of mast-heads and beyond that a channel of water running between the headland on the far side and a clutch of small hotels and pubs on the near.

'Sea view,' he murmured.

'Indeed,' said Furnival proudly. 'It's perfect really. I find the sea air and the view just cheers them up – as it should.'

Brennan turned. 'I'm very impressed. Tell me – do you have vacancies at the moment?' Brennan gestured around the empty room pointedly, as if staking a claim.

'This is due for occupation next week, I'm afraid. It all depends on how urgent your father's needs are.'

Brennan narrowed his eyes. 'Are we talking "turnover" here?'

Furnival forced a patient little smile. 'Well, we have a natural wastage rate obviously, though not too dramatic, it has to be said. I'd guess that in the normal run of things we have a couple of vacancies every two months or so . . .'

Brennan nodded. 'And no waiting list?'

'Well, we have a few names pencilled in. It often happens that our existing guests, and their visiting relatives, suggest us to others, so one never knows when there'll be a surge.'

'Shortly after most Christmases, I'd have thought,' Brennan joked to no effect.

'Anyway, I'll furnish you with a brochure and a tariff and perhaps you could let us know within a few weeks whether your father is interested?'

'Sure.'

Furnival invited Brennan to leave the room ahead of him. Brennan watched as he allowed the door to click shut.

'You seem quite hot on security here?'

'Of course. During the spring and summer there's a highly transient population. Young people mostly. Homes like this are vulnerable – not just to burglary, but to the risk of vandalism, or worse. We have alarms wired up to all corridors at night.'

They sauntered back down towards the main building.

'So may I ask how you came to find us, Mr Dunlop?'

'You described it perfectly before, I think. My father remembered a couple of old friends who'd retired down here a few years ago. Well, they were more neighbours rather than friends, I gather.'

'Do you remember their names?'

'Yes – er, Denton, I think he said. Ring any bells?'

Mr Furnival stopped walking and assumed a grave expression. 'I'm very sorry – but they've passed away.'

'Oh – oh, dear. Recently?'

'I think it was about two months ago. Nice couple. One of those classic cases where one goes, and the other follows very quickly. Some of our nurses seriously believe in the idea of a broken heart as a cause of death. Can you understand that, Mr Dunlop?'

'Yes, I think I can,' Brennan said.

Furnival retreated to his office for a few moments leaving Brennan alone. The disjointed singing was still going on:

> Give me, give me what I sigh for,
> You know you've got the kind of kisses
> That I'd die for . . .

Brennan moved to the door of the lounge and watched, despite the sour odour of stale piss which hung over the room. The average age of the 'guests' must have been at least seventy-five. Those that weren't attempting to sing were either asleep or reading. One of these was a thin-faced man, in brown slacks and cream-coloured shirt. He had a surprisingly vivid bush of grey hair. Brennan smiled at his indefatigable attempts to proceed with his book. Furnival appeared behind Brennan.

'I'd be grateful if you didn't disturb the guests . . .'

'Sorry,' Brennan said, pulling himself away. 'I was just watching them sing – or not—' Brennan pointed across to the old man trying to read.

'Not one of life's joiners in, is Mr Green,' Furnival said. At that point, Green looked up and peered across at Brennan, screwing up his eyes in an attempt to focus. He raised his right hand and gestured for Brennan to come closer. Furnival's arm prevented Brennan making any forward movement.

'His eyes and ears are failing him a little anyway.'

Mr Green gave up the struggle to focus and sat back in his chair. Furnival now escorted Brennan across to the front door and unlocked it, handing him a glossy folder. 'All you need to know is in there. Any further queries, don't hesitate to ring me, Mr Dunlop.'

'I won't. Thanks.'

'Do *you* have a card I could take?'

Brennan made a play of feeling in his top pocket.

'I think I may have left mine at home. Day off for me, you see.'

'What is it you do?'

'Management consultant – freelance.'

'No substitute though, is it . . . ?'

Brennan put on a broad smile to disguise his utter blankness.

'I suppose not . . . for real life!' When in doubt, agree was one of Brennan's endless rules of engagement.

Brennan stepped outside, grateful for a few lungfuls of fresh air after the artificial fug of the home. The rainstorm had blown itself out and patches of blue sky were breaking through the cloud cover. Brennan turned to take one more look at Chestnut Grange. It had seemed an innocuous enough place, though the modernity and obvious expense of the extensions jarred. Quite a bit of money had been invested – pity they hadn't spent some on getting the piano tuned. Brennan realised that Furnival was standing in the bay window. Furnival suddenly offered a salute, military style, to which Brennan responded with a jaunty wave.

Inside the home's lounge, the piano playing stopped. Furnival put his hand on the woman pianist's shoulders.

'What kind of "businessman" is it who turns up in a taxi, and who doesn't know he's wearing a regimental tie?' he asked, rhetorically.

Brennan walked the few hundred yards down to West Bay. He knew he'd gaffed somewhere or other – he was almost certainly unconvincing as a management consultant. But for now, it didn't matter. Plausibility wasn't the first object of the exercise. He wanted to unsettle them, just a little. If there'd been any residual nervousness after a wrongdoing, he wanted to exploit that. Stuart Gill had often told him that his style of investigation could be like looking for a gas leak with a lit match. But then Brennan had always taken that as praise, not criticism.

Little huddles of holiday-makers were coming out from under the awnings of the few souvenir shops, and walking around the small harbour. Locals were taking their dogs up on to the beach for an afternoon run. Brennan crunched his way up the shingle path which lay between the shops and the harbourside hotel. As it rose to a crest, he saw the metallic-blue sea stretching out below. The beach, a mixture of rough sand and stones, sloped steeply down and the waves, breaking in short, choppy movements, gave a sense of a great undertow.

Brennan watched the water claw at the beach. He'd not expected Furnival to fall over and convulse at the mention of the Dentons' name, incriminating himself and all his staff. But the muted, overly professional response had, perversely, conveyed no sense of shock or agitation. He'd reacted with the upright formality of a funeral director. Maybe death was such a feature of the home that it required a detached manner of those who worked there? Or maybe Brennan's sudden gambit had stiffened Furnival like a shot of strychnine to the gut?

Brennan returned to the harbour, and spotted his restaurant for that night perched on a small island in the river which ran into the bay. Brennan could see people moving inside – he crossed the foot-bridge to the main door. The staff were mopping floors.

'Will I be okay for a table tonight – about eight?'

'How many?' asked one of the girls with a mop.

'Just me . . .'

The waitress looked at him wearily. 'No problem, sir. One at eight.'

'Sorry. I just wanted to make sure – big treat for me, this. The name's Brennan.'

The waitress looked at him as though he'd just been released into the community. Brennan backed out, walked across the foot-bridge and headed for the cluster of public phones opposite. Five minutes later, his taxi reappeared, with the same driver as before. Back into Bridport was Brennan's instruction.

'What did you make of it then, mate?'

'Seemed fine. Bit worried about the death-rate there, that's all.'

The taxi-driver wheezed an asthmatic laugh. 'What, not fast enough for you to get your hands on the inheritance, you mean?'

'I'd prefer my relative to *live*, actually.'

'Sorry.'

'Do you know who'd deal with funerals from there?'

'No. But there's only two firms in town – the one with the cheapest coffins'd get the job, I suppose?'

'I'm beginning to see why your parents pissed off and left you!'

'I wasn't like this before! They made me, they did!'

Brennan got 'Mad Bollocks' to drop him at the nearest of the two funeral parlours. In a two-horse race, though, it was Brennan's role to back the wrong one. He urged the taxi round to the second funeral company and squeezed in the door just as they were putting up the closed sign – it flashed through Brennan's mind that there may be a market for jokey signs here, with a coffin and its lid displaying either 'open' or 'shut'.

'I'm sorry to disturb you at such a late hour, but my parents were friends of Mr and Mrs Denton who died recently at Chestnut Grange nursing home. I understand that you would have conducted the service, so I wondered if you could grant me the comfort of letting me know where they rest?'

'Your name, sir?'

'Mr Dunlop . . .'

The funeral attendant crossed to a filing cabinet and pulled out the top drawer. He began to leaf through a wedge of invoices. Brennan looked around at the still-life – dark blue flowers, a varnished desk, a Dickensian-style blotter, a brown leather Chesterfield, a display catalogue of coffins. Why did twentieth-century death have to aspire to Victorian decorum?

'Mr and Mrs Denton were laid to rest jointly at St Bartholomew's . . .'

'That's here – in Bridport?'

'Indeed.'

Brennan stretched out a hand, apologetically.

'Look, I happen to know that they weren't too well off. Are there any charges still to pay?'

The assistant didn't even deign to look at the invoice.

'Everything was taken care of by Chestnut Grange, sir.'

Brennan nodded. He recognised a brick wall when he saw it.

'St Bartholomew's, then?'

Brennan returned to The George to change out of his business suit. The bar was quite full when he came down – estate agents on their way home to their wives and kids, a couple of brewery executives, two Americans on a cycle tour, four girls on their way to a summer rock festival. The mix was as eclectic and relaxed as before.

Brennan perched on a stool right in the corner by the door, isolating himself from the other customers. He'd had enough talking for the day. This was drinking and thinking time.

After three pints of Palmer's, he decided he was fit enough to walk the mile and a half down to West Bay. The stroll would do him good. The wide street out of Bridport was quiet now as the sunset lit the houses on the far side. Brennan stayed in the shade, walking steadily, humming to himself, not forcing thoughts, but allowing them a chance to run around.

In a town like this, he guessed that most people knew one another, and especially so where the circles of work interconnected. A scandal in a retirement home would threaten other businesses too – catering supplies, laundries, a bank, medical services, funeral parlours. Brennan tried to guess where the chain of money might be weakest, but the beer and the strain of the walk had gone to his head by now and pushed all further thoughts from his mind.

Even as he passed Chestnut Grange, seeing the orange wall lights glowing in the empty lounge, knowing that the poor, dying bastards were being shunted back to their rooms for the night, he managed an unexpected detachment. Maybe that's all it took – a few stiff drinks and you didn't care how they lived or died.

The waitress at the restaurant had obviously remembered Brennan, because she instantly escorted him round to a table behind the door, virtually out of sight of any other diners in the room. Brennan took the side of the table looking out in retaliation – if she didn't want people eating to look at him, he didn't want to look at other people eating. But after the argy-bargy, the food turned out to be terrific – he had a huge salade Niçoise to start and a fat slice of grilled John Dory for main course. A half-bottle of oaked Californian Chardonnay set both dishes off well, he thought.

Outside the light was fading, with a great streak of grey cloud streaming in from Lyme Bay. The gulls had found their perches for the night – mastheads, the island outside the restaurant – and the fishing boats were moored until morning. All life was ashore now – families out strolling the harbourside, lads cruising around with the top of the Escort down. The pub opposite the restaurant seemed to have most of its drinkers outside, so humid was the night.

Brennan watched aimlessly – if there'd been a suspicious death or two, he could rule out visitors. West Bay was benign and cheerful. And Chestnut Grange was thoroughly secure – if anybody wanted to get their hands on drugs or valuables they'd be unlikely to hit an old people's home. So it was the inner community of the town who must know what had happened. An inside job – if it had happened at all, of course. Brennan wondered how he could have sold this story to Stuart Gill in the old days – 'Only clue is a letter . . . still no idea what really happened'. Gill would have had him on the first train back to London. 'Dead *old* people? Where's the surprise in that, son?'

Brennan's mind switched back to the present. Cathy Aldridge, out of her nurse's uniform, was making her way into the pub opposite. Brennan rose, found £40 from his wallet and handed it to the waitress.

'I'm not doing a runner – I've just got to see a friend in that pub. This should cover what I've had so far. And I'll be back for a pudding!'

Brennan swerved out of the restaurant and strode purposefully across the foot-bridge. The pub had a large L-shaped bar. He couldn't see Cathy Aldridge at first, so he bought a brandy and began to make his way through the drinkers, trying to make it look as though he had a date. As he rounded the angle of the 'L' he saw her propped against the bar in the far corner, throwing back what looked like a large whisky. Then she bought another and sluiced that down as well.

She was alone. And now she was crying. Brennan stopped watching and began to walk towards her. When he was ten yards away, she looked up. It took less than a second for her to recognise him, despite the change of clothes. And it took her less than five to pick up her handbag and slip out of the door nearest to her. Brennan walked at the same pace, still pretending to look for his missing partner. He opened the door. She was already fifty yards away and running like her life depended on it.

CHAPTER SEVEN

Janet made a last-minute adjustment to Lester's school tie. He could just about do his own Windsor knot if he put his mind to it, but that rarely happened during the five days on which he went to school. Janet stood behind him, trying to retrace the moves and folds which her father had once demonstrated to her, claiming that it would be a social asset when it came to finding a husband. Janet cursed his memory under her breath as she struggled with the tie.

'Doesn't make sense, wearing these. Not in July!' Lester moaned.

'If you're going to wear a tie, you may as well wear it properly. Tony Blair might spot you on Highbury Grove looking a right scruff-bag and the next thing he'll be calling for the restoration of National Service!'

She turned Lester around. The knot didn't look too bad, though undoing it would be a problem.

'Let me look at your face—'

'Mum!'

'Breathe on me . . .'

'Haa-aaa-aah!'

'Dog's breath. Have you been smoking?'

'Do me a favour!'

Across the hall, the telephone rang. As Janet went to answer it, Lester made good his escape, waving triumphantly.

'Hello . . . ?'

It was Frank. Masked by a stream of electronic blips, and the noise of a vacuum cleaner, he was barely audible.

'Frank? Where the hell are you?'

The blips disappeared and, seconds later, so did the cleaner. If not loud, he was now certainly clear.

'Sorry, Janet, it's the pay-phone in a pub. You have to press a button to speak, and I forgot.'

'You're in a pub at eight-thirty *a.m.*?'

'I've got a room here . . . and I'm staying on another night. Things are – how shall I put it? – interesting.'

'Tell me what you can,' Janet pressed eagerly. She could hear the handset being changed from one ear to another. Brennan's voice now sounded quieter but closer.

'There's definitely something dodgy going on – though what precisely, God knows. I've got a few more people to see today, which may help.'

'Did you find your letter-writer?'

'No. Impossible really – most of them are in a world of their own. I can't see me getting individual handwriting samples from the patients. Look, what I wanted to ask was, shouldn't a coroner's report have been made if the deaths were in any way suspicious?'

'Only if the doctor certifying death asks for it, or if the police were called in. Were they?'

'I don't know. I doubt it somehow. Could you find out who the coroner for this area would be?'

'Sure. Phone me back this afternoon. But you find the doctor who certified them dead – that's the next step.'

'I can't exactly swan in to the health centre with a megaphone . . . and the people at the home certainly won't tell me. I've got an angle on this nurse though . . .'

'Sorry, Frank?'

'She works there. At the home. Saw her in tears last night, after she'd finished.'

'Careful, Frank, it might be something else completely.'

'I know . . . look, money's running out. I'll call you later. How's Lester?'

'Just left.'

'Shit – I wanted to speak to him.'

'Then don't stay in pubs all night, Frank!'

Janet heard warning blips again and then silence. She replaced the phone. Along the hall she could hear the first stirrings of her in-laws. Brennan's mother and father had been only too pleased to take her and Lester in after the marriage had appeared to collapse. Their house – a modest Victorian semi – had enough room to accommodate the two families, but the achievement of privacy was only occasional. Janet felt obliged to help them with meals and general chores when she'd rather be finding some work, and the dinner table had tended to become a two- or three-hour marathon of family reminiscences. Lester, at least, felt secure here. His grandparents had always treated him generously. But each day brought closer the possibility of the death, or infirmity of one of them. Sending the survivor off to a home was too awful to contemplate – almost as bad as leaving him or her alone here, or having him or her come to live with the family. Janet sighed with the burden of it all – ringing around to find the right coroner in Dorset would come as light relief today.

Brennan took his breakfast in the window table of The George, enjoying the undeniably furtive thrill of being in a pub before opening time. Another tape of a jazz concert was already on the stereo – Miles Davis live in New York, 1964. Brennan couldn't help playing the piano breaks of 'So What' on the table with his fingertips.

Laurie, the waitress with the tattooed hands, wandered across from the kitchen range with another pot of coffee, a jug of hot milk and a rack full of thickly sliced wholemeal toast

'You a Miles fan, Mr Brennan?' she asked.

'Who couldn't be, save the deaf and the dead?'

Laurie smiled. Brennan gestured to the seat opposite him, not entirely innocent of intent.

'Join me in a coffee?'

'Sure, thanks.'

Laurie collected another large green and gold Apilco cup and saucer from the kitchen and installed herself opposite Brennan. He poured the coffee and the milk together, blending the two until a foaming meniscus formed at the lip of the cup.

'It's Frank, by the way . . .'

'I'm Laurie . . .'

'I know, I heard. Toast?'

Laurie shook her head.

'I like it here. It's different. Relaxed.'

Laurie nodded her head to acknowledge the compliment.

'I sometimes feel we're out of step with what most people really want.'

'You don't seem short of customers.'

'It's the same circle of about fifty or sixty people. Plus the drop-ins such as yourself. This is still quite a staid kind of town.'

'Much the same as mine.' Brennan planted.

'Where's that?'

'Bradford-on-Avon.'

'Oh, yeah, it's lovely there.'

'Maybe – it's like most English county towns though, you only see the half of it. The heritage angle, the touristy bits, that sort of thing. I'm sure it has its darker side. Just as Bridport must have?'

Brennan applied a question mark to this last phrase and a rising, inquisitive tone. The smile vanished from Laurie's face.

'Are you a copper?'

Brennan laughed out loud.

'Well, you suddenly started to talk like one . . .'

'Sorry. I was – I *am* – a journalist. I'm trying to write too. One of the ways I find things out is by asking people. In a roundabout way.'

Laurie drank some of her coffee, unsure of him now, where five minutes ago she'd had him pegged – slightly sad, single or divorced, looking for a new home, perhaps flirting a little.

'So you're down here working, is that it?'

'In a silent way,' he answered, seeing if she registered the borrowing of another Miles Davis title.

'If you're trying to fuck me over at all, I've got plenty of big lads who come in here. Rugby players. Farmers. Fishermen.'

'Please – I'm not after you, Laurie. Promise. This is a refuge. I wouldn't want to spoil it.'

'What are you doing here then?'

'It may be nothing. The old people's home – on the left as you go into West Bay. Chestnut Grange . . .'

Laurie shrugged.

'Can't say I've noticed it.'

'There's been no talk about it, has there?'

Laurie shook her head.

'Nothing. But this isn't exactly the sort of pub where you'd expect to hear it. The suits and the wrinklies stay away from us – we're a bit too threatening, you know.' She flicked her right ear-lobe, which was pierced with three gold rings.

'What about doctors?'

'You'd best try The Bull. They'd all go there. Dry sherry, roast beef, trifle, golf talk.'

'Have you heard of a Cathy Aldridge at all? Married. Mid-forties. Mousey. Likes a drink.'

'The name means nothing to me, Mr Brennan.'

Laurie left her coffee unfinished and returned to the kitchen.

'Is it all right if I stay another night?' Brennan called out. But Laurie just turned up the music. Brennan finished his breakfast, went to the hall of the pub where the pay-phone was mounted and returned with a local directory, divided between Business and Private numbers. Within fifteen minutes he had the addresses of four doctor's surgeries in the Bridport and West Bay area, and all the details of the five entries under the name of Aldridge. It would be a busy day.

It had just gone nine when he emerged from The George, feeling refreshed and purposeful. There was a chill in the air, thanks to the cloudless morning sky, and a chorus of seagulls screeched a welcome. Fifty yards down the street, the bookshop with 'Olde Curiosity Shoppe' windows was just opening. Brennan breezed around it, finding what he needed with ease – a town map and that week's local paper. He checked inside and found a branch office listed for Bridport on page two. The paper had been published only the day before, so Brennan doubted that its staff would be rushing into work today. St Bartholomew's was first call.

Brennan found it on the map, marked The George, and traced a route with his biro. It looked about ten minutes' walk. What the map didn't tell Brennan, though, was that the church was at the head of a long slope which drew up into the hills above the town. Ten minutes became twenty, and by the time Brennan reached the churchyard gate, his lungs were heaving and his shirt clung damply to the small of his back. Most of the time he was glad he'd been breathalysed and lost his licence, because at the time it had felt like disarming a lunatic. He'd felt no self-righteousness at the cause of the police's intervention – doing 40 in a 30 m.p.h. zone – because he knew that he could, in criminal parlance, 'put his hands up' for several less innocuous offences. In the eighties, a journalist on a drink-driving charge was fêted by his colleagues. Those days, rightly, had gone now. Brennan had vowed to himself that he would be a paragon of sobriety when the licence returned in about six weeks' time. And this morning, particularly, he missed the car like hell.

Brennan recovered his breath and walked in through the lich-gate. The church was eighteenth century, built of a dullish brown sandstone, and Catholic. The graveyard looked well tended as he began to move among it, wishing that the dead, as in the newspaper classifieds, were filed in alphabetical order. The whole of the southern side of the plot, he soon discovered, was made over to the nineteenth century and whatever headstones were left from earlier times.

He moved round the back of the church. The yard opened out up on to the hill, the elevation now yielding a fine view of the town. Brennan noted the twentieth-century dates appearing and stopped to try and anticipate the pattern of growth in the stones.

'Can I help you at all?' a loud voice called.

Brennan looked up. The priest, a tall, heavily built man in his fifties was making his way across the tufted grass towards him. He wore his black cassock, with an old woolly cardigan over it against the morning chill. As he drew closer, Brennan recognised, all too easily, the red-veined toper's nose. The eccentric look was completed by the sight of a pair of green wellies poking out from the fraying hem of the black gown.

'Morning, Father,' Brennan offered.

'Do I know you, sir?'

'No – I was just visiting. Mr and Mrs Denton – ring any bells?'

The priest raised an eyebrow.

'Are you taking the mickey, son?'

'I'm sorry, Father, I wasn't thinking.' Brennan felt a tug in his guts, a churn of childhood fear and tearfulness. Remarks like that would have got him a good three cracks on the arse with a cane from the brothers who ran the first school he'd attended.

'I'm here to pay my respects to Mr and Mrs Denton. I believe they were laid to rest here?'

The priest pulled at a shaving scab on his jaw line, unwittingly releasing a thin bubble of blood.

'I'm not too good on names, sometimes. They couldn't have been regulars, certainly.'

'No, no – they were from the home. Down in West Bay.'

'Oh, yes, yes – that was a day. Two coffins and only one mourner – the dead outnumbering the living!'

The priest broke to his left.

'I think we put them over here . . .'

Brennan followed, watching the dew gather on his shoes. The priest hesitated a moment then made a decisive move towards a plain, grey marble headstone.

'Here they are!'

Brennan walked round and stood alongside the priest as they both silently read the briefly etched details.

'After a lifetime, only a day apart,' Brennan mused out loud.

'Yes. Quite efficient from our point of view – my lad would have chucked his shovel into the next county if I'd had to ask him to widen the grave again, right after filling it in!'

'There was only one mourner, you said?'

'Yes – silly blubbering woman from the home.'

'Mrs Aldridge?'

'I think that was her.'

'Did you minister at the home ever?'

'I think I went one Christmas-time about five years ago, but they tend not to get people of our faith. If they want me, they know where they can get me!'

'So you didn't know Mr and Mrs Denton at all, then?'

'Never clapped eyes on them.'

'Odd, them going so close together?'

'Oh, I don't know. They must have been good people to be so blessed. No one left mourning, no sense of loss, leaving the world hand in hand as it were.'

'You've no idea how they died, I suppose?'

The priest looked at him, darkening suddenly.

'Who are you to ask such questions?'

'They were friends of my father's. He didn't find out till recently. He was a bit worried that they might have been . . . well, that they might have suffered, shall we say?'

'Isn't that what we're put on the earth for?'

Brennan felt like smacking him one in the mouth. All that vile certainty that had fucked up his early adolescence came flooding back. The mysterious prayers, the fierce warnings, the cant and the rant.

'Maybe they had another purpose, Father,' Brennan said tartly, before setting off for the gate.

'The church is open if you want to light a candle for them, Mr . . .'

The priest's voice tailed off as Brennan kept moving without a backward look. He took the descent briskly, fuelled by irritation. Back on the main street, there was a hint of bustle, as shopkeepers arranged their window displays and pavement signs. Brennan walked west, back past the junction for West Bay, and found the newspaper offices at the end of a whitewashed alley behind a complex of tea-rooms. Brennan stepped inside the small front office, where a girl in her early twenties was seated behind the desk. She wore a telephone headset with microphone and was typing into a desktop computer as she confirmed details with a caller.

'Is that one "ess" or two?'

She caught Brennan's look and raised her eyebrows in a weary gesture.

'You've gone over the thirty-word limit now, ma'am, so the price will go up. You could have a fifty-word box for ten pounds fifty, you know? Okay – look, I'll store your details until you've decided . . . er, by five tomorrow. Bye.'

The girl flicked a switch on the telephone and lowered her headset.

'Good morning, sir, my name's Joanna, how can I help you?'

Brennan smiled politely at the Citizen's Charter-speak.

'And my name's Frank. Do you have any editorial staff on the premises?"

'The editor's based over in Dorchester. That's our head office.'

'Yes, what I meant was, your local reporters, correspondents, whatever. Are they here?'

'We've only one – Mike Watkiss . . .'

'May I have a word with him . . . ?'

'He's not in yet. I can give him a message if you like.'

'That's very kind of you. May I?'

Brennan gestured towards Joanna's headed notepad, which she handed over. Brennan took his biro out and began to compose a message.

'You deal with all the classified advertising, I presume?' he asked as he wrote.

'That's right, yes. Just for the town and immediate area.'

'So if I wanted to place a death notice, you're the person to speak to?'

Joanna's face immediately assumed a sorrowful look, as if her favourite pet had just been run over.

'Yes, sir, I'm sorry to hear about your bereavement.'

'Distant friends, really. They may already have been commemorated actually – by the home.'

'Home?'

'Chestnut Grange – West Bay.'

'Oh, yes, we do a lot of theirs.'

'Is there a way of you checking whether there's already been an entry?'

'Yes, sir, provided it was in the last four months. We store details for that time before . . . before . . .'

Joanna groped for the most seemly expression.

'Dumping them . . . ?' Brennan offered.

Joanna gave a little private smile, a glimpse of humanity behind the robo-speak.

'Well, they died in early April so we might be in luck . . .'

'What was the name then, sir?'

'Denton.'

Joanna's fingers clicked over the keyboard.

'Can't see anything, sir. Sure it was "Deaths" not "*In memoriam*"?'

Brennan shrugged. 'You could try that one too, for me, please?'

'They're not there either.'

'Oh, dear. Gone *and* forgotten, then?' Brennan said as he tore off the top sheet of the pad and folded it in half, before handing it back to Joanna.

'If you can make sure Mr Watkiss gets that as soon as he comes in, I'd be most grateful,' Brennan said, applying as much charm as he could muster.

'Surely,' said Joanna, writing 'M. Watkiss' on the note as a reminder to herself.

'I may be back to place a classified later . . .'

'We close for lunch between one and two, then finish at five.'

'Very civilised,' Brennan said, as he looked around at the framed photographs on the wall – giant marrow competitions, school fêtes, somebody handing over a giant cheque to a charity, everybody's idea of small-town life. There'd be no place for an ugly or unhappy story on these walls.

Brennan paused for a half-hour in the tea-rooms which fronted the newspaper office and, under the guise of doing the crossword puzzle in *The Independent*, began to construct a pattern of names and notes, almost as if he were trying to solve an anagram. Indeed the same processes applied – Brennan found that mental calculations could often founder on his brain's inflexibility to respond to anything other than ordered, linear directives. That's how he'd been taught – from 'two plus two equals four' at school, to the 'big intro, three pars, recap and out' structure of writing for newspapers.

But with the mental images made physical and movable, the thought processes took on a new flexibility. So almost as soon as he'd written down 'letter from home – patient?', 'Dentons', 'Cathy Aldridge' and 'Furnival', new possibilities appeared. He'd seen Aldridge crying in the evening after his visit. She'd also run away from him as soon as she'd seen him in the pub – what if *she'd* written the letter, hiding behind the scratchy handwriting for safety? Brennan's arrival, unannounced, would clearly have had her on edge, especially if Furnival had suspected her of provoking it. And if this was the case, perhaps she was even in danger?

Brennan scrubbed out the word 'danger' almost as soon as he'd written it, recognising the potential for unhelpful melodrama. Brennan returned to his town map, and to the list of doctor's surgeries. Of the four listed for the area, only two were within a mile of Chestnut Grange. Brennan assumed that convenience would be a key factor here, and marked the locations on his map. There was one just along the main street, near the junction with the road for Chard. Brennan finished his pot of tea, took two more bites from the stodgy croissant that he'd allowed to go cold, and left, via the toilet.

The stream of shoppers and holiday-makers had become a flowing river on the pavements outside, as the sun rose higher and promised another warm day to them all. Brennan threaded his way through, expecting any minute that one of them would spot his own lack of identifiable purpose. He had no shopping bag, nor was he dressed for a holiday. He certainly wasn't retired, and looked too well dressed to be unemployed. But he didn't look like a professional man – the day's plain blue cotton jacket, with white button-down shirt, probably suggested a lecturer or teacher. In which case they'd be asking, 'Why isn't he at school?'

As Brennan drew closer to the Chard junction, the shoppers and trippers thinned out. He crossed a short bridge over a rather turgid river and saw a two-storey mill conversion which had the unmistakable look of the modern, fund-holding practice, right down to the named parking spaces for the doctors. Scott, Allsop and Sutcliffe. Brennan walked in, composing himself, trying to order his mind.

The trill of the phone at the reception counter was almost non-stop – was there an epidemic nobody had told him about? Eventually after several mouthed and gestured acknowledgements from the smartly dressed woman behind the counter, the phone was laid to rest.

'Do you have an appointment, sir?'

Brennan put on a hesitant smile and tried to look as vulnerable as possible.

'Look, this may sound strange, but I don't know.'

The receptionist smiled blankly, with her pencil poised over a packed register.

'I wanted to see someone about my father, you see.'

'Ah, and he's registered here?'

'Well, that's just it, I'm not sure. He's at Chestnut Grange, the nursing home on the road towards West Bay,' Brennan said, pointing roughly in a southern direction, to hasten a reaction. 'I was told that he was on the list here . . . Denton's his name.'

'I think you'll find you've come to the wrong centre, Mr Denton. We certainly don't have patients from Chestnut Grange on our books.'

'I knew I'd botch it. Terrible with names . . .'

'Shall I ring the home for you, to check?'

Brennan's head swirled at the complications this might provoke.

'No, no – I'll do it. I'm sorry to have disturbed you. Really.'

Brennan backed away, making a contorted face to signify his apparent embarrassment. Once outside, his demeanour changed. Chance had given him a dry run at bluffing his way into a doctor's surgery. The performance would be much more polished next time.

It would have to wait until after lunch now, though, because Brennan had invited the journalist Watkiss to meet him in the lounge bar of The Bull, between twelve and one. The timing was strategic – even a fragment of that hour might prove useful in gleaning information, with the option of moving on to lunch if the bloke proved particularly forthcoming. Brennan had unquestionably pulled rank in an attempt to lure Watkiss out – the apparently modest construction of 'you may have seen some of my work in . . .' was an infamous attempt to let the local boy know that a national man was in town.

The ploy had worked more often than not in the past, mostly for reasons of self-interest rather than Brennan's image or personality. A local journalist, if he or she was the right age to still have ambition, would generally calculate that a helping hand to someone from a national paper might result in a return favour somewhere down the line – at its most basic there might be a fee, and beyond that there could be a word in the ear of the local editor or proprietor. A note with a daily's mast-head saying 'you've got a good lad/girl there' was like an American Express traveller's cheque, bankable anywhere.

And if the contact proved particularly helpful, there could even be an invitation to become the national's stringer for the area, charged with putting the bigger local stories up in return for an exclusive retainer. And perhaps, in their wildest dreams, the local journalist might expect a call from London to offer the big break.

Brennan perched on a bar stool in the lounge of The Bull and watched the door, waiting for the power play to produce a result. He'd ordered a mineral water, partly because that morning's walk had reminded him he was drinking too much, and partly because he didn't want Watkiss to think he was setting a beery trap for him to walk into. Brennan needn't have worried. The instant that Watkiss walked in, at half-past twelve, he knew he was on a loser. It wasn't just the two-tone shirt and the golf-club tie which shouted 'establishment man', but the curl of contempt on Watkiss's mouth as he looked across at Brennan.

'Are you Brennan?'

Brennan got off his stool and offered his hand.

'Thanks for coming over, Mike. I appreciate it. Drink?'

'No thanks, I can't stop.'

'You free for lunch, then?'

'Sorry, no. What is it you want exactly? I thought you'd been canned recently?'

'Right. I'm discovering the joys of freelance work.'

Watkiss picked a few peanuts from a bowl on the polished bar and tossed his head right back in order to drop them into his mouth.

Looks like a fucking pelican, Brennan thought to himself.

'I have to say that I've never liked your stuff, Mr Brennan,' Watkiss said, grinding the nuts with his back teeth.

Brennan smiled patiently. He noticed the pager strapped to Watkiss's gold-buckled belt, the identity bracelet dangling from the wrist – did the berk have a faulty memory or what? – and the small gold chains which ran across his slip-on shoes. This was a prize twat among journalists.

'Maybe you can help me improve my output then, Mr Watkiss? I need some help on a local story I'm investigating.'

Watkiss shrugged, picking a small silvery cocktail onion and thumbing it into his mouth.

'Sorry. I already have an arrangement with the *Mail*.'

'Okay, so I'll leave off your credit to protect you. This is just a small favour – paid, of course. I wouldn't dream of trying to pick your brains for nothing. The union would frown upon that.'

Watkiss looked at Brennan incredulously.

'I'm not a member of the NUJ, Mr Brennan. Bunch of job-wrecking, Marxist infiltrators opposed to any form of private success.'

'Actually, I think I'm lapsed myself, now I come to think of it,' Brennan said ingratiatingly. Watkiss could sense the tone, however.

'I'd rather you didn't patronise me, Mr Brennan. I'm part of a thriving group of papers. We all work hard at bringing people uplifting and life-enhancing stories. We don't like rubbing their faces in the shit. Just so you know.'

'Thanks for dropping by then. I'll put the peanuts on my bill!'

Watkiss gave him the iciest of smiles and dusted his hands on a small paper napkin from a tray on the bar.

'You people really think you can roll into any small town and have us all on our knees licking your boots, don't you?'

'I don't wear boots, Mr Watkiss. These are boat shoes,' Brennan said, pointing to his raised foot. 'They give me a softer, quieter tread, and I never slip up.'

'Enjoy your lunch,' Watkiss said as he moved away without a handshake.

'If I get my story, your editor's going to be asking you why you had your head up your arse at the time. And I'll have to tell him it's a permanent condition!'

Brennan saw Watkiss's right fist clench momentarily, before he lifted it to smooth out a wrinkle in the sleeve of his jacket. Brennan ordered another mineral water immediately. He wanted to throw back a few Scotches to wash Watkiss away, but decided that the bastard wasn't worth drinking about. What angered Brennan more than the attitude was the realisation that a turnip-headed berk like Watkiss could probably stymie him for good in a small town like this. In fact, Watkiss would almost certainly spend the afternoon ringing round the great and the good of this corner of Dorset to warn them that one of the nation's prime trouble-makers, as Brennan would no doubt be described, was in the area, making himself busy.

Brennan cursed his own vanity for allowing him to think that he'd be able to put a pliable local journo to work on his side. It wasn't just vanity either. It was sheer fucking laziness as well. Brennan either had a story or he didn't – and if he did he should just get on with it himself. Despite the water, the ice and the slice of lemon, Brennan seethed with self-recrimination.

Stalled and becalmed, he tried to restructure a plan for the day. Making meaningful contact with Cathy Aldridge was on the agenda, but he'd have to time his approach as well as moderate it. She'd probably steer clear of the pub at West Bay having seen him in there already. But first he needed to find the doctor who ministered to Chestnut Grange's inmates. He'd try the second of the two nearest practices after lunch.

Brennan eased himself off the stool and wove his way through the tunnel of low wooden beams and creaking, red-carpeted floors to the dark-panelled restaurant. A *maître d'hôtel* in morning suit stepped out to greet him.

'Lunch, sir?'

'For one only, I'm afraid.'

'No problem, sir. Would you like a smoking or non-smoking table?'

Brennan sagged – the tide of health-conscious fascism had swept over even this old coaching inn, where less than two centuries ago you could probably have had a cock-fight and a wench thrown in with the table d'hôte lunch.

'Well, non-smoking while I'm eating, but smoking afterwards with coffee and Armagnac. How's that?'

'You can adjourn to the lounge for coffee, sir!'

Pleased with his solution, the *maître d'hôtel* led him through into the beamed room, past a shining, silver-plated carving-trolley from which great heat shimmered. Brennan guessed that a well-done slab of roast beef hid under the dome and made a mental note to order any fish available.

But his foul mood changed in an instant as he saw the table adjacent to the one the *maître d'hôtel* was now standing over. Furnival was seated there, sipping a glass of red wine. And opposite him was a well-groomed man in his mid-forties. Furnival's face stiffened as Brennan was installed not more than four feet from himself and his dining companion. Brennan nodded across briefly.

'Small world, Mr Furnival,' he added with a smile.

The *maître d'hôtel* assumed that an engaging business connection had been established and beamed with delight at his social dexterity. He brought his hands together in matey self-congratulation.

'Now then – Mr Furnival, Dr Simmons. Are you ready to order?'

CHAPTER EIGHT

Brennan tore the plastic wrapper off the phonecard, slammed the card into the slot, and began dialling even before the flashing message could cue him. The High Street had fallen quiet, with most of the shops closed for the half-day, and there was little traffic noise to penetrate the booth. Brennan heard the ringing tone and, with the phone cupped between his left ear and shoulder, took out his notebook and biro. All he needed now was Janet to answer the phone.

'Hello?'

'It's me. I'm in Bridport still. Look, I think I've found the doctor who looks after the old people, but I can't go in empty-handed. Did you get anything out of the coroner's office yet?'

'There was nothing to get, Frank. The deaths were never reported to them, by the home, by the doctor or the police. Unless there's evidence to suggest something unusual, they can't act.'

'Where was this?'

'Dorchester.'

'Is it worth me going over?'

'You'll just get the same response. Maybe worse if they think you're wasting their time. What's the doctor's name, then?'

'Simmons.'

'Right. I've got a couple of hours before Lester gets home. I'll get down to Kingsway and see if I can get a look at the death certificates for the Dentons. What were the dates again?'

Brennan flicked through his notebook, scanning the various scribbles.

'He went on the 7th of April, she died on the 8th.'

'Have you got a number I can call you at, Frank?'

'Well, there's this public phone, or the one at The George . . . the numbers are—'

'You really are a wanker, Frank, if you had a mobile none of this nonsense would be necessary!'

'If I had a mobile, MI-fucking-5 would spend all day listening in to it, Janet! At least I have to make the bastards work this way! Look, I'll call you between, what, four and four-thirty. See how you've got on, okay?'

Janet hung up. For all the exasperation she caused him, there was no denying the excitement of working with her again. She was often two steps ahead of Brennan, partly because he worked slowly, and thought before each move, and partly because she just had a more organised and more practical mind than he did. She was prone to mistakes through over-eagerness, of course, but he could usually spot them before they became too disastrous.

Brennan walked back to The George, his thoughts on Janet turning to how much he'd like to have spent that afternoon with her up in The Bull's King Charles Suite, with its four-poster bed and mini-bar. There might even have been horse-racing on Channel 4 to go with it! Brennan quelled his fantasy by thinking of Cathy Aldridge – was she still at work, was she still tearful and vulnerable?

Brennan sat at the bar of The George, thanked Laurie for her tip about the 'suits' patronising The Bull, and ordered a coffee. In his head he replayed the excruciatingly enjoyable forty-five minutes through which Furnival and Dr Simmons had had to sit over lunch. Their conversation had been as free-flowing as the heavily floured parsley sauce which had accompanied Brennan's cod steaks. Simmons had soon picked up on Furnival's body language and eye contact, which had practically screamed about the unwanted intrusion of Brennan at the next table. And despite Brennan's determined efforts at *bonhomie*, Furnival hadn't once responded with anything beyond a grunt or a pained smile, let alone an introduction to Dr Simmons.

Yet Brennan knew that he couldn't move in obliquely on Simmons – for one thing, Furnival would have warned him of this strange Mr Dunlop by now, but more importantly, Simmons could hide behind his professional status by withholding private information, or threatening legal action if his ethics were questioned in any way.

Brennan finished his coffee and moved into the hall to ring through his list of Aldridges – the half-day gave him a better than even chance of finding one or two of them at home. He got three – two had never heard of a Cathy and he was able to scratch them off his list; the third call caused a momentary flutter when Cathy was acknowledged, but when it was revealed that she wouldn't be home until school finished, Brennan was able to plead a wrong number and leave them be for the rest of their lives. This left two potential addresses – one in Bridport, one in West Bay. He could look at both within the span of an hour's stroll.

Brennan went upstairs to his room to change into more casual clothes. He couldn't help noticing that the odd item – a guidebook, some receipts, the envelope containing the notes, photocopies and brochure on Chestnut Grange – had all been moved from where he remembered them last. Brennan preferred to put the disturbance down to whoever had cleaned the room. Nothing had been taken, and anyway, Laurie, as distrustful as she had become about him, knew all there was to know so far. Short of leaving his old NUJ card and a map of his movements, he couldn't have done much more to accommodate the enquiring mind.

Brennan passed Laurie on the stairs. She avoided his eyes. Brennan called after her.

'I'll be out for about two hours.'

'You're free to come and go as you please, Mr Brennan.'

'My, uh, wife might phone – to leave a message, if you don't mind.'

'No problem.'

'Laurie, this doesn't involve you, I promise.'

'So you say.'

'If you've got secrets, they're safe where they are.'

Laurie smiled cynically, and disappeared up the staircase.

Brennan found his way round to King Street, a long, three-storey terrace of neat Victorian homes, with front doors opening right on to the pavement. Opposite each house was a small enclosed garden – similar to the arrangement with Brennan's own cottage high up on Tory. Brennan found the number listed for Aldridge. The outward signs were non-committal – there were no feminine touches such as hanging baskets or china ornaments in the window. Brennan rang the doorbell to allow himself a look through the front window. It looked spinsterish inside – a chintz-covered sofa square on to a restored fireplace, little watercolours on the walls, dried flowers either side of the hearth. Brennan rang again to complete the pretence, then moved away before anything other than a casual call could be construed.

He moved on down to West Bay, taking a different road off the bypass roundabout, which brought him down to the harbour on the opposite side from the restaurant, pub and shops. The road had become unmade a short distance down from the bypass as the hillside steepened and the grass became coarser. The dwellings here were more modest than the large, solidly built premises on the other side of the valley. These were mainly wooden bungalows with small verandahs, some of them not much bigger than a summer house. They were well kept, nevertheless, free of rot, and boasting, if not fresh paint, then certainly intact coverings of it. The colours too were in the jolly, seaside spectrum – leaf greens, a pillar-box red, even a bright Suffolk pink at one point.

Brennan imagined a good living could be earned renting these places out as summer holiday homes, but shivered at the thought of what they must be like in the winter, when the winds would lash off the bay and straight into the valley. He found 'Ashvine' nestling in a little hollow, with a fine view down over the harbour. Brennan swung open the sprung, wooden gate, noted the presence of a woman's bicycle on the verandah and rapped on the glass panel of the door. There was no answer.

Brennan moved to one side to get a look at the window but a white, lace curtain spread across the full width of the frame masked his sight.

'Can I help you, squire?'

Brennan walked back to the gate, where a bearded man in a singlet and jeans was now standing. His forearms were heavily tattooed, and though there was a beer belly dangling over the belt of the jeans, the bloke had that convincing demeanour of hostility which hard men reveal from the outset. Brennan offered a hand and a smile.

'Hello, there. My name's Frank Brennan. I was looking for Cathy. Cathy Aldridge.'

Neither of Brennan's gestures of conciliation were acknowledged.

'She ain't here, mate. Can you come out of her garden.'

'Sure.'

Brennan opened the gate and moved outside, allowing the man to close it and flick across a small latch, as though that would prevent further intrusion.

'Whatcha want?'

'To speak to Cathy.'

'She's at work.'

'At Chestnut Grange?'

'If you knows where she works, whatcha calling here for?'

I thought this was her day off . . .'

The man moved a foot closer, bringing Brennan into the sickly, sour aura of his armpits.

'You the guy that's been pestering her?'

'*Me?* No! I saw her at the home yesterday, and just had a few questions to ask her, that's all.'

'If you're fucking DSS, mate, I'll bury you right here!'

Brennan took a pace back. He'd been smacked around enough times in his career to know that violence was not his strong suit. Avoiding it wasn't exactly his best hand, either.

'Could I ask you to give her a message, perhaps?' Brennan offered, guessing that the bloke had probably not progressed much beyond fridge magnets.

'Who said I lived round here?'

'Well . . .' Brennan balked at the prospect of a further challenge to such formidable logic. 'Okay – I'll try later, maybe.'

'If I see you round here again, you'll end up in Lyme Bay with a pocket full of rocks!'

'I'm being buried at sea now, am I?'

The fist curved inexorably into Brennan's solar plexus, felling him in an instant.

'Dumb, dumb, dumb!' Brennan said to himself as he doubled up on the grass. He saw the guy's right boot lift and rolled over quickly, taking the blow just above his bottom. He scrabbled over the ground on all fours, trying to regain his feet, but another kick took his right leg away. Brennan pitched down the slope and rolled up against the chicken-wire fence of the house below Cathy Aldridge's.

'Look, I'm going off the area, rapidly. I promise not to come back, okay?' Brennan panted.

The bearded man slid down the slope towards him, like the giant coming down the beanstalk. He bent over Brennan, giving him a close-up of the right fist, which had the letters 'f-u-c-k' etched across the four, banana-thick fingers.

'You leave her alone, *completely* – understand?'

'What if I'd come to tell her she'd won the *Reader's Digest* Prize Draw?'

The fist jabbed forward into Brennan's nose, sending a shaft of pain throbbing through his head. Blood spurted instantly from both nostrils. He would have to shut his mouth before Big Daddy filled it with his hand.

'All right, all right. Enough. Please!'

The man backed away a few paces to allow Brennan the chance to stand. The blood was dribbling down over his mouth, running off his chin on to the front of his shirt. Brennan felt his legs shaking, not from fear, but from the shock waves of the blows. He hung on to the top rail of the garden's fence to steady himself. The man stayed still but poised. Brennan edged away from him, back up towards the track. He watched Brennan but didn't follow. Brennan covered fifty or so yards before he dared to look back. The man had disappeared from view. Whatever had troubled Cathy Aldridge to tears couldn't have been for the want of a guardian angel.

Brennan made a detour down to the river and scooped out what he hoped was clean water to wash the blood from his face. He pressed his forefinger gently down the line of his nose. There were no lumps or protruding bones as he had feared, just a sense of inflammation. He soaked his handkerchief and used it to wash his chin and neck, then held his head back for several minutes with the cold, damp cotton pushed up against his nostrils.

Brennan felt humbled and angry. Try as he might, he'd never been able to deal with the humiliation of not being a good fighter, right from the first dust-up in a corner of the school yard. The occasions when he'd copped it in the line of duty, as it were, had usually been made worse, as had happened this afternoon, by his attempts to assert some sort of verbal superiority over his aggressors. But, Brennan tried to remind himself once and for all, it was, both literally and figuratively, a language the violent didn't understand.

With the pain easing, and the dust and grass stains brushed off by hand, Brennan made it back across to the bypass. He should have retreated to The George for a bath and stiff drink but the thought of conceding victory to the tattooed warrior brought bile to his throat. He turned back down the road on the other side of the valley, and was quickly outside Chestnut Grange.

He walked up to the main door and rang the bell with a prolonged push. He saw Cathy Aldridge emerge from the lounge and then pull up short. He locked his eyes on to hers as she stared back at his bruised and swollen face. Aldridge moved slowly across to the door, but made no move to open it.

'What do you want?'

'I want to make a booking for twenty-five years from now,' Brennan said, his face as close to the glass as he could manage without triggering another nosebleed.

'Mr Furnival's not here,' Aldridge replied with dumb logic.

'Can I talk to you, Mrs Aldridge?'

'No – go away. Whoever you are.'

'You know about Mr and Mrs Denton, don't you, Cathy?'

Aldridge blinked rapidly then looked to both sides.

'Please go away, or I'll call the police.'

Brennan smiled victoriously.

'Go ahead. I'd love to tell them what I'm enquiring about!'

Behind Aldridge, the plump woman who had been playing the piano appeared from the administrative corridor. She marched up and moved Aldridge firmly to one side. She eyed Brennan with distaste.

'Your name isn't Dunlop is it, Mr Brennan?'

'Not when you put it like that it isn't, Mrs . . . *Mills*, would it be?'

'Never you mind. Whatever you're trying to do, you should know this is a well-run home. If you write anything other than that, *we* won't hesitate to sue. We will not put up with your sort! Gutter press!'

'How about opening the door, then?'

Brennan caught sight of a halo of wrinkled faces in the bay window to his right. They were looking at him with the bewildered expression of kittens expecting a random act of cruelty. Brennan suddenly felt shamed. He wished these old people no distress, but it was becoming obvious that the world into which they had been abandoned was as fragile as a bubble.

'I will try to talk to you on the phone, if I may?'

'You can try, but all you'll get is our solicitor's number. Now go away!'

Brennan nodded and walked down the steps. The eyes in the window followed him, but when he reached the gate and turned to look, the plump pianist was drawing the curtains to keep out the sinking sun.

Brennan found a phone box on the way back to The George, but couldn't get an answer from Janet. It was the day for his parents to walk down to Steve Hatt's in Upper Street to treat themselves to a bit of fish. Ten to five. Lester was probably booting a ball around Highbury Fields. The phone booth began to boil up as the sun caught it full on. Brennan felt prickles of sweat forming on his forehead. What the fuck was he doing here, chasing a non-story that nobody had commissioned in the first place? He felt grim and alien and alone. The thought of Janet diligently padding along the racks of files at the Census Office in pursuit of death certificates depressed him even further. He put the phone down. He pushed open the door to let in cooler air and trudged off back into Bridport.

Brennan spent an hour soaking in The George's ball-and-claw-footed Victorian bath, and then lay on his bed in the towels and fell deeply asleep. When he woke he could see that the sunset was fading. It was gone nine. He then realised that the reason he'd woken was that there was a repeated knocking on the door. He wondered for a minute if he'd left the bath taps on. Or maybe the tattooed armpit had another dose for him.

'Just a minute,' Brennan called as he pulled the towels up around him. He padded over to the door, then as an afterthought, came back for the brass table lamp which he unplugged from its wall socket. Holding it behind his back with his right hand, he turned the key of the door with his left. Janet was standing on the landing looking at him impassively.

'How did you get the face – fancy shagging?'

Brennan eased the door open and tried to look as natural as he could with the table lamp in his hand. Janet sauntered in.

'Neighbour of Cathy Aldridge's took exception to me visiting her house.'

'She's the nurse, is she?'

Brennan nodded, then winced as his head throbbed.

'I thought that might have been him on a follow-up call. It was a toss-up between the lamp and the Gideon Bible.'

'How about "nice to see you, Janet, what brings you down here?" '

'Sorry – I must have been asleep for nearly three hours. I'm still a bit dozy.'

'I've got a Bloody Mary waiting on the bar downstairs when you're ready.'

'Right.' A cloud of doubt passed across Brennan's face. 'You *didn't* really think I had a woman in here, did you?'

Janet shrugged. 'I've got copies of the death certificates. Both signed by a Dr Simmons. Causes of death are given as respiratory failure for him, heart attack for her.'

Brennan tried to log the information, scouting for significance. He frowned at her.

'So what's the urgency?'

'Well, I just fancied being with you for an evening. Is that all right? Or should I have made an appointment?'

'No, Janet. It's fine, honest. I'm really pleased to see you.'

Janet looked far from reassured.

'Get your kit on then – you're taking me out for some seafood.'

Brennan gave her a warm, wide smile.

'I'll be down in five minutes!'

'By the way, who died first, him or her?'

'The Dentons, you mean?'

Janet nodded patiently.

'Well, according to Furnival, and the gravestone, him, then her.'

'That's what I thought. It's probably nothing, but the serial number on *his* death certificate is several numbers back from the one on hers.'

Brennan and Janet took a taxi down to The Riverside restaurant in West Bay and took advantage of the fact that few of its customers dined at the metropolitan hours of nine-thirty onwards. Indeed, while everyone else

around them was sipping coffee or tucking into puddings, they ordered
aperitifs, feeling deliciously decadent and depraved.

'I'm glad you came,' Brennan said, now fully awake and alert. 'It's
turning into a bit of a slog, this one.'

Janet eyed him beadily.

'So I'm down here primarily as your research assistant to ease the load,
am I?'

'No – not primarily, secondar . . .' Brennan struggled to get the syllables
past his swollen lip. 'You know what I mean?'

'Do I?'

Brennan fingered his bruised nose.

'Can we not have one of those jagged evenings where we just keep
taking shots at each other?'

'We can *try* – but I wouldn't want to bet on it!'

Their first courses arrived, and the bottle of white wine. Brennan pushed
it across to Janet to taste because of the cracks in his lip – tonight would
be one time when he could slug it back legitimately.

'What have you got, then?' Janet asked, returning to business.

'Nothing concrete – just lots of very defensive people. Well, aggressive
in one case. The nurse is the key, if I can get to her.'

'What do you reckon it is, then – straightforward neglect? A tragic act
of carelessness which they all want to hide?'

'I guess it's something like that. It's going to be desperately hard to get
anything though. If we assume it was a patient who wrote the letter, who
saw or heard of something going wrong, then I can't march in and expose
him or her to the gang that runs the home.'

'Have we established whether the Dentons had any next of kin or close
friends?'

Brennan shrugged.

'Doesn't look as though they had. Chestnut Grange had to pay for the
funerals . . .'

Janet laid her fork aside.

'That's interesting.'

Brennan looked at her, waiting for clarification.

'Most of these homes are financed by a mix of local-council funding
and the private or state pensions of the patients. But the drift is towards
getting the old people to pay themselves, rather than being a burden on
the state. Very American.'

'So what's interesting precisely?'

'Well, if the home paid for the Dentons' burials, it suggests that they had control of their money – their savings, which are now their legacies.'

'You're suggesting that the home could have arranged to inherit whatever money the Dentons had left?'

'Sure. Which complicates matters sufficiently to justify a cover-up, yes?'

Brennan tried to slow the speed of the thoughts, fearing mistaken assumptions and false trails. He was also a little frightened of finding a second line of enquiry when his mind had just about settled on one.

'Hang on, hang on – this is potentially a bit hysterical, Janet. An old people's home with a vested interest in their clients dying?'

'It's possible . . .'

'But the implications of that are . . . terrifying!'

'I know. That's why I brought it up.'

'Look, can we eat while I have a think about this? My head's sore enough as it is.'

Janet conceded defeat. They chatted on about Brennan's new house and Lester's plans for the summer, skirting around any mention of their own future.

It was nearly midnight when they left the restaurant, brimful of physical contentment, if not spiritual. The pub had long closed and the harbourside was eerily deserted, with the rigging of the fishing boats clanking in the warm night breeze.

'Can I see the sea?' Janet asked as she put her shoulder under Brennan's left arm.

'Well, seeing as you've come all this way . . .'

They walked up the shingle bank, hearing the rhythmical whisper of the waves on the shoreline. As they reached the crest of the bank, they saw several wood fires lit along the beach, surrounded by shadowed figures. The dull thump of rave music wafted across.

'Ee – time was when you came to a beach to shag! Not to dance and take funny chemicals!' Janet said in self-parody.

Brennan looked affronted.

'Sorry – I don't ever remember you doing it on a beach with me!'

Janet let out a little laugh.

'Clacton – 1982. Staff summer outing.'

'Oh, Christ, yes – I was drunk presumably?'

''Fraid so.'

'Seems a lifetime ago now, Janet. What happened to our youth? It's just gone so fast!'

'Come off it, Frank, you're not ready for the Zimmer frame yet. Youth is a state of mind.'

'The state of your body comes into it too.'

They looked out into the night. A thin trail of coloured lights marked where Lyme Regis was.

'What are we going to do, Frank?'

'Well, I think, on balance, we should take the letter and the circumstantial evidence to the police and let then decide what to do. I've got no . . . no mandate to be looking into this.'

Janet watched him carefully, trying to decide whether it was avoidance or just plain insensitivity which had led him to misinterpret the question.

'I was talking about us – *primarily* . . .'

'I don't know – you tell me first.'

'How can I do that when so much depends on what you've decided for yourself? You're not being fair to me.'

'No. No, I suppose not. Well, in the best of all worlds, I'd like us to be together. All three of us. But I happen to like where I'm living now, so moving back to London's out of the question.'

'What about your work?'

'Not so sure. I know I won't be able to write fiction – it's wishful thinking in both senses. But I'd like to try my hand at books. You know, factual ones. Case histories, profiles – that sort of thing. I think I'm finished as a journalist.'

'So everything has to be done according to your own revised life.'

'I beg your pardon?'

'You selfish bastard, Frank. You've really no idea what you're saying, or what the implications are for me and Lester!'

'Yes, I have – I've said I'd like you to be with me.'

'But as what, Frank? Housewife and horse-racing companion? Can't you see that your work and my life have a direct impact on each other if we're going to get back together?'

'I know that – but I've said I'm changing. The nights out on the piss are all over now. I'll be calmer. More regular!'

'But if your work is self-contained, there's no place for me! I can pick up all sorts of research contracts from television companies in London, but if I move to nowheresville, I'm brain dead!'

'I thought you liked it in Wiltshire?'

'For a short visit, yes. But if I'm to live there, I need something more meaningful than coffee mornings with other women to sustain me!'

Brennan took a few paces away from her, running his hand through his hair in a gesture of frustration.

'What happened to people just loving each other? Wanting to be with one another for no other reason?'

'Don't be so fucking naïve, Frank! Attitudes like that belong in the last century! People get together today as much for what they *do* as for who they *are*! I was attracted to you because you cared about people getting turned over, and did something about it!'

Brennan turned to look at her. Even in the faint light that the night yielded he could see the tears flowing down her cheeks.

'But if I go back to papers, the same old destructive cycle will start up again!'

'Go back on *your* terms, Frank, not theirs. Do the stories that still matter. In your own time. If they don't want them, take them to the TV documentary firms. I can help you – we can work together! I mean you *do* find me useful at times, don't you?'

'Yes, of course I do. I was only thinking this afternoon how . . . how good it was to have you on my side. Covering my blind spots . . .'

'Doing the legwork?'

'No, I genuinely think you add to what I do. I just question whether this sort of case is still worth our attention . . .'

Janet looked at him and shrugged.

'Okay – well, you know what's at stake. It's your decision.'

Janet began to clamber down the shingle bank and walk back to the harbour. Brennan caught her up and put his arm round her shoulder. They walked past Chestnut Grange wondering what secrets it had yet to give up. Laurie was still wiping down the bar when they got back to The George. Janet's presence seemed to soften her attitude to Brennan. She made them all hot chocolate and brought the bottle of Armagnac to the table. They all talked jazz for at least an hour, before Janet decided it was time for bed. She and Brennan lay awake alongside each other for what seemed a long time without speaking, their thoughts being too tangled to articulate. Eventually, first Janet, then Brennan drifted off into profound sleep.

When Janet woke, just after eight, Brennan was no longer alongside her. Indeed, the side of the mattress where he lay was already cold. She sat up and drew the sheet to her chin. His clothes had gone too, although his holdall lay on the floor. Janet felt a sudden onset of irrational panic. She'd pushed too far and said too much.

The door to the room eased open. Brennan, fully dressed, clean-shaven and bright-eyed, peered round the angle of the door.

'Sorry, I woke up with my head buzzing, so I went down for an early breakfast. Do you want me to bring yours up to you?'

'I'll come down. Thought you'd gone for good when I first woke.'

Brennan came across, sat on the side of the bed, took her hand and pressed it to his mouth.

'We're going to crack this bastard, Jan. Both bastards, in fact!'

CHAPTER NINE

Brennan was surprised by the ease with which he was able to make an appointment to see Dr Simmons. Indeed he was obliged to reintroduce himself again half-way through the phone call when it crossed his mind that Simmons might think 'Frank Brennan' was a patient of his. But Simmons remained calm and courteous and showed no reaction to the fact that the Dentons were the subject of Brennan's enquiry. Short of sending a uniformed chauffeur for Brennan, Simmons couldn't have been more accommodating.

Brennan reported the highlights of the conversation back to Janet as she was finishing her breakfast in The George's dining-room.

'Don't sound so grateful, Frank. Doctors are trained to be professional liars in all kinds of situations. He'll just attempt to baffle you with medical terminology, same as they all do!'

'All right – it just wasn't the reaction I was expecting, that's all.'

'Exactly – designed to throw you off balance. Well, I know how to retaliate – I'm coming with you.'

'I didn't mention that to him. Isn't it a bit unfair?'

'Tough shit – if he knows he's got questions to answer, does it matter how many people are asking them?'

Janet went upstairs to change into more businesslike clothes while Brennan spent ten minutes with her make-up bag, powdering over the worst excesses of the previous day's beating.

Then Janet sat him down to talk through his notes and between them they kicked around five or six questions which they felt would at least shed light on the Dentons' last hours, and perhaps reveal a strategic crack in what had so far been an impregnable brick wall.

Simmons's surgery was on the way out of town on the Beaminster Road.

Brennan and Janet decided to walk, partly to prepare more questions, partly because the fine morning dictated it.

The surgery was located in one wing of a large Victorian Gothic rectory, which was serviced by a gravel drive from the main road. Mature poplars and oaks were dotted around the ground, creating an air of isolated calm.

'Must have a lot of private patients to pay for this,' Janet observed tartly as they approached the house. Two other partners were enshrined on the brass plaque next to the surgery's door, and Brennan and Janet assumed one of them was providing moral support for Simmons, because there was another, smartly suited gentleman sitting to one side of Simmons's desk as they were ushered into his room.

Simmons rose to offer his hand to Brennan, who felt for any signs of clamminess as he took it. But the gesture was both cool and firm.

'I hope you don't mind, but I've brought my wife Janet along. She's my research assistant.'

Simmons looked to the man in the chair, who nodded his assent.

'Well, as we're batting with runners – let me introduce you to my solicitor, Martyn Roche.'

Brennan briefly caught sight of Janet's 'I told you so' expression, before shaking Roche's hand.

'I'm here for your benefit just as much as my client's, Mr Brennan. I'm sure none of us wants to get involved in an expensive misunderstanding.'

'Perish the thought,' Brennan said with the minimum of charm.

Simmons gestured for them to sit down, at which point Roche produced a small cassette-recorder which he placed in the centre of Simmons's desk.

'I'll be happy to provide a copy if you require one at a later stage,' Roche said with the smile of a grandmaster who'd just secured check with his first move.

Janet produced her notebook in retaliation and settled herself.

'My shorthand's in good order, actually.'

Roche switched on the tape, announcing the day, time and names of those present as a prologue, before he himself posed the first question.

'Now let me just clarify what we're dealing with here. You are an investigative journalist of some repute, Mr Brennan, and for reasons best known to yourself, you have seen fit to make enquiries at the retirement home called Chestnut Grange in West Bay, for which my client, Dr Philip Simmons, is GP, those enquiries being conducted initially under a false name?'

'I'm ashamed to give a short answer after that, but "yes".'

'May I ask the reason for the subterfuge?' Roche consulted a yellow legal pad on his lap. 'The use of the name "Dunlop".'

'Yes. I felt that as my enquiries centred on a sufficiently serious subject, it was better for me to find out as soon as possible whether there was any substance to my . . . well, to my suspicions.'

'So you admit this initial deceit?'

Janet intervened, her face tautening with anger.

'With respect, I'd like to move on to the questions we have to ask your client—'

'Not until I've established a framework for them, Mrs Brennan.'

Janet spotted the patronising, 'you're just a dumb housewife' smile which accompanied the use of her marital name.

'The framework is simple, Mr Roche. We'd like to ask your client, Dr Simmons, about his involvement with the deaths of two patients at the home – Mr John Denton, and his wife Irene.'

'Define involvement,' Roche said quickly.

'Professional duties,' said Brennan.

Simmons took a breath and sat forward, but Roche was not ready to let him speak for himself yet.

'On what grounds are you asking these questions?' Roche pointedly leant forward and moved the tape recorder six inches nearer to his inquisitors.

'I have reason to believe that the deaths of Mr and Mrs Denton had suspicious circumstances . . .'

Roche stood up, agitated.

'I caution you to be very careful in what you say from now on, Mr Brennan . . .'

'I'm never anything but—'

' . . . because you're moving into deep water.'

'Can we put the questions now, please?' asked Janet.

'Wait a minute . . . I want to know the grounds for your use of the phrase "suspicious circumstances" first.'

'A letter from someone at, or associated with, the home, requesting that I investigate the deaths.'

'Written by whom?' Roche asked, making furious notes.

'It was anonymous . . .'

'Terrific! Can I see it?'

Brennan gave Janet a look – she shook her head.

'I guess that whoever wrote it, did so in fear,' Brennan said, 'so the answer's "no", I'm afraid.'

Roche leant across and whispered into Simmons's ear, before turning back to them.

'I'm sorry, but I've just advised my client that this interview must terminate now. It's predicated on entirely spurious grounds. Possibly even fictional given the state of newspapers today!'

'Careful, Mr Roche,' Janet said, 'straying into slander, I'd say!'

'I'm sorry – I withdraw that remark. But really – I must ask you to leave . . .'

'Did you certify them dead, Dr Simmons?' Janet asked, looking directly across the desk to avoid Roche.

'I really don't think you have to answer any questions, Philip . . . this is just too ridiculous—'

Simmons pushed his feet under his chair and sat forward.

'No, it's all right. I'd prefer to set the record straight, Martyn, please.' Roche made a gesture of futility and sat back in his chair.

'Yes, I was called out to examine both Mr and Mrs Denton, and yes, I certified their deaths. It is, regrettably, a frequent element of my work when dealing with a retirement home.'

'Did either of their deaths give you cause for alarm or suspicion?' Brennan asked quietly. If Janet was going to take on the hard-cop role, he'd best be the soft one.

'No. But it was distressing. It isn't always. But seeing her grief, her sense of loss, and then discovering she'd died the following morning . . . well, yes, that was disturbing, just in a human sense, do you understand?'

'Of course,' Brennan said sympathetically.

Janet produced photocopies of the death certificates from her document case and handed them across the desk to Simmons.

'Come on, what's this?' Roche asked, with a hint of disdainful laughter.

'I'd like to know why the serial numbers on the certificates don't relate to the chronology of the two deaths?' Janet asked, drawing up her shoulders.

Simmons and Roche both looked at the certificates to confirm the discrepancy.

'You'd have to ask the registrar that – I don't complete these things, you realise, I simply forward written confirmation to him.'

'But in the right order?'

'Well, yes, of course. But you have to remember that Mr Denton passed away on a Sunday evening, Mrs Denton the following morning. So there was some potential for misunderstanding in the bureaucracy. You'll find that a registrar's busiest session is a Monday morning!'

'You have no doubts about your diagnoses, though?'

'Well, no – I knew their medical histories from the time they first came to the home. He'd always had chest and lung problems, he'd been an eighty-a-day man he once told me—'

Roche raised a hand.

'Aren't we getting into dodgy areas with patient confidentiality here, Philip?'

'Well, yes, but their causes of death are public.'

'So you saw *no reasons* for post-mortems or inquests, Dr Simmons?' Brennan asked with emphasis.

'No. Not at all.'

Roche leant forward and switched off the tape, then stood up.

'I think we've gone as far as we can go to help you now. Unless you have some startling evidence, in which case you should take it directly to the authorities.'

'Okay,' Brennan conceded, 'but I'll ask one last question, which Dr Simmons can leave unanswered if he wishes.' Brennan turned to Simmons and fixed him with a stare. 'Are you sure that neither of the deaths could be ascribed to any sort of negligence or malpractice within the home?'

'Look, I'm sure. Apart from urgent calls, I went, I *go*, to Chestnut Grange once a week to check on any of the patients' ailments or whatever. I promise you, they are well looked after. I'd be the first to say so if they weren't!'

Brennan and Janet exchanged looks, but Brennan was the first to rise.

'Thank you for your time, Dr Simmons. I'm sorry to have troubled you, but I hope you can sympathise with our concern.'

'Well, in some ways. But I have to say I'm mystified by the way you've gone about this. I mean, do journalists really respond to every anonymous letter they get?'

Brennan smiled and shook hands with both Simmons and Roche.

'If I say any more I'll be giving away trade secrets.'

Janet stood, anxious to dispel the male *bonhomie* that had descended upon the room.

'If we have any more questions may we . . . ?'

Roche moved towards her, taking a business card from his wallet. Janet held out her hand, and he gave her the card, but then talked directly to Brennan.

'You file questions to me, in writing. Needless to say, I'll be watching out for anything you might write, Mr Brennan.'

'We'll be in touch about a copy of the tape,' Janet said before opening the door and leaving. Brennan followed, nodding his thanks to both men. He caught up with Janet on the path.

'What a fu—'

'Two minutes,' he interrupted. 'It's like leaving the pictures. You don't talk about the film until everybody else is out of earshot.'

'Why the hell not?'

'Because you end up sounding a prat if you're not careful.'

'Hey, look, we're not talking about a work of art here – all we've been watching is a highly professional, carefully orchestrated snow-job!'

'You think so?'

'Frank, you're the one who used to have a season ticket to Whitehall press briefings! You can't seriously believe that was a sincere attempt at co-operation?'

'I wasn't saying that – I was just asking you . . . us to reserve judgement. If you jump to an instant conclusion—'

'It saves time . . .'

'It also prevents you from thinking about other possibilities.'

'Such as?'

'Well, how do we know that that was Simmons's solicitor?'

'I've got his card . . .'

'Yes, yes, I know he *is* a solicitor, I just wonder how long Simmons has been a client? I mean, they seemed like complete strangers to me – at cross-purposes. Simmons wanted to tell us what had gone on – Roche didn't. And forgive me being "regionalist", but how come a small-town doctor in Dorset can just happen to have a brief with such media savvy? I mean, it's supposed to be just old ladies' wills and farm sales down here!'

'Well, Dorchester's not exactly Manhattan, is it?'

Janet thrust Roche's card at Brennan, pointing at the solicitor's quaint address. Brennan registered it absently, refusing to give ground on his point.

'I don't care where he's based – it's who brought him in we should be worrying about. And I don't think it could have been Simmons.'

Brennan's point finally silenced Janet, who frowned at him in exasperation.

'So you *do* agree with me?'

'Yes, but for the right reasons!'

They walked slowly back to The George together, feeling both encouraged and discouraged in equal measure. The case – if there was one – seemed to be increasingly subordinate to the machinations going on around it.

'Did I embarrass you at all?' Janet asked suddenly.

Brennan seemed shocked by the suggestion.

'You're kidding! I was bloody glad you were there! I think I'd have struggled taking them both on. My only doubt is that we may be generating more mystery than there actually is.'

'How do you mean?'

'Well, without being arrogant – my name *can* create an aura of trouble without there actually being any. I mean, can you imagine what it's like for an ordinary, innocent shopkeeper suddenly finding that TV bloke Roger Cook at the counter, trying to buy a pound of cheese? The shopkeeper's probably thinking, "Christ, what have I done wrong? Has the sell-by date on that Camembert expired yet?" And Roger Cook will probably be thinking, "Why is this man panicking when all I want is a piece of cheese?" Do you see what I mean?'

'It still doesn't explain the letter. You didn't invent that, did you?'

'No, but I can't help thinking sometimes that it's all a wind-up.'

'What for? I mean, who'd do a thing like that?'

Brennan gave her an old-fashioned look. Janet quickly recognised its significance.

'You can't be serious? The security boys wouldn't waste time on something like this?'

'They're not – *I'm* the one wasting time. Potentially digging myself into a deep hole. They'd have a lot of fun watching me do that.'

'I don't think you got enough sleep last night, Frank, you're beginning to hallucinate!'

'Buy me a coffee then . . .'

They wandered in through the now open doors of The George. About half a dozen people were taking coffee or orange juice. Brennan signalled to Laurie, who was down in the kitchen area, working the Gaggia machine. A few minutes later she brought two coffees over.

'Somebody rang for you while you were out, Frank.'

Laurie reached into the back pocket of her jeans and took out a folded scrap of paper.

'Cathy. Wants you to call her at the home. That make sense?'

Brennan took the note from her.

'I have to say, Laurie, that after the last few days, it makes no sense at all . . .'

Laurie retreated to the kitchen, leaving Janet and Brennan to deal with this bizarre reversal.

'Have I missed something?' Brennan asked Janet. 'I mean, it's not

National Have-a-Chat-to-Frank-Brennan Day, is it?'

'Maybe she found out about you getting beaten up, and wants to apologise?' Janet suggested in earnest.

Brennan sipped his coffee thoughtfully, then trudged off towards the pay-phone in the hall. Janet watched him through a serving hatch behind the bar. His face was expressionless whatever was being said. He hung up the phone and returned to the table.

'I don't have a good feeling about this.'

'What'd she say?'

'She wants to meet to try and explain things.'

'That's it?'

'Yeah.'

'So what time does she get off?'

'She doesn't – she wants me to go to the home at two o'clock.'

'But they wouldn't even let you in the front door yesterday!'

'Like I said – I don't have a good feeling . . .'

Brennan invited Janet to accompany him to the home, but she felt that if Nurse Aldridge was in a volatile state, it might just tip her over the edge if a team of interrogators turned up. Brennan took her point but asked her to come with him as far as the house, just in case she saw something that he'd been missing.

They arrived just before two, after a light and alcohol-free lunch. As they approached the door, the plump piano-playing lady opened the door and moved down the steps to greet them.

'Mr Brennan, thank you for coming so promptly. I'm Liz Jobson, by the way, I help run the home.'

Brennan shook her hand and introduced Janet.

'Would you mind if my wife waited here for me?'

'No, no, not at all. In fact, why don't you come to my office for a cup of tea?'

'How kind!' Janet said, forcing a smile.

Jobson closed the main door and security locked it before leading Brennan and Janet across the hall.

'Right – if you go down to Mr Furnival's office on the right, your wife can have a cuppa and a natter!'

'Thank you very much,' said Brennan, moving down the corridor. Meanwhile Jobson held open the door of her office for Janet. A vague, surreal thought struck Brennan – that both he and Janet were about to be murdered, or drugged and kept in the home for the rest of their lives. The notion brought a brief smile to his lips as he knocked firmly on Furnival's door.

'Come!' said Furnival's clipped voice from behind the door.

Brennan opened the door and tried hard to make it seem that what he saw was what he expected. Behind the desk, Cathy Aldridge was seated between Furnival and Martyn Roche. Standing to one side with a huge smirk on his face was Mike Watkiss. Suddenly the town felt even smaller.

'Take a seat, Mr Brennan,' Watkiss slurped, enjoying the moment of surprise.

'I hope your paper knows you're taking an afternoon off?'

'I manage my own time, thanks. They can always bleep me if there's a Martian invasion.'

Brennan managed a smile.

'I've got news for you – I think it's already happened!' Brennan nodded at the foursome lined against him to emphasise the joke.

'Mr Watkiss has offered us his valuable assistance, Mr Brennan,' Furnival announced unctuously. 'We have no experience of dealing with sharp media men such as yourself, so he's here to prevent our panic and your confusion.'

'How considerate of him. *And* Mr Roche – solicitor to the newspaper group based in Dorchester, at a guess?'

Roche preened himself.

'I believe it's what's known as synergy,' he said, utterly at ease. 'The situation is much as this morning, Mr Brennan. Mrs Aldridge has volunteered to deal with any reasonable queries you may have, but I'm here to ensure that you don't stray.'

Brennan nodded. He looked at Cathy Aldridge. Immediately, her eyes looked down and away. She was out of uniform, dressed in a drab, cheap floral dress which made her look ten years older. Her face, when he'd had a chance to see it, looked careworn. He couldn't help thinking, as Furnival and Roche flanked her, of a wild flower having the life pressed out of it.

'You may begin, Mr Brennan,' Furnival said. 'Take a seat, why don't you?'

'Actually, I think I'd rather stand.'

Brennan began to pace the room, parodying an American prosecution attorney.

'In the circumstances, I feel my questions will be fruitless. So I don't wish to subject Mrs Aldridge to any pressure whatsoever. I will just reiterate the nature of my enquiries – that somebody associated with the home alerted me, no, *asked* me, about the nature of the Dentons' deaths, the inference being that there might have been something suspicious about them. That's all I have to say. If Mrs Aldridge feels that she can enlighten me in any way, she can contact me at this telephone number.'

Brennan patiently transcribed his new phone number on to the back of a receipt and handed it across the desk to Aldridge. Furnival nodded for her to take it, and her thin, bony hand reached out to swallow the scrap of paper.

'Gentlemen, thank you!' Brennan shot them all a superior smile, saving his last look for Watkiss, a poacher-turned-gamekeeper.

'I hope you won't be overcharging Mr Furnival for your services, Mr Watkiss?'

Brennan turned and left the room. As he reached the hall, Janet emerged from the patients' lounge, with Jobson at her side. Brennan nodded to the door. Janet took the hint and paid her thanks to Jobson. She followed Brennan out of the door and down the steps.

'What happened?'

'I've told you! Two minutes! Probably five in this case! Don't look anxious or angry – I don't want them to think they've won! I'll tell you about it on the train!'

'What train?'

'The one we're getting out of here!'

Brennan walked on at a furious pace and turned off the drive back on to the road into Bridport. They packed their clothes at The George and then Brennan settled up with Laurie, reassuring her again that though she might have heard unpleasant things about him around town, he was only doing a job. Laurie had given him a smile of trust which was about the only warm memory he would take away. He ordered a taxi for Dorchester West station, and caught a train heading north within half an hour.

Brennan sat slumped in a stupor of disappointment throughout the journey. Janet watched him, knowing it would be a bad move to probe or provoke. So instead, she took out the notes and photocopies and began to browse through them. But even this antagonised Brennan.

'You're wasting your time, Janet. These people are dead.'

'But it's still *how* they died that—'

'I was talking about the *living* dead – Furnival, Watkiss, that fat Jobson bitch, Aldridge – pathetic cow. There's nothing we can do to punish them – God's done it for us already. They're mean, miserable, shrivelled gits, with no lives. Let 'em rot, whatever they've done!'

'No need to be so constructive, Frank.'

'Fuck off!'

Janet registered the embarrassed looks of the other passengers. The sweltering summer countryside passed by unnoticed as Brennan spread a black gloom throughout the carriage.

They changed trains at Westbury, with a twenty-minute wait for the service up to Bradford. Janet lead him across to the buffet, which didn't seem to have changed since the age of steam. Apart from the prices. And the giant poster of the French Train-de-Grand-Vitesse, which looked like a subversive comment on British Rail, or whatever it was called now.

Brennan slurped his coffee, avoiding Janet's look.

'Shall I get Lester to come down? Have a family weekend.'

'If you like,' he muttered. 'I can't promise my mood will improve.'

'He knows you well enough by now.'

Brennan took this as a dig and scowled at her. Janet vowed not to speak again unless prompted.

The Bradford train pottered in fifteen minutes late and then stood clattering at the platform for a further five minutes. Janet could see Brennan's temper rising to volcanic levels. All it needed now was some dumb announcement from the conductor and he was likely to go ballistic.

Mercifully the train pulled away. Janet dug her head back into the files, flicking idly through what now looked like dead material. They hadn't come up with anything new, other than exposing a bunch of nervous people, whose first line of defence was the law. Janet tried to see a way in which Brennan's interest in the case could be revived.

The train was just leaving Trowbridge when she began a last trawl through the details of the holding company which ran Chestnut Grange. The directors were listed as Reginald Arthur Furnival, Jane Hough Furnival and Elizabeth Linda Jobson. Jane was presumably Mrs Furnival – Janet checked the addresses, they were the same. Jobson was listed as living at the Old Rectory, Beaminster Road. Janet's heart flipped over.

'Frank!'

'What?'

'Frank, look!'

Janet thrust the page of the Companies House document at him.

'Liz Jobson lives at the same house as Dr Simmons has his surgery!'

'So? It's a big house!'

'It's a big coincidence – the doctor who looks after the patients in a home, sharing living space with a director of the same home!'

'As I have found out to my cost – it's a small town, Janet!'

'But it establishes a non-business connection between the two of them. Which neither of them acknowledged in the "open day" they laid on for our benefit!'

'Okay, so it's a connection. But I'm not dashing back to challenge them again. It's a detail, that's all.'

'No, it's not, Frank, it's more than that. It gives them both a reason to lie!'

Brennan registered Janet's point. Unfortunately, they were so intense in their consideration that they missed the stop for Bradford-on-Avon, and found themselves carried on to Bath to complete the day.

CHAPTER TEN

'Bristol Rovers?' Lester said with incredulity. 'Bristol *Rovers*? Are they in the League then?'

Brennan looked at him patiently.

'They're quite a decent little side. Second division.'

'But I don't want to go all the way to Bristol, Dad. I've just spent two hours on a train! I'm travel sick.'

'You don't have to, Lester, their ground's in Bath. We can be there in half an hour by train and taxi.'

'Why are they called Bristol Rovers when they play in Bath?'

Janet smiled across the kitchen table – here was living proof that the enquiring mind and a pedantic attention to detail were hereditary.

'Because their original ground closed,' Brennan said, his patience ebbing. 'So they borrowed one in Bath. Your beloved Arsenal were once called Woolwich, you know, because that's where they were based!'

'Never?'

'You just think it's about the latest shirt design, or what boots Ian Wright is wearing this year. Football is – well, it used to be – about communities. The only people who went to watch a team were those who lived in the area. After they'd finished work on a Saturday morning. There was none of this swanning up and down the country to follow the team most seen on television!'

'So what's this got to do with Bath Rovers or whatever they're called?'

'Because they're one of those clubs who've kept their core support, despite playing in another town. Nobody in their right mind would *choose* to support them, but the people that do are still linked with the community that the club sprang from. Do you get me?'

'You mean they're a sort of historical item?'

'If you like . . .'

'So who are they playing?'

'It's a pre-season friendly. Against Yeovil Town.'

Lester shook his head to display incomprehension. The names might well have been from a foreign country as far as he was concerned.

'Well, it's either that or Bath Races, okay?'

Lester pulled a face.

'Horse-racing? Bor-ing!'

Brennan scowled at him.

'So go to the game with your dad. I've got shopping and cooking to do, so I don't want you under my feet all afternoon,' Janet said, clearing the table.

'Isn't there anything else to do round here then at weekends?'

'Such as?' Brennan asked, raising his eyebrows like a dissenting headmaster.

'Well, tenpin bowling? Movies?'

'You can find all that in due course, Lester,' Janet said over her shoulder. 'It's a summer's day, you should be outdoors.'

'We can have a quick look round Bath afterwards, if you like?' Brennan offered as a truce.

Lester wiped his hand in front of his face to indicate his blank indifference.

'Go and get changed then,' Brennan said with a nod upstairs. 'And that doesn't mean your Arsenal shirt – I've been beaten up once already this month!'

Lester trudged out of the kitchen and clumped up the stairs towards the top floor of the house.

'He's determined to punish me for this move, isn't he?' Brennan asked with a shake of his head.

'Well, you've got a chance to talk to him now. To explain. He thinks you're giving up – you can tell him you're not.'

'I'm not sure I'd get past a lie-detector on that one, actually . . .'

Janet came across from the sink and put her arms round Brennan's shoulder.

'Just try to relax and enjoy the weekend, Frank. We've got enough to know that things aren't kosher down at that home. All we need is a few pieces of hard evidence. And they'll come! They're probably all sitting around this weekend congratulating themselves on getting away with whatever it is they've done – so when you turn up again, they'll fall apart!'

'Almost convincing, Jan,' Brennan said rising. 'Right, better go and dig out my scarf and my rattle . . .'

Brennan headed for the staircase.

'What do Robert and Alice eat, by the way?'

'I dunno. But I'd guess you'd better steer clear of meat and wildlife.'

Brennan walked Lester down to the station, pointing out those few features of the town which he thought Lester might appreciate – the video shop, the library, the swimming-pool, the playing fields and the country park. There was no major response.

'Is there an arcade or something?'

'What, you mean with one-armed bandits and stuff?'

'Dad, get real! I'm talking about Stealth-Bomber simulators, intergalactic warfare pods!'

Lester grinned in triumph at his father's cultural unease.

'You might get the odd game of dominoes breaking out,' Brennan said in retaliation.

'Is there a youth club then?'

'Haven't seen one yet. Bound to be one, though.'

'Bet you it's run by some vicar who wants to get you into the choir,' Lester said dismissively.

'Look, Lester, you're twelve, not twenty-two. This is a key time for you now, son. You've only got a handful of years left at school. This is when you decide to compete or give up. To expand your mind, or just let it rot on junk culture.'

'I don't think I've got a chance of doing *either* in this town, Dad!'

'Well, I think if you give it a try, you'll find it both stimulating *and* calm here.'

Brennan gestured around him. 'Can you not see that this is a less hostile planet than Holloway Road?'

Lester sniffed and shrugged.

'I've never had any trouble in London, Dad. Yeah, this is pretty. But then what?'

Brennan tried to grapple with the cloud of negativity surrounding his son. Surely, at the same age, Brennan had had some sense of purpose and a basic grasp of aesthetics? Or was he just kidding himself? Or was he committing the ultimate crime of all those who are the first successful generation of an ordinary family, in placing a burden of expectation on their children, when none had been placed on themselves?

Fortunately the train arrived in time to cut short the agonising, but the doubts provoked Brennan into shuffling off the premeditated attempts to manipulate Lester into happiness and just having genuine fun with him instead. He bought hot dogs for them both outside the ground. They laughed together at the frequently dislocated pattern of the football, and then fantasised out loud about the possibility of having seen a new star here in this humble stadium. The promising kids were all called Marcus, Bradley and Dylan now, a generation on from the Waynes and the Darrens.

After the game, they walked back into Bath and Brennan bought Lester a summer blouson jacket at Gap. It was the fag-end of the Saturday afternoon and the shopping frenzy had ebbed away, allowing him to feel that the purchase was an act of free will and not one of consumer compulsion. The city was beautiful, there was no doubt of that, but the honey-coloured Georgian amphitheatre still seemed to be playing host to the eighteenth-century idea of a gentrified life. Fine clothes, fine food, and luxury goods were on the same shelf as music, theatre and art. It was life as the old Social Democratic Party would have had it – a ruling class possessed of tasteful wealth, serviced by constantly cheerful and completely grateful artisans. Brennan had felt uncomfortable every time he'd visited the city, and was happy to get back to Bradford as soon as possible.

Lester, however, had enjoyed his first glimpse of an alternative to London. He'd logged all the crucial designer shops. There were plenty of would-be American diners with pretty teenage girls either sitting or serving in them. There were record shops for every taste, posters for gigs and clubs on every corner, and the distinct buzz of a Bohemian life was in the air. There was even a guy at the station selling *The Big Issue*, so maybe the area was all right after all! Not that Lester would be confiding this to his father just yet.

As they walked back up Market Street together, Brennan wished Lester could scale the heights of sixteen sooner, so he could smuggle him into the Dandy Lion for his first under-age pint, while Lester was wondering if he could get the new Schwarzenegger video out for the night.

'Do you want to go for a quick pint while I have a look in the video shop, Dad?' Lester asked, calculating his move.

Brennan could hardly believe such serendipity. He gave Lester a fiver and crossed to the bar on the opposite side of the road with a new spring in his step. When they both arrived back at the house, Janet could almost see the silly little male bond between them which had been absent for so long. She didn't know whether to celebrate or despair at its return.

'I've done a vegetarian lasagne, and a fruit salad, how's that?'

'Sounds perfect,' Brennan said, ruffling Lester's hair. 'Show Mum your jacket . . .'

Lester lifted the blouson out of the carrier bag. It wasn't to Janet's taste but she certainly wasn't going to say so. The moments of genuine harmony among the three of them seemed so few over the years. Now here they all were, on a Saturday night, all in the same house, without an editor ringing up screaming for Frank's whereabouts — the normality seemed overwhelming.

'You're not half growing up, love,' she said with a sudden catch in her voice as Lester paraded the jacket, instantly looking two years older.

Brennan put on a CD of The Temptations' greatest hits while he laid the table and Janet went upstairs for a bath. He'd first heard and danced to these songs, full of innocent longing and teenage pain, thirty years ago. He could still remember every word, but their meanings had changed between then and now.

Robert and Alice arrived at eight, bearing wine and a gift each. He had a volume of H. L. Mencken's waspish writings for Brennan (a bookseller who remembers his customers' tastes!), while she had a little jar of fragrant oil for Janet, labelled with gold-pen writing 'Alice's Potion: Expand Lungs, Awake Mind!'. Brennan brought out wine from the fridge and while Janet sat back to quiz Alice about aromatherapy, Robert gently interrogated Brennan about the process of settling down.

'Yeah, I think I'm over the worst now,' Brennan suggested. 'It felt a bit like changing down from fifth to second gear in the fast lane of the motorway. Now I'm beginning to realise that, in reality, my brakes were failing.'

Robert smiled enigmatically. Brennan hadn't got a handle on him yet. He seemed so gentle, so contented, it was almost as if he didn't exist compared to the rampant carnivores with whom Brennan had usually associated.

'How's the work going?' Robert asked in a tone devoid of envy or competitiveness.

Brennan scratched his head, wondering if he could, or should, articulate his feelings about the Denton investigation. Robert watched him placidly.

'I don't know, to be honest. It could be nothing, or it could be something quite big. It definitely isn't something in between.' Brennan laughed at his fumbling phrases.

'Do you mean there *is* such a thing as a hunch for a journalist?' asked Robert.

'I suppose there must be. I've no idea what it looks or feels like, but I'm sure I've got one!'

'Do you meditate at all, Frank?'

Brennan shifted his feet, uncomfortable for the first time, as though he'd invited a Jehovah's Witness in by mistake.

'Well, I *think* a lot.'

Robert wagged a finger at him gently.

'It's not the same thing. Meditation is a clearing of the mind, not an inventory of what's already there.'

'Well, if I cleared mine, I'd be worried about getting the stuff back again!' Brennan said, looking for a way to change the subject. Lester's arrival from the bathroom, freshly scrubbed and in his pyjamas, provided it.

After ten minutes of conversation about the merits of the local school, Lester was allowed to retreat upstairs with his tea on a tray and the video under his arm. Brennan almost envied him. But the evening passed without too much more New Age spouting. They contented themselves with the usual liberal party games. They discussed whether Keats was better than Dylan – Brennan insisted Dylan was better than Keats, but that Smokey Robinson was better than both of them put together. And they decried government cronies and the metropolitan arty élite, in which the likes of Kenneth Baker and Danny Baker were spiritually linked.

'Have you noticed how all these London wankers' – Brennan by now felt comfortable enough with Robert and Alice to use such expressions – 'begin every sentence with "It seems to me"? You listen the next time *The Late Show*'s on – I wish I had a quid for every time it was used. "It seems to me"! Whatever happened to "I think"?'

Janet sensed that Brennan was becoming dangerously unwound, fearing that even somebody as innocuous as Robert might come in for a verbal assault if he touched on the wrong subject, or traduced one of Brennan's few, but intense, passions in life.

'Anybody for coffee?' she asked, rising from the stylishly cluttered table.

'Decaff if you have it, please, Janet,' asked Alice.

'Me too,' added Robert.

'Can I have a Greek coffee, love? The full works – glass of water and a cigarette?' Brennan asked in retaliation. Janet's eyes narrowed – she was wise to the wind-up.

'So why didn't you tell us about your break-in?' Alice asked, catching Brennan completely off guard.

'I, er – well . . . how did you hear about it?'

Robert smiled enigmatically.

'Not much goes unnoticed in this little community. If you leave a box of broken china out with the rubbish, people will put two and two together.'

' "People" meaning Moira Backhouse?' Brennan asked with a knowing look.

'You should have told us – we could have helped,' Alice offered.

Brennan stiffened a little at the simpering.

'Well, not so actually – the break-in took place while I was giving that bloody talk, which Moira conned me into, and which you attended. Had you all been at home that night, then yes, that might have helped prevent it.'

'I meant that we could have helped you afterwards – spiritually,' said Alice.

'Well, I'm sorry – I didn't see it in those terms. The people who broke in were after something which threatened a contact of mine – they didn't get it, so spiritually, I didn't give a shit about it!'

'Frank!' Janet chastised.

'Sorry, Robert. Alice. I'm just a bit wound up by aspects of this case. I'm bad company tonight.'

Brennan sipped his drink, wishing they'd take the hint and go. But he'd opened the door to their overwhelming well-meaningfulness. Alice rose from her seat and moved round behind Brennan in an instant, laying her hands on his shoulders and kneading the neck muscles.

'Let me take the weight off your head. Let it drop back.'

'Go on. Relax, Frank,' instructed Janet.

Brennan shot her a betrayed look, and lay back his head into Alice's hands. She began to massage his scalp with her fingertips, a square millimetre at a time.

'May I ask what's the main problem with the case, Frank?' said Robert, admiring his wife's handiwork.

'Getting somebody to talk.'

'Somebody in particular?'

'I suppose so, yes.'

'And why won't he talk?'

'It's a she. Fear, I'd guess.'

'Of what? You?'

Brennan fell silent. He hadn't thought of it that way before. The justness of his cause occasionally blinded him to the fact that the innocent could still see him as a threat.

'It *may* be me personally. It's more likely she fears what I represent. Exposure. Publicity.'

'What if you took away her fear?' Robert probed. Brennan was beginning to feel like a member of an audience pulled up on to the stage to be the victim in a magician's stunt.

'I'm not sure I can do that. Especially if she's done wrong herself. Besides, I don't think she's afraid as such. She has protection. Physical, I mean.'

'Then you should show her that what she sees as protection is worthless. The only real protection is the truth.'

This sounded like a good line, whatever its provenance. Brennan would try to remember it, assuming his brain didn't go to sleep in Alice's wondrous hands.

'Thanks – I may use that.'

Janet returned to the table with a tray laden with *cafetière*, cups and chocolate mints.

'I think she's more afraid of the people she works for than she is of you, Frank,' Janet suggested.

'Ah,' Robert sighed, 'then if you want her to talk, *you* must become her protection.'

'I'm not sure I'd fancy my chances over three rounds,' Brennan said with a private look to Janet. But the notion of re-presenting himself to Cathy Aldridge as a saviour not a tormentor certainly registered.

'Does that feel better, Frank?' Alice asked.

'Much. Thank you, Alice. You're an angel.'

They drank coffee and gossiped about the secret goings-on of Tory, and its sister terraces, Middle Rank and Newtown, for another hour or so. Then they left, Alice inviting Janet over for a massage the following morning, and Brennan promising Robert he'd spend more time browsing in the book barn whenever he could manage some time off.

Brennan and Janet crept upstairs to find Lester asleep on the couch with the video channel flickering blankly. Janet covered him with a blanket where he lay, while Brennan unplugged the set. Once in bed, they lay awake while they discussed the eeriness of getting to know new people when life had already thrown too many at them.

'They're more than "nice", Frank. "Nice" is a nothing word,' Janet said analytically. 'They're spiritual – without the religion.'

'You don't think they're setting us up to join some loony sect with them then?'

'Your mind's only got one mode – suspicion. I just think they radiate . . . well, peace of mind for want of a better phrase.'

'You can get that with a lobotomy.'

'Stop being so fucking cynical. They enjoy what they do. There's a harmony about their lives. They're not stressed, or competitive, somehow.'

'You sound envious?'

'I didn't say I wanted to emulate them. I'm just interested to see that it's possible to live without shit in your life!'

'And excitement, and variety, and mystery . . . ?'

'How do you know they haven't got those?'

'Come on! She's an investigative aromatherapist, is she? He smuggles stolen gems inside his rare editions?'

'Frank, you moved here for more balance! They've already got it. I was just seeing if there was anything we could learn from them!'

'I *feel* pretty balanced now, thank you. I just can't see life as a state of passivity, that's all.'

'It seems to me tha—'

'*Janet*, please don't use that bloody phrase!'

But further conversation was abandoned as they gave in to the lure of each other's bodies.

The next morning, while Janet went over to Alice's for aromatherapy, Brennan took Lester out to a canalside cottage where they hired mountain bikes and set off along the towpath towards Avoncliff. While Brennan huffed along at a steady pace, Lester couldn't resist the temptation to get 'radical', throwing his bike at every improbable path he could spot. They rode under the great aqueduct which took the canal across the valley and found a riverside tea-shop. They sat outside at a picnic table, the mid-morning sun evaporating the sweat on their faces as they feasted on hot tea, scones and carrot cake.

Though the outing hadn't been a calculated move by Brennan, Lester's breathless satisfaction couldn't help provoke thoughts of a strategic discussion.

'You know that your mum and I would like you to move down here with us, don't you?'

Lester looked as though the sun had gone behind the clouds in an instant.

'I guessed as much.'

'Not that we're trying to pressurise you . . .'

'Dad, don't bullshit me! I know what's at stake. If I don't want to move here, then Mum will have to stay in London to look after me. And if she can't move, then maybe you'll have to come back to London too. Which you don't want, do you?'

'Probably not. But then I'd have to put your interest first . . .'

Lester shot him an accusing look, which Brennan read only too well.

'Maybe the best solution is for us all to stay in London and keep this place on for weekends?' Brennan suggested.

'You – the fearless reporter – still living at your mum and dad's?'

Brennan smiled.

'It'd be a novel twist! Anyway, we'd have to find a place of our own.'

'What if we lived here, but went back to London for the odd weekend . . . ?'

'Like when Arsenal were at home?'

Lester smiled sheepishly as the transparency of his motives was exposed.

'Just a thought, Dad.'

Brennan sat forward.

'You said about living here . . . ?'

'Well, I can see it's a nice place. And I liked Bath.' Lester hesitated.

'Go on – tell me the "buts". I'm here to listen not to persuade.'

'Well, there's my friends . . .'

'Do you not think they'd like the chance to come to the country at weekends and half-term to see you?'

The thought silenced Lester for a moment. He hadn't seen it from that point of view at all.

'Maybe . . . then there's school of course.'

'It's only your first year there – how settled do you feel?'

Lester shrugged.

'Dunno really. I always knew I was going to go there so I never thought too much about other places.'

'The school in town's supposed to be very good. Lots of facilities – playing field, music centre, gym, computer building.'

'I'd still be a Cockney git to all the other kids though, wouldn't I?'

'Well, there's gits and gits. They might well be bowled over by your street sharpness and your jazzy clothes.'

Lester pulled a resentful face.

'Dad, you're doing that trick on me now . . . what is it, pat-something?'

'I'm sorry, son – I was. I apologise. It's just that while you might think they'd see you as an outsider, they might see you as a welcome arrival. It's possible.'

'Maybe. I suppose footballers' kids have to keep on the move all the time.'

'But then their fathers are instantly famous people in whatever town they move to.'

'Well, you're famous too . . .'

'Now who's patronising who, Lester? Look, I'd like you to come down for as much of the summer holiday as you want. We can get to the coast from here in an hour. Give yourself the six weeks, and then you can decide!'

Lester nodded slowly.

'Is there a girl you'd miss in London?'

Lester blushed full with embarrassment.

'It's all right,' Brennan joshed, 'men don't talk about women!'

They finished their morning tea and crossed the valley on the aqueduct, before setting back for Bradford on the road which ran beside the railway line. With the canal, the river, the railway and the aqueduct, Brennan couldn't help but think of the spot as a real-life version of those Hornby-Dublo landscapes which accompanied the train sets of his youth. What would Lester see it as – the jungle haunt of a mythical computer predator?

Janet was flopped out on the couch in bliss when they got back to the house.

'Enjoy that?' Brennan asked solicitously.

'She's wonderful. I don't think I've felt so in touch with my bones and my muscles . . .'

'Two hours on the train will do much the same.'

Brennan made lunch for them all – tagliatelle with pesto sauce – before walking Lester and Janet down to the station for the mid-afternoon train to Waterloo. It was running late.

'You know, I think the collective noun for trains should be "an apology",' Brennan suggested with irritation.

They sat on one of the wooden benches and looked along the line as it disappeared down the valley.

'Don't want to go back, really,' Janet muttered as she leant a head on Brennan's shoulder.

'It's only for a week. Then we can be together for the summer . . .'

Janet lifted her head to give him a sceptical look.

'It's all right. Lester and I have been talking.'

'I'll tell you on the train, Mum,' Lester said defensively, hoping she'd forget.

'What are you going to do about Chestnut Grange then, Frank? Want me to call Simmons tomorrow and ask what Jobson is to him?'

'No, I think we should save that for later. All you'd get now is a bland apology. Or another Mike Watkiss press conference.'

'Anything you want me to do in London?'

'Yes. Try and find out some more about the Dentons. We've only got hearsay that they had no family. Maybe they were dumped there by relatives too embarrassed to leave a forwarding address. Anything else on the home itself might be useful – you know, annual income, local authority reports.'

'What about you?'

'Me, I have to try another way to reach Cathy Aldridge.'

The train arrived a few moments later and whisked Janet and Lester off. Brennan felt bereft and depressed all the way back to the house. While once the family had been just a burden of obligations to his work – and his carousing – it was now becoming the steady centre of his life. The thought of returning to a split existence appalled him. But now it was all down to Lester.

In the evening, Brennan put in a call to Erlestoke Prison and asked to leave a message for his former cellmate Tommy Preston. The Visiting Order arrived in the first post on Tuesday, valid for that afternoon.

Brennan walked down into Bradford and did a shop from memory of Tommy's favourite things. Booze was out – that had to go in through the unofficial channels. But Tommy was allowed to smoke cigarettes in the visiting hall. Brennan bought two packs of Gauloises – Tommy fancied himself as a bon vivant – and two rolls of strong mints. At the chemists, Brennan struggled to remember what he could and couldn't take in. Aftershave was out because of the alcohol, and opaque containers – whether for soap, shampoo or shaving foam – were also *verboten* for obvious reasons. Brennan selected an expensive shampoo, a new face flannel, and a roll-on deodorant. None of which reflected Tommy's level of hygiene as a cellmate. In fact he'd been meticulous about what he'd called his 'body whiffs' while Brennan had been in with him. Brennan just knew from his time inside that any hint of luxury did the head good.

Brennan returned to the house to pack up the goods in an easily inspected carrier bag – the screws would have it away with anything that demanded their attention – and ordered a cab to pick him up at the Conigre Hill car-park, opposite the Zion Baptist Chapel.

'Just visiting,' he told the cab after he'd confirmed the destination. Twenty-five minutes later, the taxi was pulling up outside the quaint Georgian lodge with its neat lawns and rows of flowers, and Brennan was soon approaching, a touch queasily, the gates he'd left behind four months earlier. He expected to run the gauntlet of comments from the screws on duty, but they processed him through to the visiting hall as if it *were* just another chore in another long day, and he was just another nobody.

The carrier bag was inspected, then tagged with Preston's name and number and taken away. Brennan was asked to turn out his pockets by one screw while another ran his hands up the inside of his legs and then up underneath his arms. Though Tommy was categorised as a non-violent prisoner, there was no guarantee he would stay that way. Once cleared, Brennan was escorted into the long featureless room, with its Formica tables and canvas-backed chairs. He chose a seat in one corner. Moments later, Tommy was admitted. The handshake and the scrabble for the cigarette packets became one continuous gesture. Brennan sat down and let Tommy slake himself on the first cigarette before demanding speech.

'How you doing, Tom?' he asked as Preston stubbed the first fag and lit the second.

'Medium, kid. You?'

'Not even that.'

'You got trouble?'

'Not in the way that you'd think.' Brennan leant in on him a little. 'Did you get the, er, food parcel from Hodges?'

Tommy nodded as he exhaled the fragrant blue smoke like a dragon.

'Sweet as a bun. Kind of you.'

Tommy Preston was in his mid-sixties, though a combination of massive intakes of vodka and, during his successful days, several years in the south of France, seemed to have kept him looking younger. The grey hair was slicked back with pomade – Morgan's only, thank you – while his fingernails were squared off and clean. Despite his record of crimes – mostly to do with thieving rich women's jewels from various hotels or shops – Tommy never regarded himself as a lag. Being sent to the 'hospital' was merely an occupational hazard, a minor detour in what was otherwise a life of style. Which didn't make him a 'ponce' or, even worse, a 'sigh' – a soft touch.

In fact, in his younger days, Tommy had told Brennan during their nights of talk, he'd run with some of London's serious gangs. When Brennan had once asked whether he'd ever killed anyone, Tommy had laughed and replied, 'No, but I could have done if it was necessary.' How much of this was braggadocio, Brennan never cared to wonder, certainly not aloud. All he knew was that Tommy had treated him courteously and that they had enjoyed their time spent together – a game of pool once a week, Brennan choosing him some good reads from the library, or mentioning the names of likely briefs for any future emergency, and Tommy, in his way, putting Brennan right about how to survive inside. They had got on – which was better than Brennan could have hoped for when he'd first been led to the cell, sickening from the gills downwards.

'I need a favour, Tommy, if it's possible . . .' Brennan began.

'Even if it's not, it's as good as done, kid.'

'I don't want to get you into trouble . . .'

Tommy gave Brennan what he could only think of as an Oliver Hardy look, disbelieving and amused at the same time.

'It can't be birds, you don't need money – so what is it? Muscle?'

Brennan nodded.

'For protection rather than action.'

'I should let them decide that, if I were you. You don't buy a whore then ask her to read poetry, do you?'

Brennan smiled.

'You got your pen?'

'I can remember it . . .' Brennan nodded his head at one of the prison officers, who was eyeballing their table.

'Oh seven one – if you're outside of London. Which you'd better be . . .'

Tommy virtually mouthed the other digits, so faint was the whisper. Brennan logged the number.

'Any particular name?'

'Don't ask — just mention mine. They'll do you a rate. One fifty, maybe two ton a day. Plus a drink if they're good. How many do you think you'll need?'

Brennan thought about the foul-smelling tattooed giant guarding Cathy Aldridge's bungalow.

'One to hold him, one to spray on the deodorant . . .'

Tommy laughed at the image this created and lit another cigarette and took a mint at the same time. Today would be a little treat. When the thirty minutes was over, Tommy stood and offered each of his cheeks for Brennan to kiss. He liked the idea of the screws not knowing it was a stylish gesture in France.

'I'll come and see you again, Tommy,' Brennan promised.

'I'd like that,' Preston said with a smile. 'And maybe when I get out, I can come and *visit* you?'

'I'd like that too,' Brennan said fondly. 'And I'll see you all right for this, okay?'

'You will not,' Tommy barked. 'This isn't tit for tat, son. If you want me, I'm there. And likewise. That's how it sits, right?'

Brennan punched him on the shoulder. Having Tommy 'on the firm' would no doubt come in useful further down the line. But for the moment, he needed other hands to help.

Brennan called the number that night, his details being taken down by a woman, as if it were dial-a-pizza. The next morning, Brennan packed an overnight bag with his change of clothes and his case notes, and set off for the main car-park next to the community hall.

On his way down, he ran into Eric the postman, probably the fittest man on the planet with this daily climb.

'Mornin', Mr Brennan. Want 'em now, or shall I leave 'em on the mat for later?'

'Let's have a look, Eric.'

Eric flicked through his bundle, bound by a thick rubber band.

'You don't want he,' Eric said, showing the brown Inland Revenue envelope with the tell-tale red inset. 'How about him?' He held up the other envelope. Brennan saw that the address of the newspaper had been written over, together with the instruction: 'please forward'. But the handwritten name had been left unchanged, in its thin black-ink scrawl.

Brennan took the envelope with a mixture of dread and excitement. He opened it on the move, seeing the Chestnut Grange letterhead as soon as he removed the sheet of paper. This time the scrawl was more aggressive in tone, and more provocative in content:

Dentons – why haven't YOU found KILLER yet? WHY?

Brennan folded the sheet into his inside pocket. He checked the envelope. He could still read the original postmark, 'Bridport, West Dorset'. If it was a Big Lads' wind-up they were going to a lot of trouble to make it look good.

Brennan came down the narrow passage of Church Lane, past Holy Trinity where the organist was putting in some early morning practice. He crossed the foot-bridge over the River Avon to the car-park, and as he crested the rise, saw a green Range Rover parked to one side, with two heavily built, casually dressed men standing by it. As he drew closer, Brennan could see that while both of them stood over six three, neither of them had much nasal cartilage left. While most people took this as the sign of a hard case, Brennan had always applied the reverse logic – that they couldn't be so hard if that had happened to them. Not that he was about to discuss this.

'Morning – I'm Brennan,' he said as he reached the car.

The driver nodded and opened the rear passenger door for Brennan, while his companion climbed into the front seat.

'West Bay still, guv?' the driver asked as he moved behind the wheel. Brennan nodded into the driving mirror and the big engine growled with life.

CHAPTER ELEVEN

Janet hated the place. As the statistical repository of the nation it became, metaphorically, a charnel house, reducing each and every citizen to just three key elements – birth, marriage, death – which were as stark and dry as bones and their dust. She'd always felt that people deserved better, perhaps being filed and cross-referenced under their individual character types – boozer, wit, gambler, show-off – rather than according to the circumstantial details of their surname and initials. Here, in these rows of shelves on several floors, life had ceased to exist in both the physical and the clerical sense.

What made Janet even angrier was that having reduced individual identity to a handful of pen strokes, and then converted these to the merest byte on a computer, the office could still get it wrong. She'd spent most of Monday trying to track down the birth and marriage certificates relating to the two Dentons. None of the three documents had been where they should have been. Her queries had been registered – 'probably a hangover from the move from Somerset House' had been the off-the-peg excuse – but now, two days later, the supervisor on this section still had no proper explanation.

'If you'd leave it with me for a few more days,' he begged.

'Was two not enough then?'

'We have other work to do, Ms Dunlop.'

'But aren't you alarmed when something like this happens? The potential for misunderstanding, for corruption, for terrorism even, is enormous!'

'I'm aware of the implications, thank you, Ms Dunlop,' the supervisor sneered. 'I take it your enthusiasm for a well-maintained system of population surveillance represents a change of heart?'

'I beg your pardon?'

'I know your work, Ms Dunlop. I've seen your name in the papers, on the TV documentaries, and on the Charter 88 petitions for citizens' rights. I wouldn't have thought you were a fan of the Census Office.'

'How did you get this information about me?' Janet demanded.

'Shall we just say it's collated. We have to know who's asking for our information and why. That's why we get you to fill in those request forms. Bit like the local library really. It's nothing sinister. I thought you'd be grateful for our efficiency and discretion.'

'Find me those certificates I asked for, *then* I'll be grateful!'

Janet walked stiffly away from the counter.

'I'll be back this afternoon,' she announced without turning.

'You want a pee or anything, guv?' the driver asked Brennan as they approached a service station outside Blandford Forum. They were the first words spoken since leaving Bradford.

'I'll wait, thanks. Don't let me stop you, though.'

'We're fine,' said the man in the front passenger seat without a glance in Brennan's direction.

'You blokes got names, at all?' Brennan asked, sitting forward.

'Better that we don't, guv. If you don't mind. Complicates things if you know. You might have to tell someone, see.'

'This is what the political parties call "putting clear water" between them, I guess?'

'Right. "Clear water" – I like that,' said the driver.

The passenger turned to Brennan, putting his arm round the head-rest of the driver's seat.

'If there's any nonsense, you see, you don't know us, we don't know you.'

'But you do. Know me.'

The passenger grinned.

'Brennan, that's a false name obviously, isn't it? You're not a Mick!'

The driver laughed and the passenger returned to staring out at the road ahead. The Range Rover powered on, though never at all above the prevailing speed limit. Brennan had to admire these blokes' professionalism. Even a humble traffic cop would have arrested them on sight, given an excuse to pull them over.

Half an hour later, they moved slowly down the main street into Bridport. Neither man had made the slightest remark about the beauty of the summer's day around them, so Brennan was surprised when the driver volunteered a comment about the neat rows of Georgian-fronted houses and shops.

'Looks a nice place,' he muttered.

Brennan guessed that there might be an element of foreboding in his voice. They were obviously way off their usual patch, knew it and felt uneasy. You could have dressed them up in cheesecloth smocks and put wisps of straw in their mouths, but their gobs would still have screamed 'Sarf Landun!' at the outside world.

'What's the story then, guv?' asked the driver.

'I need to find a bank to get you your readies. Unless you want to wait.'

'Best now, guv, if you don't mind. Might be in a rush later, if you see what I mean?'

'Take your point. Park up then, please.'

The driver steered the Range Rover into a small Pay-and-Display car-park just down from the turning for West Bay. Brennan couldn't help but smile, privately, as he watched the two men try to figure out the intricacies of the ticket machine. The bank took only a few minutes to clear his cheque and handed the £400 over in eight £50 notes. On his way back to the car-park, Brennan popped his head round the door of The George. Laurie was at the bar. She smiled as she saw him.

'Can't keep you away, can we?'

'Many have tried, none have succeeded. Am I all right for a room tonight?'

'Single or double?'

'Single.'

'I'll put you in the book.'

'See you later, Laurie, thanks.'

Brennan, though tempted by the prospect of a morning coffee, didn't fancy leaving Bill and Ben alone too long. His reservations were justified when he returned to the car-park to find them still standing at the ticket machine, baffled by the instructions.

Once inside the car, Brennan handed the money over in two bunches of £200.

'Any extras, I'm sure you'll let me know.'

'Thanks, guv. So what's the score then?'

'I need to talk to this woman. Only she's got a large friend who takes Neighbourhood Watch a bit too seriously.'

'Will he be carrying anything?' asked the passenger.

'About two stone overweight. I think he's just a local head-banger whose way of expressing his affection for this woman is to beat up anybody who comes near her.'

'And he got you, did he?' the passenger said, looking at Brennan's nose.

'I'm afraid so.'

'Do you want us to give him a coating then?'

'No, no – I just want time to talk to her alone. Restraint is the word.'

'Understood, guv. But if he gets shirty, we may have to deck him.'

'I'll leave that to you, thanks. Okay. Out of here, left at the lights, then straight down to the roundabout.'

The driver gunned the engine and the Range Rover followed Brennan's prescribed route down to the bypass roundabout. Brennan pointed out the turn-off, and the car slowed and set itself for the slow climb towards the coast.

'It gets a bit "off-road" up here, if you know what I mean?'

'No worries,' said the driver.

The Range Rover gobbled up the path as it turned from tarmac to loose stone and tufted grass. Brennan sat forward, eyeing the bungalows for signs of life.

'Next one up on the right, please.'

The driver nodded and parked the Range Rover directly outside the gate of Cathy Aldridge's house. The passenger and the driver both stepped out quickly, eyes scanning the full 360 degrees of landscape, then opened the door for Brennan. As the driver slammed the door behind him, Brennan saw the Giant Armpit emerging from the bungalow on the slope below, alerted like a spider by the movement on its web.

'Sorry. That's him,' Brennan sighed.

'Easy,' said the driver, opening his shoulders and moving out front of the car. The passenger moved with him, pulling a two-foot-long tyre lever from the lining of his jacket. The giant paused, confused by the scent of opposition. Brennan stepped forward.

'Look, I'm just going in to talk to Cathy. She'll come to no harm, I promise you. My friends here would like you not to cause a fuss, okay?'

The giant pointed and grimaced.

'I'll fucking kill 'em! Then *you*!'

'That's *not* the attitude my friends want to hear, I'm afraid! If you go back to your home, have a quiet cup of tea, we'll be out of here in twenty minutes. For good. Promise!'

'Fuck off, mister!'

The giant began to move up the slope. The driver and the passenger took a brief look at one another, then moved towards him. The driver pushed off the giant's first swing with his left forearm and slammed a

right-hander into the mountainous belly. At the same time, the passenger
swung the tyre lever in a low arc, smashing it on to the giant's knee. He
went down in a tumbling heap with a yell of pain. The passenger gave
him another whack across the shoulders with the lever to keep him down.

Behind Brennan, the front door of the bungalow burst open and Cathy
Aldridge ran out screaming.

'What are you doing? What are you bastards doing?'

Brennan held up his hands.

'It's me, Mrs Aldridge. Remember me. Frank Brennan. I just want to
talk.'

Aldridge saw the two heavies standing over her now wingless guardian
angel, and quailed.

'What did you have to do that for? He's harmless is Clive!'

'Not quite, Mrs Aldridge. I have the bruises to prove it. These gentlemen
are just ensuring that I have the right environment in which I can put my
questions to you. May I come in?'

'I'll call the police!'

Brennan sighed wearily.

'We've been through all that, Mrs Aldridge. If they come here, I'll
have to tell them what I'm looking into. And you don't want that, do you?'

Aldridge paused. Her bottom lip began to tremble.

'Look, a cup of tea and a chat will do us both good. I know you won't
believe me, but I'm here to help you.'

'Got a funny way of showing it,' she stuttered, nodding at her prostrate
neighbour.

'Listen, that's nothing to what the other lot will do when they come to
shut you up. You do know who I'm talking about, don't you? Furnival.
Jobson. Simmons.'

Aldridge turned and retreated into her house, leaving the front door
open. Brennan opened the gate, then closed it carefully behind him. He
looked across to his companions for the day.

'That's enough now, okay, lads?'

The driver nodded and put his right boot on the giant's neck as a last
reminder. Brennan went up the short path and went indoors.

The single-storey dwelling had one large living-room, with a small
kitchen at one end and a bed at the other. In between was a sofa and a
table, both of which looked as though they'd been purchased at a jumble
sale. Cathy Aldridge was filling a kettle with water.

'You'll be able to get a better job, you know. Better money than they
pay you at the home.'

'If I talk to you, I'm finished,' she said, wiping her nose with the back of her hand. She placed the kettle on the stove and lit the ring beneath it. There was a brief whiff of Calor gas before the whoosh of ignition.

'Is that what they told you?'

Aldridge nodded. She sat down on the sofa. Brennan perched on the arm furthest from her, trying not to make her fly away.

'The truth is the best protection you've got, Mrs Aldridge,' Brennan said, cynically quoting the bookshop philosopher. Aldridge looked at him. The phrase, like those on a cheap greetings card, had struck a chord. It sounded both noble and hopeful. No wonder 'Desiderata' had once topped the charts, thought Brennan.

'I've no idea what happened. Nobody's ever told me. Other than it probably being an accident. All I know about is the gas—'

'Gas?'

'From the fire. That's what killed 'em. Like putting a dog to sleep, you know. One of the old girls on the corridor came and got me about seven in the morning. I could smell it about ten yards away. Soon as I got in their room I could tell they were goners. Seen a few in my time, like. I opened all the windows. Then locked the door on 'em till Mr Furnival could come in.'

'And the gas was still coming out of the fire?'

'Oh, yeah. Must have been on all night. I managed to turn it off though. I was worried 'bout an explosion, see. Some of them old buggers still start the day with a fag, you know.'

'There you are, you see, you're a heroine, Cathy. Not a villain. You've got nothing to be afraid of.'

Aldridge didn't look too reassured. She went to rise, but Brennan gestured for her to sit down.

'I'll make the tea.' Brennan crossed to the stove and turned off the flame, then began to assemble teapot, cups, milk and teabags.

'So who came first then – Furnival or Dr Simmons?'

'Furnival. I called him at home. We have an emergency routine for nights, see. He was round inside quarter of an hour. Told me not to panic.'

'And did you take him to the Dentons' room?'

'Yeah. It was still pretty smelly, but the wind had sort of sucked most of the gas out of the room.'

'What did he say?' Brennan put two teabags in the brown china pot and filled it with the boiled water.

' "Jesus Christ" – they were his first words! Never heard him swear before! He asked me not to tell anyone else – patients, like. Didn't want to scare 'em.'

'Then what happened?'

'He went to his office. I had to get a few of 'em round to the breakfast room, and while I was doing that, must have been about ten minutes after he'd gone to the office, Dr Simmons turned up. Parked round the side – came in that way too.'

'And did you speak to him at all?'

Aldridge shook her head.

'Furnival took him down to the room, and then the two of them disappeared into Furnival's office.'

'So Dr Simmons didn't talk to you at all that morning?'

'Nor since.'

'Was anyone else called. Fire brigade? Police?'

'I was due off at nine, but stayed on for an hour in case they needed me. All I saw was the gas-fitter turn up, and go down to the room. When I signed off, Furnival made me go in his office and told me it had been a tragic accident.'

'That's all?'

'Well, no. Said there'd been a fault in the fire's pilot-light thingy. Ignition something. He just asked me not to say anything to anybody. Said we'd be in trouble if word got out. They'd close the home, like.'

'And that's all that was ever said?'

'Apart from when he realised you'd turned up, yeah. He just said the same thing again – said nobody would ever know now. Nothing was going to bring 'em back, like, was it?'

Brennan poured two mugs of tea.

'Sugar?'

'Two, please.'

Brennan put three in, and one for himself. He brought the mug across to Cathy and handed it to her like a communion cup.

'The blood of Christ,' he suddenly said, the words coming from nowhere. Cathy looked startled.

'Are you religious, Cathy?'

'No way – shitty marriage was all I got out of the Church and its wedding vows.'

'You don't think you've done wrong then?'

'White lie, that's all. People die all the time. In accidents. It was nobody's fault, was it? I knew what Mr Furnival meant about the home closing if it ever got out.'

'And did he threaten you at all?'

'Not until last week. Told me I shouldn't talk to you on no account. Said you were a shit-stirrer. An' you are!'

'Was that why you ran away when you saw me in the pub?'

Aldridge nodded. Brennan sipped his tea and walked around the room. Through the lace curtain he could see the driver and passenger standing over Clive, lighting cigarettes.

'What you going to do, then?' Cathy asked, suddenly reversing the roles.

'I don't know. I didn't realise you knew so little about the real story.'

'What story?'

'Did you find any note in the Dentons' room, any sign that they might have taken their own lives?'

Cathy frowned.

'No. They were tucked up. Sleeping like babies. There was nothing on their faces – no fear or anything.'

'But if you smelt gas when you were in bed, you'd wake up, wouldn't you?'

Brennan opened the wooden cupboard beneath the sink, revealing the blue gas canister.

'Well, I bloody well hope so!'

'Why didn't they then? If they wanted to live?'

Cathy dropped her head. Brennan tried to guess why. It came to him with a jolt.

'You'd given them a pill or something, hadn't you? To make them sleep?'

She didn't look up.

'They all have it! Whether they like it or not. Most of 'em are happy to take them. Those that aren't don't get to know about it. They'd be wandering round all night, moaning and groaning, if you didn't give 'em a little something with their cocoa!'

'I hope you die before *you* get old, Cathy. Otherwise you'd know what's coming, wouldn't you?'

She looked at him, beaten and scared. Brennan unfolded the latest letter from his pocket and held it in front of Cathy's face.

'Do you see that word in big letters – KILLER – is that you, then?'

'Where'd you get that?'

'You tell me – whose handwriting is it?'

'I dunno!'

'Don't you? How do the patients send letters?'

'They leave them on the table in the front hall. Postman comes about four every day to collect 'em.'

'What about stamps? One of the wrinklies staggers down to the West Bay shops on his Zimmer frame, does he?'

'No, they never go out without supervision. Miss Jobson keeps a pile in her office. They get 'em from her. Put 'em on the table, and that's it. Gone. Wouldn't have got out otherwise, would it? Not with *your* name on it?' Brennan was shocked by the first sign of intelligence and logic.

'What about pensions and all that? They must have to sign their names.'

'I told you. Miss Jobson takes care of that side . . .'

'When she's not playing the piano and being married to Dr Simmons, that is!'

'You what?'

'They'll make you take the whole fucking rap for this, you know, Cathy! They'll deny everything and blame you. You're in shit up to your eyeballs!'

Cathy sat forward and buried her face in her hands.

'What do I do, then? What do I do?'

'Find out who wrote this letter to me. I don't care what it takes. The sooner you let me know, the sooner I can try and get you off the hook!'

Brennan watched her. He hated doing this to her, bullying and comforting in rotation, but it was his only way to the truth. He walked over and put a hand on her shoulder.

'There's no need to cry, Cathy. You didn't do anything that was too bad. You won't be punished for this – I'll make sure people get to hear what they asked you to do. Promise.'

'Thanks.'

Brennan put the letter in her hand.

'I'm trusting you with this. I know you won't let me down. If you can't get into the office to have a look at the files, get the patients to write you a little poem, or sign a birthday card for someone. Do you see what I mean?'

'Even I could manage that, Mr Brennan.'

'And as soon as you know – call me. I'll be at The George in Bridport. If it's difficult to phone, drop a note in for me, okay?'

She nodded meekly.

'Will you get them to leave Clive alone, for me? He's a big daft lump, but he's all I've got round here.'

'I'm going right now. Cheer up. You'll feel better once this is all over. It's been a burden on you, hasn't it?'

'You're not kidding . . .'

'One last thing you may have to do for me . . .'

Cathy raised her face. Her eyes were red-rimmed.

'What's that?'

'You'll have to make a statement. An affidavit they call it. In front of a solicitor . . . but not in this town, okay?'

Cathy nodded. Brennan made his way out, closing the door behind him as quietly as he could. Outside, Clive was still lying face down on the ground, as Bill and Ben took it in turns to circle him and remind him they were still there. They stubbed out their cigarettes when they saw Brennan coming, an act of civility which seemed so at odds with their potential for violence.

'Is he okay?' Brennan asked.

'He'll be a bit sore, guv. But he was quick on the uptake, so there was no lumps taken off him.'

Brennan bent low so that he could see Clive's face.

'You'll be all right now, Clive. Just got to learn to stop hitting people.'

'I'll fucking kill you . . .' Clive muttered with his face in the grass.

'Attaboy, Clive . . . and Cathy's fine, by the way. If you ask her nicely, she'll probably tend your wounds.'

Brennan moved back to the Range Rover. The driver ran to open the door for him, while the passenger kept the tyre lever hovering over Clive. Once he saw Brennan and the driver installed, he raised the lever high above his head. Brennan dived forward between the seats and smashed his fist on the horn. The passenger stopped the lever in mid-arc and stared at Brennan with contempt. Brennan waved him back into the car with his index finger. The heavy bent over Clive and hissed at him.

'Your luck's in, shithead. Now stay face down for five minutes, or we'll drive the fucking motor over your legs, understand?'

Clive nodded. The heavy moved quickly back to the car, and even before he'd closed the door, the driver was reversing at speed. Brennan saw Cathy come out of the house and kneel down by Clive's side, then the car lurched into a sweeping turn, and sped away, scattering stones all over the track. They rejoined the road up to the roundabout, and took Brennan up towards Bridport. Brennan got them to drop him some way short of The George, and said a curt thanks before slamming the door shut. The Range Rover moved off in an instant, business done. Brennan walked briskly towards the pub, but for the first time in his life, he wanted a bath more than a drink.

'Any luck?' Janet asked the supervisor, leaning on the counter as if it were the bar of the local.

'I'm afraid not, Ms Dunlop. You seem to have unerringly put your finger on our Achilles' heel.'

The supervisor looked pleased with his contorted image.

'So what happens now?'

'We'll report on your findings – or lack of them – and see what can be done.'

'And you'll let me know?'

'Well, we're not meant to be quite so helpful. But call me at the end of the week and I'll see what I can come up with. I've got the names, so that's a start! You'd be surprised at some of the people we have to find with nothing more than a nickname to go on!'

'Maybe that's the trick, then?'

Janet gave him one of his trademark supercilious smiles back and left. The supervisor promptly crumpled Janet's search request in his hand and dropped it into the nearest waste-paper bin.

Miss Jobson was surprised to see Cathy at the door on her day off, and opened the locks quickly, fearing a crisis.

'Cathy? What's the matter?'

'Sorry to trouble you, Miss Jobson, but a friend of mine had an accident this afternoon—'

'Oh, dear – and you want time off?'

'No, no – he's not in hospital or anything. I just wondered if I could get the patients to sign this get-well card for him, you know, cheer him up a bit.'

'Well, yes, of course. They know him then, do they?'

Cathy tutted and patted her own forehead in self-admonition.

'Sorry, I should have said right away. It's Clive – you know, the big bloke who was our Father Christmas last year! So they do know him, but they don't, if you see what I mean?'

'Oh, yes, of course. Go right on through then! Can I get you a pen?'

Brennan listened carefully on the phone, despite the early evening bustle in the pub. It wasn't often that he'd heard Janet so confused and angry. While she ranted about the cynicism of bureaucracy, he knew that she was really having a go at her own failure to get a result.

'There's probably a simple answer,' Brennan said, hoping to placate her. Some chance.

'Frank, if there was a simple answer I would have found it by now, you prat!'

'Sorry, stupid remark. I've had a long day.'

'Any progress?'

'Well, I know some of what happened now . . .'

'Tell me!'

Brennan looked around, the hall was too busy with people criss-crossing between bar and dining-room to risk a detailed explanation.

'Sorry, Jan, it's a bit difficult at the moment.'

'All right, but just give me a one-word answer. Have we got a case or not?'

'Yes, probably two, in fact . . . look, I'll call you later, when it's quieter, okay?'

'Say if you want me to come down, won't you?'

'I want you to come down—'

The pips started to sound.

'Call me, Frank.'

'I will.'

Brennan moved round to the bar. There was not much he could do that night, other than sit and hope for some word from Cathy. And as the chances of running into big Clive in town were quite high, it doubled the attraction of a quiet dinner in the pub. He ordered a Dover sole, and seated himself in the tiny alcove which featured the only table for one. He cursed himself for not having had the foresight to buy a book to read, but knew that even if he had, he'd have been too twitchy to concentrate.

So he settled for reading and rereading the menu, watching Laurie's movements round the bar and kitchen, and keeping an eye on the door for Clive. The thought struck him that he'd probably be able to smell him before he could see him. Brennan smiled to himself. And then Cathy Aldridge walked in, looking around the room, blinking nervously. Brennan pushed the little wrought-iron table forward and stood up. But she was already turning to go.

'Cathy!'

She swung round, alarmed. And then offered a half-smile as she saw Brennan. She moved across. Brennan pulled up a spare stool from the adjoining table.

'Would you like a drink?'

'Scotch, please.'

'I should have remembered. Sit down.'

Brennan got to the bar just before a big order went in, and returned quickly with a double measure. He placed it in front of Cathy. She drank it in one go.

'You okay?'

'I think so. I'm not sure they believed my story.'

She fiddled with the clasp of her handbag and then took out the get-well card. She handed it across to Brennan.

'Get well soon, Clive! It's an ill wind!'

Brennan scanned the assorted messages, scribbles and signatures, initially confused by the use of the same pen for all.

'Have you got the letter?'

Cathy brought it out and handed it over.

'I've not had a chance to look myself.'

Brennan held the letter above the card, his eyes dancing between the two as he searched for a match in the handwriting. And then there it was – down in the bottom left-hand corner of the right-hand side of the card. The same thin wavering lines that had formed the word 'killer'. He jabbed a finger at the signature.

'What's that say, who is it?'

Cathy peered at the card. 'Joseph Green.'

'What's he like – could he have written this?'

Cathy looked at the letter again, trying to square it with her image of the quiet little man who always had his nose in a book.

'If you want my honest opinion, never in a million years.'

Brennan sighed and hung his head in despair.

CHAPTER TWELVE

Brennan bought his morning papers, including a copy of the *Racing Post*, at the harbourside shop in West Bay and found an unoccupied bench on the little green in front of the pub. 'Glorious Goodwood' had started, and though Brennan preferred the jumps to the flat, the top quality summer meetings at Newmarket, Ascot, York and Goodwood always drew his attention. Especially so today, when he felt that all the effort he'd spent over the last few months had come to more or less nothing. Sure, he had enough ingredients for a minor story: a doctor who was prepared to lie about causes of death so his wife or girlfriend's business could enjoy a quiet life; a cover-up by an old people's home over two embarrassing deaths; a behind-the-scenes look at its practices, including the drugging of patients and the annexation of their finances. He could almost see Stuart Gill's face, stifling a yawn. So this morning would be the last act, before handing over his notes to the local health authority and letting them decide what to do about Chestnut Grange.

Brennan began to cross-reference the form pages with the odds listed by the various bookmakers in their trade advertisements. His instinct would always push him towards a runner with longer odds if form lines read about equal. He had little time for backing likely favourites as it seemed a pursuit of the obvious. Brennan preferred the strictly occasional satisfaction of winkling out a dark horse at a decent price, whose subsequent win would obliterate any memory of his failures in the immediate past. He knew, and secretly enjoyed, the fact that he had chosen many of his assignments on roughly the same basis. Well, this one now had all the hallmarks of a complete loser, so maybe the gods would be kinder to him with the horses today.

Brennan looked up to scan the corner around which Cathy Aldridge would come if she succeeded in her plan. She'd made no promises, and given only an approximate idea of times – between half-ten and half-twelve – as she'd downed her last drink with Brennan at The George the previous night. Maybe it had been the booze talking, or the relief at finding someone with whom she could share her guilty secret? It crossed Brennan's mind, as eleven o'clock, then eleven-fifteen, came and went that she may even have woken this morning and decided on a comprehensive runner as her best option. He imagined her driving across the country with Clive at the wheel of his pick-up truck, a maudlin country and western number on the stereo, ready to hole up in a trailer park for the rest of their misbegotten lives. Brennan fidgeted, discomforted by this notion. It would be the last insult if his chief witness were to disappear now.

These dark thoughts blurred his vision momentarily, so that he imagined that when he saw her walking towards him, pushing Joseph Green in a Bath chair, it was simply a product of wishful thinking. But Green was real enough, even offering a smiling wave now as he drew closer. Brennan remembered that he'd done exactly the same when he'd first taken a look in the lounge at Chestnut Grange. Then, Brennan had seen it just as a vague gesture of excitement at the presence of an unfamiliar face. Now, as Green smiled broadly at him, he knew that it had been personal all along.

'Mr Brennan, at last we meet!' Green said with a wheeze.

Brennan stayed seated on the bench as he shook Green's almost powerless bony hand. Cathy applied the brake to the chair and sat down next to Brennan.

'How long have I got?'

'About half an hour, I should think. Furnival's out playing golf, so I just told Miss Jobson that Mr Green had wanted a quick look at the sea.'

Brennan took out the two letters from the inside pocket of his jacket. He unfurled them before Green's face, watching the dark eyes, dulled by the advance of cataracts, as they peered towards the twin sheets of paper.

'Did you write these, Mr Green?'

Green turned his left ear to Brennan and cupped it forward with his hand. Brennan repeated the question at a greater volume and a slower pace.

'Yes – yes, of course!'

'And you sent them to me?'

Green nodded.

'You were the only person to trust, Mr Brennan. I have read your paper for many years!'

Brennan gave him a patient smile. There was an over-formal construction to the old man's English which jarred with Brennan, giving an echo of those old movie villains who gloated at the capture of James Bond. He almost expected Green's next line to be 'What took you so long, Mr Brennan?' but he was busy clawing at the pocket of Cathy's tunic. She took out her packet of cigarettes, lit one and put it into his mouth.

'And why did you send them to me, Mr Green?'

Green exhaled the smoke with relish.

'Because I wanted you to know!'

'About the deaths?'

'Yes! Of course. I had to let somebody know.'

'But why me? You could have told Mr Furnival, or Nurse Aldridge here?'

Green spat on to the grass.

'What would they do?' he exclaimed with a rising tone. 'Tell me to forget about it. Go back to sleep. But I knew you wouldn't let me down, Mr Brennan!'

Brennan's smile was more genuine this time, as he couldn't help being touched by this bizarre endorsement.

'Why didn't you sign the letters, Mr Green? It would have saved me a lot of trouble.'

Green waggled his hands in apology.

'I knew that I would have to make it . . . *interesting* for you . . . so that you would come. The mousetrap needs cheese, yes?'

Brennan began to sense a note of triumphalism in Green's voice, at odds with his apparent motives.

'Is that why you put the word "killer" in the second letter? To intrigue me?'

'Yes, a little – but also because it was true!'

Brennan gave Cathy a weary look.

'Mr Green. Nurse Aldridge has told me about how she found the Dentons. How they died. How the doctor wrote that they'd died from natural causes, on different days. I know all this now, okay?'

'But you remember my first letter? I asked you "why?", Mr Brennan. Do you know that, yet?'

Brennan looked to Cathy again, then shrugged.

'Nurse Aldridge has told me all about it. It was an accident. The fire in their room was faulty. They were too deeply asleep to know, to save themselves.'

Green threw the remains of the cigarette away and slapped both palms down angrily on the arms of the chair.

'Don't let them fool you, Mr Brennan! They will tell you everything but the truth!'

'What is the truth then, Mr Green?'

Green looked around him, ran his yellowed tongue along his lips to generate moisture. He leant forward a little.

'It was I who killed them, Mr Brennan!'

Cathy stood up, agitated.

'You mustn't say such terrible things, Mr Green!'

Brennan gestured for her to sit down again, and gave her a reassuring look.

'So you wrote to me to get me to find out that you had killed Mr and Mrs Denton, is that it?'

'Of course!'

'But you couldn't just tell me straight, huh?'

'What would you have believed? Some old nut-case writing to you? You would have thrown the letters in the bin!'

'You *are* an old nut-case, aren't you, Mr Green? Pissing me about? Imagining things that didn't really happen. Wanting some attention?'

Green glowered at him with an intense hostility.

'No! No! No!' Green banged his palms down again. Cathy stood up to take hold of his wrists.

'You'll kill him if you get him too wound up, Mr Brennan!'

'Roll up my left sleeve!' Green barked.

'Not the old tattoo again. Must have seen it a hundred times!' sighed Cathy wearily.

Brennan gestured for Cathy to undo the cuff buttons on the shirt. She fiddled with them for a moment. Then pushed up the sleeve to reveal Green's forearm. Brennan leant close to have a look. It wasn't a tattoo in the conventional sense, more of a crest, an eagle with a crown hovering above its head, and it seemed to be etched in white. On closer inspection, Brennan could see that the white lines and colouring were in fact scarred skin. The crest had been branded on to Green's arm.

'Do you know what that is, Mr Brennan?'

'A crest, a national symbol . . . ?'

'Whose, Mr Brennan?'

Brennan shrugged. 'I'm sorry, I can't say. Central Europe?'

'Poland, Mr Brennan! The Land of the White Eagle!'

'How did you get this, though? It looks as though it's been *burnt* on to the skin.'

'It was!'

'And who did this to you?'

'My fellow-officers! As I did to them! It is a crest of honour, Mr Brennan! Of the most élite cavalry regiment in Poland's history!'

Brennan looked to Cathy and saw her face filled with confusion.

'Has he ever said anything about this before?'

'I'd have remembered,' she said, shaking her head.

'Are you making this up, Mr Green?' Brennan asked. 'Because if you are, I can get you a pile of trouble!'

'What trouble could *you* bring me that I haven't already had in my life? Torture? Nightmares? Death?'

The milky eyes were fixed on Brennan's now, defying him to raise another challenge.

'Can you get us all coffee from that shop, Cathy?' Brennan asked, partly because he needed one, partly because he wanted her away for a moment. He gave her five pounds and she moved off, hesitantly, her professional instincts jarred by the act of leaving a patient with a stranger. Brennan turned to Green.

'Your real name won't be Green then, will it?'

'Josef Granowski, Mr Brennan. I wanted a new identity and a new life when I came to this country!'

'When was that?'

'Nineteen forty-five. Can you imagine what it was like to have fought the Germans for five years, only to find the Russians marching in to possess you? Those of us left alive fled, to Czechoslovakia first. Then to Vienna. We had nothing. Only the clothes we stood in and an identity card. And this—' he tapped the white eagle crest again.

Brennan nodded. The lucidity of Green's speech and memory had intensified. Brennan recalled how his own father, though vague about the present, could summon precise, almost photographic details of his life in London during the thirties and forties.

'And is this connected to why you killed the Dentons?'

'Of course. I've killed many times, but only in battle. With them, for the first time, I felt pleasure!'

'Why was that?'

'Because of who they were and what they had done! They must have believed that they had escaped justice, and then God delivered them to me for retribution!'

Green looked up at the clear blue sky above. Brennan took out his notebook and made a brief summary of their conversation so far.

'Mr Green, are you talking about a death camp or something?'

Green scowled at him.

'Other people suffered as well as the Jews! They had their own country within three years! *Three* years, Mr Brennan! We didn't get ours back for thirty-five!'

'Tell me what the Dentons did?'

Green looked out across the harbour, his face pained by the summoning of the memory.

'Every country has them, Mr Brennan. Even here. People with evil in their hearts. All they wait for is the opportunity. For when people stop looking, or caring. And when people don't care enough, terrible things happen! Terrible!'

'Tell me,' Brennan said quietly.

'My regiment was decimated in the first months of the German invasion in 1939. We were on horseback against Panzer tanks, armed only with a lance and a pistol! Like out of the nineteenth century – your Valley of Death, Mr Brennan! It was a glorious slaughter if there can be such a thing! Horses exploding as they were hit by shells, and still we got through! In fact, the nearer you are, the safer you are!'

Green wasn't even looking at Brennan now. He was staring at some imaginary country between here and the sea, but one which plainly existed with clarity.

'Those of us who survived and escaped capture retreated to our villages. Waiting for a day to come again. The Germans found local fascists to help administer towns and to process the Jews – Jan and Irena Dantowicz were such people. They were supposed to have worked at Majdanek, a death camp, Mr Brennan. When I first met them, they had been put in charge of a small town near Lublin in eastern Poland. I and some of my colleagues were organising resistance in the area, partisans, you understand?'

Brennan nodded, his pen moving along the page without a pause.

'This was in the spring of 1944. The Germans had been beaten back from Russia. It was our job to harass them, to break their morale, to loosen their grip on our country before the Russians could come. One night, we attacked a German patrol, killing ten soldiers, and blew up a bridge they needed for retreat when it came. Two days later, a squad of the Waffen SS was brought into the town to take revenge. Dantowicz and his wife selected those who were to be rounded up. Two hundred men, women and children were taken to the woods outside the town . . .'

Cathy returned with the coffees, but Brennan held up his hand so that she didn't derail Green's train of thought. But Green showed no sign that he even knew she was there.

'We heard the sound of the machine-guns. It lasted for nearly fifteen minutes and then silence. Not even a bird to sing. That night, my unit found the bodies lying in a hollow. The Germans were not even going to bury them. One man was still alive. We gave him water. Held him in our arms. Before he slipped away, he told us that Dantowicz had insisted on firing the first shots. On his *own countrymen*!'

Brennan took one of the polystyrene cups off Cathy, removed the lid and held the coffee out for Green. He took it in his right hand and lifted it to his mouth for a series of short sips.

'We vowed to kill them, more so than any German or Russian who took Polish lives. But they left the town before we could get them. Then the Russians pushed in from the east. And all was lost.'

Cathy caught Brennan's eye and tapped the glass of her wrist-watch with two fingers. Brennan gestured for just a few more moments. Green seemed on the point of exhaustion, weak with the exorcism that was being wrought.

'Forgive me, Mr Green. But I have to ask this. How did you know it was the Dentons, the Dantowiczes, when you saw them at the home?'

Green looked at Brennan in astonishment.

'You think it's possible to forget such faces, such eyes? We age but we don't change!'

'Do you think they recognised you, then?'

'Why should they? I was just another peasant in the town. I wished I had kept my pistol. I would have loved to have woken them, then emptied it into their heads! They deserved more than gas.'

'How did you get into their room, Mr Green?' Cathy asked, fearing further implication.

Green smiled apologetically.

'I took your key, my dear. My son had a new one cut and then I put it back on the floor of your office . . . so you would think you had just dropped it.'

Cathy's dark look at Green confirmed this treachery.

'Mr Green, you realise that if what you've said is true, I will have to report you for murder?'

'Of course! That's *exactly* what I want, Mr Brennan! To let the world know that these bastards cannot run for ever. Governments can wipe the slate clean, but those who were involved cannot!'

'There is such a thing as legal process, Mr Green. Even for war criminals,' Brennan said, folding his pad away.

'Not in England! Your wonderful Houses of Parliament voted that such trials were not possible now! Even though they *know* how many hundreds are still living here! Who escaped, like the Dantowiczes, and pretended to be refugees or heroes!'

'But how could testimony be reliable after so many years, Mr Green?'

'Like I said, Mr Brennan. If you were part of it, you can *never* forget!'

Green threw his coffee on to the grass in a gesture of disgust and impatience. Brennan ran his hand through his hair.

'I really ought to be getting him back, Mr Brennan.'

Brennan nodded, then looked at Green again.

'What do you expect me to do now, Mr Green?'

'To write the truth! To let the world know!'

Cathy moved behind the chair and released the brake. She swivelled it round and set off back towards the home. Brennan swore violently under his breath as he rose to his feet. This case seemed never-ending.

'Publish it now!' Janet urged as she joined Brennan at the bar of The George that evening.

'There is the minor inconvenience of checking the facts, Jan!'

'Publish the allegations then!'

'Oh, fine! That's the right-on alternative to proper reporting, is it?'

'There's nothing political in this, Frank, I'm just arguing for expediency. Somebody else could be on to this story any day now. And they won't hang around for the niceties of double-checking! Ring Stuart Gill tonight – tell him you have something big for him! Look on it as a way of announcing your new persona!'

'I haven't got a new "persona", Janet! I just drink less than I used to!'

'You know what I mean! It'll demonstrate your independence, show that you can still cut the mustard without the aid of an expense account and a team of researchers!'

'It'll demonstrate how I can fall arse over tip if I write something as lurid as this without proper confirmation. The old bastard's been *using* me shamelessly for his own purposes, Janet! What if he turns out to be a fantasist? A nutter who's read too many war stories?'

'Does he strike you as such?'

'No, but he's still not my idea of Santa Claus! I need to check his history, *and* theirs, before I can print anything.'

'Okay – but doesn't the absence of the Dentons' records from the OPCS at least suggest there was something decidedly iffy about the two of them? And that somebody knew?'

'It suggests it, but it doesn't prove it. It also suggests inefficiency, or a simple cock-up, or sheer coincidence!'

'Frank, the Home Office knows who these war criminals are! They may have given them shelter for innocent reasons fifty years ago, but there's nothing innocent about finding the truth and then doing nothing about it! That's just complicity.'

'But it's the law of the land – they couldn't get the War Crimes clause past either House. Because a majority couldn't be convinced of the integrity of the evidence. And look at what happened with John Demanjuk? If even the *Israelis* have doubts . . .'

'The French seem to manage it all right!'

'They have a lot more to be embarrassed about than we do, that's why!'

'So whose side are you on here, Frank? The Bosnian Serbs who raped and slaughtered with impunity? The Rwandan government militias?'

'That's different, there's tangible evidence to hand, living witnesses, videos, United Nations soldiers – not just one old man's questionable testimony.'

'So what now – do you leave it alone or try to corroborate it?'

Brennan sipped at his mineral water absently.

'I need to talk to Mark . . .' he said quietly.

'Mark?'

Brennan looked alarmed at his slip, even in front of his own wife.

'Forget the name, Jan. I never mentioned it. You don't know. Okay?'

'That's him then, is it? The guy you gave up six months of your life for?'

'I said *forget* it!' Brennan hissed at her. 'I'm compromising you by even acknowledging his existence!'

'Say I don't mind?'

Brennan didn't answer. He finished his drink and looked around for Laurie. She was behind the kitchen range, loading four fresh sole on to the grill.

'Shall we eat here tonight?' Brennan asked Janet.

'Don't you want to move on? You know – back home? Or London?'

'I've never felt more like sitting still.'

'Frank, we can tie all this up in days!'

Janet fished in her handbag and pulled out a folded photocopy.

'Look, while I was in there, I found Dr Simmons's marriage certificate – Mrs Simmons is Liz Jobson as we suspected. So that's nailed down, isn't it?'

Brennan smiled, a touch grudgingly, but it was a smile none the less.

'So what else do we need to do, regarding the home itself?'

'Get Cathy Aldridge to swear an affidavit on what happened, how they covered it up.'

'I can do that tomorrow—'

'But not round here, Janet. You never know who's connected, you understand? I need to get her statement typed for signature anyway.'

'Leave it to me,' Janet said confidently. 'Is there another route to Mr Green's story, other than your man on the inside?'

'When I was talking to him, he said his son helped him get a key cut for the Dentons' room – I forgot to ask Cathy if this was true or not, the existence of a son, I mean. The bit about him stealing her key obviously was – she'll blame herself for that.'

'He doesn't exactly sound like a pleasant man, this Mr Green.'

Brennan shrugged.

'He's every right not to be if his life was the way he said. I'm more worried about what might happen if I *do* sell this story, assuming it holds up. You know – from the point of view of stirring up old hatreds. Or giving licence to people to take the law into their own hands – not *even* the law, in fact. Murdering on the basis of their own self-righteousness!'

'What would you want from the son, if he'll talk?' Janet asked, preparing herself for the task.

'The truth about his father's background. Anything he knows that may have been said about the Dentons. Anything which throws light on how the Dantowiczes and Mr Granowski came to meet up again – I mean, after all they've lived through, they're thrown together in the same old people's home? Green said it was God who had delivered them to him . . .'

'You want me to try and contact *Him*, too?'

Brennan was cheered by Janet's practicality, her ability to deconstruct a problem in terms of doing things rather than just thinking endlessly about it. And the result was always the same. Despite his reluctance to share the burden – and he guessed that this went back through generations of rough-and-ready Brennan males – when he finally gave in to Janet's help, his shoulders would always feel instantly lighter.

They bagged the last two of Laurie's Dover sole, served with thick, buttery mashed potatoes and crisp green beans, and finished with a helping of bread-and-butter pudding each. It was shameless comfort eating, but by God it worked.

When Brennan woke at just before eight the next morning, there was no sign of Janet. Down in the The George's dining-room, Laurie confirmed a sighting of her in track suit half an hour earlier. Brennan ordered the full fried breakfast as a retaliatory strike. At about ten to nine, Janet reappeared in the hall of the pub, looking flushed, and perspiring heavily. Laurie thrust a glass of freshly squeezed orange juice at her which she downed in one, slowly recovering her breath. She unzipped the bum-bag strapped to her stomach and took out her lightweight camera with its built-in zoom lens, plonking it on the table in front of a highly amused Brennan.

'If you're passing a chemist's put the film in with them, will you. One-hour processing if poss,' Janet said panting.

'What's on it that's so urgent – sleeping seagulls caught by early rising human?'

'Dr Simmons giving his wife a kiss on the doorstep of their home, as she left for the one she runs . . .'

Brennan chuckled.

'Janet! Have you been trespassing?'

'I was only *just* inside their front wall. It'll save whoever runs the story sending down some clodhopping news photographer from London. Besides,' she said, lifting a piece of toast off Brennan's plate and popping it into her mouth, 'it means I can get paid as well!'

'I'm impressed,' Brennan said genuinely.

'There's more. I've been down to Cathy Aldridge's bungalow. We've arranged to meet at lunchtime – go through the statement together. She's going to get an address for Green's son, too.'

'What about a solicitor?' Brennan queried with a frown.

Janet looked at the digital watch on her wrist.

'I'm about to ring my friend Jill at Amnesty – she'll find me the nearest sympathetic firm,' Janet said, giving a self-mocking right-fist salute.

'It'll probably be in New York!'

'Frank,' she said skittishly, 'this is a strong Lib-Dem area . . .'

'Tories without their kicking-boots,' he scoffed, in a playful attempt to burst her balloon of self-confidence. But she was impregnable.

'So what did *you* do this morning to sustain your meaningfulness?' Janet probed with a smile.

Brennan lifted his copy of *The Independent* from the seat beside him.

'I've been deciding what I should see next at the theatre . . .'

The pressure of time meant that Brennan had to take a shortcut to Mark Fraser-Williams. He was aware of the potential risk, but was gambling on the fact that, since the break-in at his new home in Bradford-on-Avon, there'd been no sign of activity from the Big Lads. He hoped this meant that they'd finally given up on him, and declared him a non-combatant in their game. Whether this was true of Mark or not, he didn't know. But Mark worked with a minor scale of surveillance – the eyes and ears of all those above and below him in the Home Office – on a daily basis. He'd been able to look after himself in the past, so why not now? Besides, it was just an evening at the theatre with a friend.

Brennan booked tickets on his credit card and then bought one of The George's own postcards, which featured its handsome frontage. Brennan scribbled the name of the theatre and the time with a brief note – 'Hope you can make it: urgent! F.' He slipped it inside an envelope and made sure that it caught the second post out of Bridport.

Janet returned to The George after lunch, brandishing Cathy's signed statement, stamped with the seal of a solicitor in Chard, whose clients included, Janet's friend Jill had boasted, a locally based overseas aid charity. This had seemed to reassure Cathy as much as it did Janet, when the affidavit had been sworn on one of the picnic tables of a pub half-way between Bridport and Chard.

'She'll need help though, Frank. When the story breaks, she'll be out of a job . . .'

'But she'll have a clear conscience. I hope you told her she has nothing to fear?'

'I did my best. Gave her our numbers and addresses for both London and Bradford.'

Brennan nodded his approval.

'I said we'd give her advance warning,' Janet added.

Brennan frowned at this.

'I don't see what good it does her. If the evidence holds up, we're talking about a murder enquiry now. It'll be the police who'll want to talk to her, not the local health authority. I'll have to hand all my notes over to them, so I can't be seen to encourage a vital witness to do a runner!'

'Where's she going to go, Frank? Poor woman's got no money. Her ex-husband never sends her a bean. She's trapped, Frank!'

'I hope you're right . . .'

'She'll stay put. I told her she might be able to make a few bob out of the story—'

'You did *what*?'

'Bloody hell, Frank, I was only giving her a bit of encouragement. If you sell this story to Stuart Gill he'll have his boys down here spraying money all over the town! You *know* that! I was just making sure she was clued up about what would happen!'

'You didn't offer to negotiate a price for her as well, I hope?'

'No, but I told her not to settle for anything less than ten grand!'

'Fucking hell, Jan, you're the biggest critic I know of the decline in the morality of newspapers, yet you're acting like the lowest creature to crawl out under the razor-wire at Wapping!'

'I was just trying to protect her. She's gone out on a limb for you. It seemed the very least we could do.'

'Can't you see what they'll *do* to her if she started asking for money? They'll tell the world about this heartless cow trying to profit from the murder of two innocent old-age pensioners who she was supposed to be looking after!'

Janet fell silent. Her thinking hadn't gone as far down as it should have done. She may have been bright, and ready to be immoral if necessary, but she didn't really know the Jacobean treacheries that could unfold on a story such as this once rival newspapers began to scramble and snarl over the entrails.

'I'm sorry.'

'We'll see how it works out. I'll try and persuade Stuart to give her some protection if it gets dirty.'

'I've got an address for Joseph Green's son – but I don't suppose you trust me to talk to him now, do you?'

'Where is he?'

'Bristol.'

Brennan looked at her crestfallen face. All that morning's eagerness and vitality had disappeared. He privately wondered why disappointment seemed to get to her so much after being married to him for so long. Surely she'd had enough to last a lifetime?

Brennan reached out and held her hand.

'How soon can you get there?'

CHAPTER THIRTEEN

Brennan and Fraser-Williams had always exploited any potential for in-jokes for their secret theatrical meetings, largely at Fraser-Williams's behest, but Brennan's latest choice had had Fraser-Williams chuckling from the moment he'd read the postcard bearing the drawing of The George – *An Inspector Calls*. He'd responded more to this than the word 'urgent', a term to which, as a high-ranking civil servant of many years' experience, he had grown immune. Nevertheless, he cancelled his planned evening at the cinema with a friend, pleading workload, then burnt the postcard to a flaky pile in a large ashtray before setting off for the brooding Home Office buildings in Queen Anne's Gate.

Brennan and Janet went their separate ways at the two Dorchester stations – Brennan to Dorchester South, for a train up to Waterloo, Janet to Dorchester West back to Bradford-on-Avon. It was a strained parting, not for reasons of professional jealousy, or the previous day's bickering, but because they had both become close to each other again. There was an unspoken awareness that they now enjoyed being together, both as working partners, and as husband and wife. It had been in the looks passing between them as they'd made love in The George the previous night. All too often sex had been a function, a brusque quenching of a thirst for one, while the other was reduced to the status of a bystander. But last night their eyes had been, like their loins, locked together, completing a perfect circle of the two minds, and the two bodies.

'I'll go up to Green's early evening,' Janet said as she climbed out of the taxi.

'Call him first,' suggested Brennan.

'I'd rather he didn't get too much warning,' Janet insisted. 'People clam up on the phone.'

'I'll leave it to you, then,' Brennan said cheekily, but Janet was in the mood to take the joke. She kissed him lingeringly on the lips.

'Take care,' she whispered.

'I'll stay at Mum and Dad's tonight. See Lester.'

Janet pictured the inversion of the recent routine, with her luxuriating in solitude in Bradford, while Frank would have to go back to being both a son and a father again.

'Give me a ring later if you can manage it,' she said, putting a hand to his face in sympathy.

Brennan took the hand and kissed it.

'Go on – that's enough soppiness. I'm going to miss my train and then you'll miss yours!'

She closed the taxi's door but watched Brennan, as he did her, until the town's traffic obliterated one from the other.

Brennan's train, coming up from Weymouth, was full of home-going holiday-makers, looking if not tanned, then certainly tandooried. Brennan, as ever, felt that he must stand out a mile – pale skin, worried expression, mismatched clothes. His biggest fear was that people might take him to be a train-spotter, so he laid aside his case notes for the journey and just sat back to enjoy the countryside and let his mind go blank.

Only as the train began to dawdle through the grim approaches to Waterloo – or 'Gare de Waterloo' as the conductor insisted on calling it – did Brennan begin to feel animated again. It was initially a defensive reflex – London was now alien territory to him. He would have to remember not to smile at anybody, or say good morning, or offer to help with a suitcase, or go up to anyone studying a map in bafflement. The courtesies of small-town life which he now observed would have to be put on ice for a day or so.

Brennan phoned Stuart Gill from the Waterloo concourse and asked if he was free for lunch. He wasn't. But he said he'd catch Frank for a drink in the afternoon. Brennan nominated his 'club', 2 Brydges Place, a small, unpretentious establishment filed away in an alley at the side of the Coliseum opera house. Gill knew of it – his liver probably contained more information than the A–Z atlas – but hadn't been there, so his acceptance was a formality. Gill's every non-working hour – and indeed many when he *was* working – was dedicated to sampling another restaurant or another bar.

Brennan phoned his parents from the club to warn them of his arrival and of his unavailability for an evening meal. He'd be back late – so Lester wasn't to use this as an excuse to stay up after ten. And, yes, he still had his own key with him.

Brennan spent the lunch-time reviewing his notes, not just to prepare his pitch to Stuart Gill, but also to prevent elements of the story reaching his ears. Gill had an old-fashioned newspaperman's instincts which actually pre-dated the 'tabloidism' of the eighties. 'Nothing new here,' he would sniff at the headlines in the *Sun* or the *Star*, then recount his early experiences on the big, lurid stories of the sixties – Profumo, Myra Hindley, Great Train Robbery. The landscape was still the same as far as he was concerned, apart from the Royals messing things up. He regretted that crime and scandal were too often relegated to the inside pages in favour of Di or Charlie's latest machinations. Gill was – and it was often his standing joke at editorial meetings – still more interested in Barbara Windsor than Elizabeth.

So Brennan's pitch had to be about crime – if he so much as mentioned social services, he knew that Gill would fall asleep. Brennan ordered the club's most popular dish, Cumberland sausages with mash, and sat back to list the key words that would help keep Gill up on his hind legs – murder, sex, violence would do for starters, though he knew he'd have to finesse the sex bit. Janet's photos of Simmons kissing Jobson would come in handy.

Brennan took coffee and an Armagnac on the sofa in front of the club's fireplace. Its regular clientele, drawn from publishing and independent television production companies, had mostly dispersed for the summer, no doubt travelling an identical circuit – Tuscany (for themselves), Cornwall (for the kids), then finishing with the Edinburgh Festival (for networking). The attraction of this last event, had always baffled Brennan – he'd once described it in an argument with Janet as 'fifty thousand people looking for a bucket to wank into', but it hadn't stopped her attending. Brennan lay back on the sofa, enjoying the privacy that other people's holidays had given him, and lit his first cigar in a few weeks.

At about half-past three, he heard the grunting and cursing on the club's narrow staircase up from the alley. Gill appeared, short of breath from the climb.

'Got to be a fucking ballet dancer to get up those stairs, Frank!'

'Armagnac?'

Gill grinned.

'Spot on!'

Gill removed his lightweight jacket, revealing the plain, white cotton shirt underneath, offset by garish red and white spotted braces.

'Want a Monte?' Brennan asked, offering his cigar case.

'Yeah, why not?'

Brennan clipped the cigar for him and then held a match to it as Gill sucked and puckered the cigar aglow. A little touch of male freemasonry would do no harm to Brennan's pitch. Brennan ordered more drinks and coffee.

'How's it going then – settled in, are you?'

'Mostly. You should come down one weekend for a break.'

'Break? You've got to be kidding! We're off to Canary Bleedin' Wharf next month! The Old Man's got us some ridiculous rent – fifty pee a square mile or something, so it's up-sticks time. Shame really.'

'They're all there now, aren't they – *Telegraph*, *Mirror*, *Independent*?'

'There'll be some weird fucking conversations in the lift. Those *Daily Mail* boys are lucky bastards – *Kensington*. I ask you? Talk about landing on their feet! So what have you got for me, Frank?'

'Looks like a murder – a double.'

'Nice!' Gill smiled. 'Anyone we know?'

'Two residents at an old people's home . . .'

Brennan could see the instant drop in interest rates behind Gill's eyes. Brennan faked a bit of 'lurk', looking around the room, falling into a whisper, to resurrect Gill's attention.

' . . . but they're *not* all that that would suggest. It goes a lot deeper.'

'Such as?'

'Can't confirm it just yet, Stuart, but it's a real "Hey, Mabel!" . . .'

Gill frowned, not understanding the reference.

'It's what American TV producers say they need in a programme to keep people watching – something which will make the husband on the couch want to call the wife out of the kitchen!'

'Hey, Mabel,' Gill repeated, amused, logging the expression for use at the next editorial conference.

'So what are we talking, Frank? A page?'

'More a centre spread.'

'Is anybody else after this?'

'Not as far as I know. But there's a witness you might need to buy up, before the other shite-hawks get to her.'

'Is she "shaggable", you know, picture-wise?'

Brennan tried not to wince, reminding himself that getting the story in was more important than attempting to impose political correctness on a gorilla like Gill. He thought of poor Cathy, in her one-room bungalow, with her downtrodden face. But he couldn't afford to let Gill see this picture. So who was the *real* hypocrite?

'Well, she's a nurse . . .' Brennan offered as bait.

Gill pounced on it.

'The uniform'll do it. So when can I see it, then?'

'Early next week, I hope. There's just this last bit of confirmation, and a few documents to get hold of. I'll call you soon as – assuming you're interested?'

'Of course!'

'What about my byline though? Won't the Old Man go ape shit if he sees my name in the paper again?'

'Easy – I'll just leave it off the story!'

It was said as if it were meant to be a joke, but that was Gill's usual way of dispensing brutal truths. But even he could see the disappointment on Brennan's face.

'Look, if it's so strong, I'll have a word with the Old Man. Tell him you want a credit or you'll go elsewhere. I mean, to be honest, do people even look any more?'

'Probably not,' Brennan said quietly, acknowledging the cynicism.

Gill drained his snifter of Armagnac and stood.

'Gotta go, Frank. I've got Billy outside doing laps of the Aldwych in my Rover!'

Gill shook hands briefly with Brennan, before he pegged the cigar between his teeth and used both hands to negotiate the staircase. In the old days, Brennan remembered self-pityingly, Gill would have told the driver to wait till he and Brennan finished their cigars. So Brennan lay back on the couch, propped himself with a cushion, and slowly smoked his cigar to the shortest of stubs.

Janet had bought a Bristol street directory in the Roundabout Shop in Bradford before returning to Brennan's house. She was supposed to think of it as *her* house as well, but that didn't feel quite right just yet. Not that she didn't enjoy it. Sitting on the sofa in the first-floor room, looking out over the town, free of all noise, was a strange experience after Highbury Grove. She checked on the address for Green's son, Stephen. It was in the Southville area of Bristol, close to where the same Avon Janet could see became an industrial river rather than a rural spectacle. Janet cross-checked with the train times from Bradford to Bristol. She could catch one at ten to six and be in Bristol by twenty past. Say another ten minutes to the house, and with luck, Stephen Green would be settling down for the night after work. Janet wrote an explanatory note for Green, giving him the Bradford phone number, just in case he wasn't in.

Janet began to map out her questions on a pad. She'd been used to doing initial, factual research for both papers and television production companies, setting up the agenda for when the reporter went in. This was a different discipline, requiring not just method but flexibility too, and the ability to think on one's feet rather than simply working from a prepared questionnaire. She was nervous, but excited at the same time. She knew, despite her sexual politics, that it was an advantage to be a good-looking woman interviewing a man. She memorised the first ten questions, filled her cassette-recorder with a blank tape, checked that there were batteries in the recorder and that they weren't too flat. She recorded a few exploratory questions to find the right volume level, and then went upstairs for a bath.

She dressed for comfort not impact, which was easier said than done. It took five changes of wardrobe before she was happy. It was now half-past five. She'd let time slip away and needed a scramble down the shortcuts Brennan had shown her to get to the station in good order. The journey seemed shorter than half an hour. She felt her heart beating faster as Bristol approached. Everybody else on the train seemed to be going home from work, meeting their families, done for the day.

The taxi threaded its way through the rush-hour traffic and slowly drew clear of the city-centre crush. She saw that the banks of the Avon were a dark brown sludge as the taxi turned on to the road alongside the river. The driver turned off the main road, into a warren of small Edwardian terraces with postage-stamp front gardens. Janet got him to drop her at the corner of Green's street – she wanted to walk by the house at least once before going to the door. The driver gave her a receipt, written on the back of the company's card. She would need the number to get a cab back into town.

Janet paced her walk past the house so she could take in as many details as possible – pausing to pretend to check the heel of her shoe. There was a satellite dish high on the front wall; and a burglar alarm below that; the small garden looked well kept; there was no sign of attack dogs. Janet crossed the road and walked for another fifty yards, faked a check of address and then walked back to the house. She opened the gate, closed it behind her and walked up the short path to the door. She pressed a bell, hearing a muffled chime inside the house. Janet relaxed her shoulders, letting them drop with a long exhalation. She could see a figure move towards the frosted glass inset in the door. A man in his late thirties peered round the door.

'Mr Green?'

'Yep.'

'I'm sorry to trouble you. My name's Janet Dunlop, and I'm doing some research . . .'

Green opened the door a little wider, revealing his blue shirt and dark blue trousers.

'You'll want the wife, love.'

'No, I needed to . . .'

Janet finally registered the blue clothing. And down the hall on wall-mounted hooks was the check-banded, peaked hat of a policeman. Janet's brain froze.

'What, love? You needed what?'

'I'm, er, I'm from the home . . . Chestnut Grange . . .'

Janet felt sure her face was burning bright red but Green seemed unperturbed by her presence.

'What's the problem?'

'Er, there isn't one. I was just asked to do some research on how people felt their relatives were being treated there . . .'

An alien being seemed to be saying these words as far as Janet was concerned. Her ears were ringing to such an extent that she wasn't quite sure what Green was now saying but it sounded like:

'Come on in then, love.'

And Janet found herself trying to get her legs to move. Once inside, she produced a stream of small-talk about the house to try and buy herself time. Gradually the implications began to sink in. Green was a serving police officer. If Janet let slip the admissions made by his father, Brennan's story would be dead in the water.

Brennan collected the tickets from the box-office without alarms. He'd looked for signs of his old enemies – 'Leather Jacket', 'Man U' and their lady 'Referee' – but unless they'd undergone cosmetic surgery and radical changes of tailor, they were not to be seen around the foyer this night. Brennan bought two programmes and stood to one side of the staircase leading to the stalls, giving Mark Fraser-Williams a good sighting of himself and, incidentally, an all-clear signal in case he was worried.

Mark arrived about fifteen minutes later, Brennan being touched by his instant reaction to the plea for help.

'I think I owe you a bottle of champagne,' Brennan offered, as he led Mark up to the stalls bar.

'Only if you can claim for it, dear boy!' Mark said with a laugh.

They took the champagne and its accompanying ice bucket to a quiet corner of the bar, and perched on stools. Brennan poured out two glasses.

'Cheers!'

'Your health,' replied Mark. 'So what's the flap? I'm *intrigued*!'

'Something I've been working on has just taken a turn for the unexpected. And I need a quick confirmation from your office to make the story stand up.'

'What's it about?'

Brennan scanned the immediate area as he lifted his glass in front of his mouth. There was nobody in earshot, but he whispered from behind the glass anyway.

'War criminals, I'm afraid . . . living in Britain.'

'Oh, Christ, not that old stuff again! I thought we'd finally thrown the key away on them?'

'I'm sorry, Mark. But it's a vital factor in this investigation – it'll make the difference between "murder by mistake" and what the Americans call "justifiable homicide".'

'Murder? These are deep waters for you, aren't they?'

'I didn't jump, I was pushed. Can you help, do you think?'

'It's not my department, as you know, Frank. And the chap who heads it up is not a great fan of mine. What do you need precisely? I seem to remember at the time of the last debate in the House that we had files on about two hundred and fifty suspects living here. There'll be fewer now of course, through natural wastage . . .'

'The two I'm interested in died *un*naturally . . . what I need to know is if their killer's story about them is true.'

'You know the *killer*? Frank, I'm not one to moralise, but should you not hand this over to the police?'

'Well, there's more than self-interest involved. There is a possibility of it being simply an old man's fantasy – a convincing one, but fantasy nevertheless. A police enquiry would mess things up, if you see what I mean? It would try to normalise something which doesn't fit into the usual pattern of crime. And there's a public issue about justice and revenge, which will certainly drop on your boss's doormat when it breaks!'

'Ah, so I'm supposed to thank you for the warning?' Mark enquired, tugging at an imaginary forelock. 'Okay, but I'll need help with a premise for when I get caught with my head in the wrong department's computer.'

Brennan refilled the glasses, trying to put himself in Fraser-Williams's elegant shoes.

'Background research on something?' suggested Brennan.

'Far too vague, old boy! I know we're supposed to be duffers compared to the FO, but there are procedures!'

Brennan thought of Granowski's story, and the long journey across Europe before finding shelter in Britain.

'Is there any tie-in with immigration? I mean, these people must have had papers, alibis, whatever, in order to be allowed to settle in Britain. It must have been chaotic to handle, I know, but . . . there must have been procedures,' Brennan said pointedly.

'This is more promising, Frank! I can wander untrammelled through our old boxes. So give me your names.'

Mark pulled a black leather note-holder from his inside pocket, followed by a matt-black Sheaffer ball-point.

'Treachery has never been so elegant,' Brennan said wryly, before spelling out the names of Granowski and Dantowicz, and their Anglicised replacements.

Janet perched on the very edge of the sofa, her pad resting on her knees. Mrs Green busied herself making a pot of tea, while Stephen Green sat on the arm of a chair listening to the faltering questions directed at him.

'So on a scale of one to ten, how would you mark Chestnut Grange in terms of its overall performance?' Janet adlibbed.

'I'd say somewhere between seven and eight. Wouldn't you, Rosie?'

His wife shouted her agreement from the kitchen.

Janet desperately groped for questions which might double as market research and corroboration for Brennan's enquiry.

'Can I ask when you last visited your father?'

'What's that got to do with this assessment?'

Green may have been only a humble traffic cop, but this guaranteed an obstructive line in pedantry.

'Well, I'm trying to find out, in a roundabout way, whether there's anything off-putting about the place. Something that makes you think twice about visiting?'

'Sure there is – my father!'

He laughed for his wife's benefit, and she joined in enthusiastically.

'Sorry,' said Janet, feigning an apologetic face. 'I didn't want to pry.'

'Not a question of prying, love – I'm surprised the people at the home didn't tip you off.'

'Well, this is meant to be independent research . . .'

'The simple fact is my old man's always been a pain in the bum, and we're happy he's there and we're here. If I see him a couple of times a year, that's fine by me. All I get is a load of demands.'

'I'm sorry to hear that. I suppose they can be quite a burden?'

'We had him living with us till a year ago! Talk about dog in a manger! Still got half his stuff cluttering up the room, ain't we, Rosie?'

'Stuff?'

'Yeah, come and have a look.' Green launched himself off the arm of the chair.

'I don't want to intrude . . .'

'No, no – when you get back to Dorset, you tell the people who run the home to let them have more possessions. It'll make our lives a bit easier.'

Stephen Green gestured for Janet to follow him. She did so nervously, but at least with the confidence that her cover had so far held up. She climbed the narrow staircase after Green, wondering if there was a charge for impersonating in front of a police officer.

Green threw open the door of the box-room overlooking the rear garden. One wall was hung with a faded Polish national flag, with the White Eagle crest at its centre. Leaning in a corner of the room was the business end of an ancient cavalry lance, decorated with red and white ribbons. All around the floor were cardboard boxes, filled with what looked like photographs or old newspapers.

'This is all his,' Stephen Green said grumpily. 'I shall have to wait till he dies before I can throw it all out.'

'What's the story?' Janet asked, trying not to sound too eager.

'Fought in the war for Poland, didn't he? Came over here afterwards. To be honest, I think he wishes the war was still on. Always saying it was the best time of his life – can you believe it?'

'I'll have a word with Mr Furnival. See if they'll put some of this in storage at the home for you – for *him*, I mean.'

'Okay, ta.'

They made their way back down the stairs again.

'More tea, love?'

'No, I must be getting back. Can I just ask how you came to choose Chestnut Grange for your father?'

'Didn't Furnival tell you?'

Janet looked vague.

'Don't think so . . .'

'Well, it's just a little trick of his – he always puts some adverts in ex-services magazines . . .'

Janet's face registered this insight, which went some way to explaining the 'act of God' whereby Granowski had met his former enemies.

'Thank you for your time, Mr Green. I'll pass on all your comments.'

'Thanks . . . bye!'

Janet could hardly believe her ordeal was over. She tried not to hurry to the gate or arouse suspicion. She imagined that, back in the house, Green the policeman was already on the phone to Furnival about this strange, gabbling woman who'd turned up on his doorstep. She closed the gate behind her, trying to remember the way back to the main road. She would have to find a phone and call a taxi quickly.

After two wrong turns, she found the road overlooking the river, but there was no sign of a phone box. A hundred yards along, however, was a pub and she dived in there. It was full of men enjoying their homeward-bound drinks. Janet ordered a large Scotch and asked for the phone. She made her way past the pool table, aware that her body was being assessed by the two youths at the table. She fumbled in her bag for the taxi's card, then remembered she'd put it in her shirt pocket. She found change, dialled, ordered the cab, then realised she didn't have a clue as to what the pub was called. She dodged back out of the corridor looking for a sign or a beer mat which could tell her the name. There was nothing.

'What's this place called?' she asked one of the pool players.

He looked her over.

'The Cock Inn,' he said with a smirk.

'Don't fuck me about, mate – what's the pub?'

The sudden change in tone did the trick, and the pool player spat out the name. Ten minutes later the cab-driver poked his head round the pub door, and Janet at last had her sanctuary.

Brennan and Fraser-Williams decided on a stroll up to The French Pub after the play. Any misgivings Brennan had about this public display were outweighed by the need to get Mark working quickly, preferably in the next few days.

'I suppose you have to be on the look-out for them even now?' Brennan probed.

'I think Stella's boys have got bigger fish to fry than me.'

'No, no, no – I was talking about war criminals. Your department still has to be careful about who it lets in.'

'Oh, I see – yes. We do get the odd Bosnian claiming to be a refugee when they could easily be mass killers on the run. Easy to see how it happened in the old days, I suppose. At least most of ours were genuine mistakes – the Yanks wanted all the rocket scientists and military technicians irrespective of what they'd done.'

They pushed into the still packed bar, with Mark using his height to attract a barmaid's attention. Moments later a bottle of house champagne was being passed over, followed by two glasses.

'Are you sure you're all right about doing this, Mark? I mean, it's not exactly a crusading issue, is it? Not like the last one.'

'No, but I can see that your case has moral implications – and I like those!'

Brennan smiled and toasted him with his glass.

'You ever thought of getting out?' he asked Mark.

'Before they chuck me out, you mean? I suppose so, yes. I'm fifty-one now. Another four years and I can take early retirement. Buy a little place on the Suffolk coast and begin my brilliant career as a watercolourist!'

'You've never mentioned your family at all.'

Mark gave Brennan a headmasterly look.

'Sorry – I shouldn't pry.'

'Not a question of prying, Frank. I thought you'd have worked it out by now?'

'I guess I had – doesn't matter though.'

'To whom?'

'Sorry – I should keep my mouth shut. Let's just say I'm honoured to be your friend.'

'That's kind.' Mark leant in close to him. 'For the record, I've not had sex for over twenty-five years!'

'No wonder you look so young!'

Mark leant back and laughed out loud.

They finished the bottle and went their separate ways, with Mark promising what he called 'illumination' within a few days. When Brennan got back to his parents' home in Highbury, there was a light on in the kitchen, but this was only to 'illuminate' the plate of ham sandwiches which his mother had left out for him. Brennan ate one immediately as he phoned Janet to see how she'd got on.

The news of Stephen Green's occupation alarmed him at first, but as Janet unfolded her tale of the visit, he could see that she had done a brilliant job in thinking on her feet, thereby preserving the story. The details of the Polish flag and cavalry lance were very welcome in the circumstances. All Brennan needed now was a confirmation of identities from Mark, and he could hand all his notes in to Stuart Gill.

Brennan went up to his bed in the spare room, but looked in on Lester beforehand. He was flat on his back in his Arsenal shirt, fast asleep. He'd break up for summer in a few days and come down to Wiltshire. Brennan could complete his story, get paid, and they could all have a wonderful time together. Maybe it was the champagne, but tonight there were no worms of doubt eating away at Brennan's brain as he slept.

CHAPTER FOURTEEN

By the Friday, Brennan still hadn't heard anything from Mark Fraser-Williams. By mutual agreement, Brennan would never phone him, but in any case, Brennan wouldn't have been able to summon the cheek to hustle a man who was doing a dangerous favour on his behalf. He guessed that the nature of the task he had set Mark would prove more troublesome than anticipated. If there was no immediate prospect of gaining details from the war crimes files, there seemed little point in Brennan hanging around in London. Mark had the Wiltshire number and address anyway.

So the moment Lester came home from school, Brennan announced that the two of them were going down to Wiltshire that night, to be reunited with Janet. Brennan's mother and father helped Lester pack his clothes into two sports bags with an alacrity which suggested that they would not exactly be dismayed to be left on their own. Brennan sympathised with their feelings – the last year had been tougher than a retired, clean-living couple had any right to expect, with a son dragged through the headlines then gaoled, and their daughter-in-law turning up on the doorstep in distress with their grandson. Brennan hugged them both lingeringly as he left – they deserved some peace and solitude before death parted them.

On the packed train down to Bath, Lester seemed bubbling, not just with the natural euphoria generated by the end of the school year, but also by the prospect of being with both his parents for a prolonged period of time.

'When will you be finished for the summer, Dad?' Lester asked as he sipped a can of Lilt and crunched on a packet of thick-cut crisps, which Brennan had brought back from the teeming buffet car.

'Don't know, son. It's not like it used to be for me now. I'm freelance – I work for myself.'

'That means you can decide when you have your holidays then?'

'Well, not quite. I have to make sure I've done everything I have to do, and that I have some work to come back to, before I go anywhere. Because I don't get paid holidays like I did when I was on the paper.'

'You're not free then, are you? So why did you say you were freelance?'

Brennan searched for the right reply to fend off this piece of undeniable logic from his son.

'It's just an expression meaning that I have more than one employer. I can sell my articles to lots of different papers and magazines now!'

Brennan watched to see if this positive reading of his circumstances had the desired impact on Lester. He could hardly have said, 'Actually, son, I have to live from day to day now, because I honestly don't know where the next penny's coming from.'

Lester though had seen the upside of the new arrangement.

'So more people than ever will see what you do?'

'If it's in the right space, yes.'

Brennan didn't like to point out that the spaces available for his writing were becoming more scarce by the week. The 'concentration of media ownership' was just a fancy way of saying that you now had to kiss the right arses if you wanted to stay in work. Lester would have to wait until his sixth-form media studies course before he discovered this fundamental truth of the nineties.

Lester and Brennan caught the connection down from Bath to Bradford just in time, and found Janet waiting for them on the station platform. Brennan and Janet each took one of Lester's bags and they made their way into the town. The air was warm and scented, and noisy chatter and music drifted out of the windows of the Dandy Lion bar, as those who'd finished school for ever packed in to celebrate. As they walked back up the hill to the house, the smell of barbecues ambushed them every now and then, so when they finally got inside, they were all ravenous. Janet had prepared a huge lasagne, with a portion of chips for Lester. Despite the snacks on the train – as insubstantial as they were expensive – Brennan and Lester demolished their portions of the meal. They ate with the front windows of the house open, as though they were abroad in a strange and foreign country, where all the usual closed-up habits of the past could be tossed away.

Lester went up to bed about ten-thirty, a special concession for the day, while Brennan and Janet moved to the first-floor living-room for coffee. Brennan dug out one of his jazz CDs – *Modern Art* – and let Art Farmer's bubbling trumpet sounds and Benny Golson's growling saxophone fill the room. The third track, 'Darn That Dream', had the two of them dancing smoochily, ridiculously across the room, but then tonight finally felt like the new beginning they'd all been hoping for.

'I can't believe we're all here, together, after everything that's happened,' Janet whispered in Brennan's ear.

'Neither can I.'

'Don't lose us again, will you?'

'Never.'

'Promise?'

'You bet.'

'I love you, Frank.'

Silence.

'I love you too, Jan.'

'Sure?'

'Why else would I be clinging to your bum on a Friday night in midsummer with my favourite music playing?'

'Because I happened to be in the room?'

'Because I *wanted* you to be here!'

Janet rested her head on his shoulder as they shuffled around the room. Through the window, the light over the town was fading, and the Westbury hills were just a grey smear on the horizon.

'Do you want to talk about what happened with Stephen Green?'

'Not till the morning,' Brennan said emphatically. 'The rest of the world can wait a few hours. We've earned this!'

They clung to each other until the disc whirred to a halt, by which time night had fallen.

The next morning, while Lester had the only major lie-in they would allow him that summer, Janet spread her notes on Stephen Green across the kitchen table for Brennan to look through.

'Must be a bit weird having your father holed up in a box-room with a lance and a Polish flag!' Brennan muttered. 'No wonder they found a home for him!'

'I don't think there's much love lost either side from the sound of it.'

'You got no sort of impression that Stephen knew about what his father had been up to?'

Janet shook her head.

'He seemed perfectly at ease. He's a straightforward, worthy but dull copper. I'm sure if he'd got an inkling of his father's mischief he'd have had no problem shopping him.'

'Would have saved him a packet on fees for the home too! Right, so he's not an accomplice in any way – despite getting that key cut for the Dentons' room?'

'I guess not – I couldn't really ask him about that under the heading of "market research", could I?'

'Nope. Now, Furnival – advertising in ex-services' newsletters? Does that stand up?'

'He's ex-military himself apparently. Might well be a selling point to certain potential patients, I suppose? Without having seen the adverts, I don't see it as sinister or anything. I think it just helps to explain a little why both parties ended up there, that's all.'

Brennan folded the notes into one of his files.

'What do you think we should do about Green – Stephen, that is?'

'Well, if you go and tell him what his father claims to have done, I think the least he'd do is call in his fellow-officers to look at the case. He might go to the papers too, I suppose. I think you should wait for your confirmation from Mark – sorry, your "unnamed source"! – then file the story, and warn him just before it comes out. That seems the fairest option to me. I don't think he'd have much to say on the subject now.'

'He'll be like Cathy though, won't he? Somebody else caught up in the shit-storm through sheer circumstance.'

'Just do the same with him as you did with Cathy – tell him the rules of engagement. I mean, the other papers would want his story as a follow-up, wouldn't they? "Policeman's Dad is Double-Killer!" '

Brennan nodded glumly.

'I wish there wasn't such a messy fall-out with this one. I like things being clear-cut. Obvious villains. Plain injustice.'

'I can't think of a single case of yours that was ever neat, Frank! They just don't happen that way. What will you do if your source can't help, or if he doesn't find any evidence to confirm the Dentons' background?'

'Then I'll just have to run with what we know – the home's malpractices, the doctor's cover-up – though I doubt Stuart Gill would buy it off me after I'd mentioned murder to him.'

'Can you not ring Mar—, your bloke, and see how far he's got?'

'Not a chance. He knows the score though. He'll be in touch . . . just a question of waiting.'

Brennan, with Janet's assistance, tried to reduce the fever of anticipation by enjoying as normal and active a weekend as they could manage. Time spent doing things passed quicker than time waiting or thinking. So they went swimming at the Bradford pool after enrolling on a family ticket. They watched a club cricket match on the recreation ground for an hour, and then had afternoon tea out. They did some last-minute shopping as the town's shops began to close between five and five-thirty. And Brennan rented a couple of videos – one for them, one for Lester – which they watched on Saturday night.

Sunday morning took the form of a walk along the river, followed by buying as few papers as Brennan could limit himself to – Janet remembered the bad old days when he bought the lot and spent all Sunday engrossed in them. And then they adjourned to the Dandy Lion for a family lunch, which would have been fine but for the fact that Moira Backhouse came in too.

'I spy strangers!' she cooed, as she sidled over to Brennan's table, forcing herself an introduction to his companions. Brennan prayed that Janet didn't give too much away about her work, otherwise she'd be next in line for a public talk to Moira's cohorts on the various arts and craft committees which tracked any sign of unusual activity in the town, and then cornered the person responsible to give an account. While Janet expertly dead-batted Moira's questions, Brennan fantasised about forming a union of writers and artists which could call upon Moira's Mob to give talks on how boring and shallow their lives were.

After lunch, they walked across town to a car-boot sale which was taking place in the car-park of a supermarket. While the event had the forced jollity of a country fair, Brennan couldn't help noticing that most of the items being sold off – second-hand toys, garden tools, ornaments, old records – had an air of desperation about them, like those markets in Moscow shown on television. The car-boot sale had gone from being a festival of distributing excess goods in the eighties, to an act of survival in the nineties.

The walk home did nothing to lift Brennan's mood. The anxiety about the story could only be suppressed for so long. Fortunately, when they got back, Brennan saw the red light flashing on the answering machine. He played back the message as Janet and Lester watched. To an unmistakable background of London traffic noise – he was calling from a public phone – Mark's voice announced:

'Frank, it's me. I may have something for you. Could you get to my place tonight? Because this is due back in the library tomorrow, if you understand. Don't call. I'll be in all night. Bye.'

Brennan looked across at Janet, to see if she'd detected any particular tone – excitement, alarm, anticlimax? But Janet was already reaching for the pocket train timetable for the connecting service Brennan would need. Within fifteen minutes Brennan was down at the station, phoning in, as he'd arranged with Janet, in order to obliterate the incoming message from Mark.

Brennan got to Paddington just after six, a delay being caused by engineering works. Why was his work – often done at weekends – always deemed more disposable than that of the cost accountants, estate agents and sales reps who formed the weekday travelling public? Brennan decided he would send the receipt for his taxi direct to Rail Track. The taxi-driver grimaced when he heard Hammersmith Bridge mentioned as the destination. It was a sure sign of the economic recovery that they felt confident enough to go back to their pre-recession stroppiness with customers wanting anything other than a guided tour of London, or a return trip to Heathrow.

Brennan seethed in silence as the driver took a tortuous route to Shepherd's Bush Green, and then down to Hammersmith. But coming off the Broadway the driver's victory was complete when he found the approach to the bridge coned off due to emergency gas works. Brennan thought about making him use one of the other bridges, but time was short. He got out there and then, paid the basic fare and no extras and insisted on a receipt. The driver shoved a blank one at him.

'Fill it in yourself, guv.'

'You're the driver who's received the money. You fill it in! It's your job, *guv*!'

The driver scribbled the fare on to the receipt and virtually threw it at Brennan, before pulling away abruptly into the circling lines of traffic. Brennan logged the cab's number in anger, but knew that by the time he settled down to write a letter of complaint, he'd have forgotten it. He stalked past the trench full of gas workers, digging away, and began to cross the bridge. The Thames was ebbing, leaving a line of debris on the banks, like the scum on an old enamel bath. Plastic bags, a shopping trolley, two traffic cones, a wheel-less bicycle could be glimpsed without even looking too hard. Brennan paused and took a deep breath – he was getting into a completely unnecessary state. It wasn't the meeting with Mark but London itself that was distressing him. He recognised that he was now not far short of being allergic to the city.

Brennan reached the far side of the bridge. Up ahead he could see a hapless pair of policemen having to turn away a line of Sunday-evening traffic on its way back into town. Brennan peeled off down the quiet road where Mark Fraser-Williams lived, in a solid, safe, brownstone mansion flat. The further he went down the street, the quieter it became. He tried to picture Mark on his way to work – what would it be, the departmental

Rover with grey-suited driver? Or did he stroll briskly across the bridge each morning, brolly swinging, to catch the District Line to St James's Park? Brennan found the block embracing Mark's flat number and approached the communal entrance.

There was a standard-issue entry phone mounted in the wall to the left of the door. No video cameras panned down over the entrance, no robotic voice requested a five-digit entry code. Brennan pressed the illuminated button labelled 'F-Williams' and placed his mouth next to the microphone in readiness. He heard no voice, just the buzzing of the door release. Brennan pushed on the door and it sprang open. He guessed that Mark must have seen him coming down the street, or that he was the only visitor expected this particular evening.

There was no lift in the building, the four floors being serviced by a wide, carpeted staircase lit by gilt, wall-mounted lights. Brennan began to move upwards to the second floor. On the first landing he could hear the muffled tinkling of a piano, but now as he reached the second landing a different music emerged. Even Brennan could recognise Mozart's Requiem. The music was coming from Mark's flat, its door half open in welcome. Brennan tried to pin down the section – he'd heard it before. Now as choral voices swelled he realised with a smile that it was the *Confutatis*. No 'Pick of the Pops' on a Sunday night for Mark!

Brennan knocked on the door out of politeness.

'Mark, it's Frank. Are you decent?'

Brennan edged round the door. The flat was pretty much as he'd expected. Elegant, in a reproduction way, and spotlessly clean. In one of the bookshelf alcoves either side of the marble fireplace stood a mini-system stereo, lights flickering as the volume of the choir swelled then fell away. They were the only things moving in the room. Perhaps he'd caught Mark taking a bath and he'd now retreated again to his fragrant suds – what would he expect of Brennan in such circumstances? To pour himself a drink, was Brennan's first guess. He moved to the walnut cabinet, which boasted a hardwood tantalus. Each decanter had a silver-plate label hanging on its neck. Brennan lifted the 'Whisky' from its frame, took a glass from the adjacent salver and poured an inch of the toast-brown spirit. He sniffed it first – it was a malt, an expensive one.

'I'm just going through your drinks cabinet, Mark, if that's all right?' Brennan called. There was still no reply. Brennan listened. In the small silence between *Confutatis* ending and *Lacrimosa* beginning, he thought he heard the splashing of water. The first chill of alarm tickled Brennan's neck as the violins opened this most moving section of the Requiem. He put his glass back down on the cabinet and moved towards the apartment's other rooms. The kitchen was empty, but the coffee-maker was on and still dribbling liquid into the jug. Across the corridor was a study – a partner's desk with green leather inlay, built-in shelves with library steps. The green-shaded desk light was on. Brennan saw the large envelope lying on the desk. From six feet away he could see 'Frank Brennan' written across it in yellow-marker ink. As he moved towards it, there was a sudden rustle of feet, running, in the corridor outside.

Brennan ran to the door and looked out. Two men wearing ski-masks were haring across the living-room, knocking furniture over as they went.

'Oi!' Brennan shouted as he gave chase. 'Bastards!'

They were out of the door now and slammed it shut behind them. Brennan got to the door, turned the latch and ran out on to the landing. They were already down to the landing below, taking the stairs three at a time. Brennan never saw their faces, but the leather jacket on one of them was disturbingly familiar. Brennan heard the front door to the mansion block slam shut two floors below. He wouldn't be able to give chase, so he returned quickly to the flat to try and find Mark.

Brennan rechecked the rooms he'd been in and then entered those he hadn't yet seen. By now his heart was thumping in his chest and his mouth had dried to sandpaper. In the bedroom, there were signs of disarray – trousers and a shirt left strewn across the duvet. Brennan saw the open door of the en-suite bathroom. He edged across the room towards it. With the Mozart now muffled by the distance between the rooms, he could again hear the faint drip and ripple of water. Brennan took a breath and peered round the door.

Mark Fraser-Williams lay dead, his head bobbing up and down in a bath full of water. He was naked apart from a black, lacy woman's négligé. On the bathroom floor, puddles of water were gathering. Brennan saw that there were photographs torn from a magazine scattered around, some glued in the puddles. Brennan bent down to get a closer look – at first the nakedness in the photographs looked tangled and innocent. And then he saw the boy, no more than ten or eleven years old. There were others in all the photographs, each being violated by adult males.

Brennan stood up, his head reeling as though the pumping heart had saturated his brain with blood. Mark's mouth hung open, the bath water which had filled his lungs lapping gently against his blue-tinged lips. Brennan retraced his steps out of the room. His first fear was that the men – and as his head cleared, he realised who they must have been – might come back for him. But then he calculated the risk factor.

They'd been disturbed, and possibly identified, so they would steer well clear. Deniability would be all important to them, even if they thought they had the sanction of their superiors. Brennan felt reassured enough to take the time to collect the envelope on Mark's desk – and a strange logic occurred to him. If he removed the offending documents it would, bizarrely, go some way to clearing Mark's name, making his killing seem all the more pointless. He knew that the child pornography had been brought in especially to blacken Mark's name. It wasn't just him they'd wanted to kill, but also his reputation. A classic Big Lads operation – which would conclude, ironically, with leaked police reports to one of the more pliant papers.

Brennan's eyes danced around the room. Was there anything else he'd not spotted? He made his way back to the living room. He suddenly realised his fingerprints would be on the whisky glass. The door handle. God, where else had he touched? Should he just call the police and try to explain what had happened?

And then the darkest thought popped out of a brain in overdrive. He was the perfect, stone-dead target while he was still in the flat – he had government files in his hand, a previous history of subversion and it wouldn't take the average plod more than a minute to think he was Mark's murderer. Christ, the bastards would have been on their mobile phones in a flash, almost unable to believe their luck. Brennan grabbed the whisky glass and threw it across the room where it shattered against the wall. He ran to the door, wiping the handle with his handkerchief. He didn't have the time to go back elsewhere. He pulled the door shut and scuttled down the stairs.

As he came out of the main entrance, he could hear the first sirens in the near-distance. Brennan turned left, away from the main road. He didn't even know if there was a through road here but he knew the direction the police would be coming from. He walked purposefully, but not too quickly. He imagined there would be faces at the curtains of many of the mansion flats already as the sirens drew nearer. The road eventually dog-legged away from the river, but then became an abrupt cul-de-sac. There was no sanctuary for Brennan, no phone box to offer him an apparent purpose, no flat he could pretend to be visiting. A woman, walking her dog, passed him. Brennan almost felt compelled to talk to her, as if in expiation. But he restrained himself, scanning the flat numbers as though he was less lost than he actually was.

Eventually, he turned and made his way back along the road, albeit on the opposite pavement from Mark's flat. He could see as he moved that

an ambulance had arrived and that two police cars were parked. A small
knot of neighbours had gathered, held back by a single constable. Brennan's
pause to take in events was not just his most natural move – he wanted to
see the scale of the call-out. There were, as yet, no unmarked Mondeos
from Special Branch. After what felt like an age of postured curiosity,
Brennan moved off, hoping that none of the local residents had ever been
his readers.

Back on the main road, he realised that the police attending the flat had
come up from the road diversion, because a chaotic jam of cars had gathered
on the southern approach to the bridge. Brennan could see a pub at the
junction. It was tempting to dive in there and throw back a few calming
drinks, but then a solitary drinker gets noticed quickly. So too would
anyone taking a cab to a station. Brennan did what he thought was most
normal and walked back across the bridge, then caught a bus, any bus, at
Hammersmith Broadway. Ten minutes later, he found himself on the
western fringes of Kensington High Street. He got off the bus and walked
a while. A few cafés and take-aways were open, with tables outside, almost
exclusively occupied by holidaying Arabs. Brennan spotted a cab heading
east and flagged it down. Paddington was a fairly neutral venue for this
area, so no interest or disdain registered on the driver's face.

The station concourse was dotted with the usual Sunday-night detritus
– backpacking tourists heading for Oxford, families rolling luggage trolleys
towards the night-sleeper to Penzance, drunks soaking up the booze with
burger and fries for the journey home. Brennan tried to remain invisible.
Even buying a magazine risked being noticed or recorded on the ever-
present security cameras. So he took up a central position and scanned the
departures board. After fifteen minutes of agonising stillness, the platform
for the next Bristol train flicked up and Brennan was moving.

He bought a coffee, a sandwich, a phone card and a brandy from the
buffet as he made his way down the train. He found a seat at the end of a
carriage and tucked himself in there. He finally released the envelope which
had been clamped, address-side inwards, under his arm for the entire
journey. The yellow lettering had been smeared and diluted by the sweat
which had flooded out of his armpits in acute anxiety. Brennan laid the
envelope aside while he devoured the sandwich and then hurled down the
brandy. As he opened the lid of his coffee and let the cup rest on the tray
in front of him, he dared to slide open the envelope for the first time.

The top sheet was a Home Office memo, dated 1992. Brennan was too
dizzy to read. He scanned the half page, looking for key words – 'false
identity papers' flashed up, then 'good grounds for suspecting', and then

in the last sentence 'suggest be added to list of war criminals resident in UK'. Brennan's head fell back in relief. He closed his eyes and tried to stop the world spinning.

He now had three deaths to write about, linked by his own investigations. He ran through any of the moves he'd made which might have exposed Mark. The night at the theatre had seemed trouble-free, but there was no way of knowing about the true level of surveillance. The circumstances of their conversations had been random, and therefore unlikely to have been vulnerable to electronic eavesdropping. Mark had called him today from a phone box – now yes, they could have put a tap on a public phone if they knew Mark was in the habit of using it.

Equally Brennan's own phone could still be in the front line, but he'd checked it for devices at least twice since he'd moved in. The likeliest source of exposure, then, was from within the Home Office itself. If Mark had got these files on the Friday, he'd have called that night, or Saturday morning. Calling Sunday afternoon suggested that he'd only got his hands on them that very day. Going into the office at weekends would certainly allow freer movement, but, perversely, create greater suspicion too. Brennan knew he was trying to get himself off the hook here, but whatever proved to be the case, he'd be burdened by guilt over Mark's death. The important thing now was to get the story out – *both* stories now.

Brennan took the envelope with him as he moved back down the train to the phone booth in first class. The section was eerily deserted, despite the 'weekend first' offer of luxury travel for just £5 extra. Perhaps people felt it was a trap, a pyramid sales device. But while the silence made Brennan's call easier, it didn't help his peace of mind, and he kept one eye on the sliding-glass door behind him, fearing the sudden reappearance of 'Leather Jacket' and friend.

'Jan? Listen – I'm on the train.'

'How did it go?'

'Just listen, will you! It's getting a bit hairy. Make sure all the windows are closed and locked and don't answer the door or the phone till I get home. If I need to call again, I'll give it two rings, hang up, then redial, understand?'

'What's the matter? What's happened?'

'*Not* on the phone, Jan! I should be back in about an hour. Okay?'

'Not really . . .'

'Just lock up and wait for me! It'll be all right!'

Brennan hung up and his phone card was ejected into his waiting hand.

The sliding door sprang open with a jolt. Brennan coiled, but it was just the conductor.

'Seen your ticket, have I, sir?'

'Yes – just on my way back to my seat.'

Brennan stepped out of the phone booth as the conductor stood to one side.

'That yours, sir?'

He was pointing back into the booth, where Brennan's envelope, with his name in lurid, smeared yellow, was resting on top of the unit.

'Thanks,' Brennan muttered as he grabbed the envelope and made his way back down the train.

Brennan couldn't be bothered with going all the way through to Bath and waiting for a connection down to Bradford. He needed to get back to Janet and Lester quickly. So he got off at Chippenham and claimed the last cab in the rank. The fare was just over £15 but it was worth it to cut down the anxiety.

The Zion Baptist Chapel had never looked so menacing as it did as Brennan passed it now on his way up Conigre Hill. The slab-fronted building seemed to offer damnation more than redemption with its glowering shadows and unlit, mesh-protected windows. Brennan turned on to Tory and made his way along it. It was gone eleven now. Nobody was out. There probably wouldn't be that many still up. He could see the lights blazing on all three floors of his house and felt instantly reassured.

He found his keys and first turned the Chubb lock, then inserted his ordinary door key. It wouldn't turn. Janet had put the snick down. He rang the doorbell in a rhythmic pattern, hoping this would alert her to his presence. Moments later he could see her at the door.

'It's me, Jan!'

Janet unlocked the catch and threw open the door. Brennan fell into her arms and kicked the door shut behind him.

'Are you both all right?' he asked anxiously.

'Yes, yes – fine. Lester's asleep. I didn't tell him anything. So what happened?'

Brennan moved into the kitchen and checked the window locks.

'I've done them, Frank!'

Brennan now drew all the curtains.

'What's happened, for Christ's sake?'

'Mark's dead. Murdered.'

Janet's face was instantly drained of colour.

'They got to him. The Big Lads. You know?'

'How did you find out?'

'Jan, I was *there* when they finished him! And now it's going to look like I did it, not them. That's what they'll be trying for!'

'What are you going to do – you can't call the police, can you?'

'Not at the moment. But I *will* have to talk to them tomorrow. Before they come after me.'

'So what can you do in the meantime? Call Stuart Gill?'

Brennan shook his head.

'What about a lawyer . . . ?'

Brennan shook his head to that too.

'There's only one thing I can do, only one way I can fight back, Jan . . .'

'What is it?'

'I write.'

CHAPTER FIFTEEN

Janet cleared the kitchen table completely, while Brennan brought his typewriter and a box of A4 paper down from his office. Janet assembled the notes and evidence which she'd accumulated, and copied, and transcribed and began to file each piece in chronological order. These were arranged opposite Brennan, where she drew up a seat. Brennan took his handwritten notes from the folder he'd dedicated to the case and put them on the right-hand side of the typewriter. To the left, he placed a lined, yellow legal pad on which he would make concurrent notes, or queries. He placed Mark's envelope on top of the typewriter and stood over it, making a check that he had all he needed.

'Got everything?' Janet asked, a little unhelpfully.

'I think so. I've got to read this thoroughly first,' he said laying his left palm on the envelope. 'So – in time-honoured fashion, despite all the urgency, let's have a coffee and a cigar before I start!'

Janet laughed. She'd seen the routine many times before in the newspaper office – the endless putting off of the start of writing. She'd given up wondering why it was like this, and just accepted it was Brennan's roundabout way of getting himself focused. She stood up.

'I'll make the coffee—'

Brennan intercepted her.

'I'll do it. And I'll get the cigar! You have a look at that,' he said, handing the envelope across to her.

'This is what Mark got for you?' Janet asked as she pulled out the papers, with their clips and memos and staples.

Brennan crossed to the work surface and filled the kettle from the water filter.

'I've only glanced at the top sheet really. Seems to confirm that they *were* war criminals. Got in on false identity papers – that would explain the absence of birth or marriage certificates, I suppose.'

Janet was flicking through the papers.

'Some of these documents are in Russian!'

Brennan turned. 'Are they?'

'There's a précis in English . . .'

'I guess the only controlling force in that area by the end of the war was the Red Army. They'd have been responsible for the bureaucracy.'

'So how did these papers end up in the Home Office?'

Brennan narrowed his eyes. 'I suppose we have to thank Gorbachev and Yeltsin for that. That top memo's dated 1992 – must have been when they were handed over. When the KGB was finally dismantled and opened up.'

'Fancy this coming back to haunt all those people who thought they'd got away with it!'

'Well, let's not be too disingenuous about this. They release stuff that suits them – papers that indict British collusion or negligence. Maybe some disinformation too – you know, blackening the name of someone who everyone thinks is a hero.'

'Look at their faces – they must have been bastards through and through!'

Janet proffered a photostat of an SS personnel file from 1943, which featured stark, black and white images of the younger Dantowiczes.

Brennan looked at the forms, which, leaving aside the death's head logo, seemed as innocent as an application for a building society account.

'It's amazing that they put so much down on paper. So much evil processed so publicly. They must have thought they'd never be brought to account!'

Janet kept flicking through the papers as Brennan put four scoops of coffee into the *cafetière*.

'It reads pretty much as Mr Green said – Majdanek camp is mentioned here.'

'Anything about the massacre of the villagers?'

Janet turned more pages, each with a memo in English attached.

'Yes, here we are!' She began to read the memo.

' "Red Army soldiers were taken by villagers to a nearby wood where they found a mass grave. Statements were taken which confirmed an SS unit, called in by Jan and Irena Dantowicz, had carried out a retaliatory execution of two hundred villagers after the ambush of a patrol by Polish partisans in February 1945." '

'Flag that, will you, Jan. I'll need every word!'

Janet peeled off a yellow note from a pad and stuck it along the top edge of the paper.

Brennan poured the water from the kettle and gave the coffee a stir.

'Jesus Christ!'

'What?'

'That's him, isn't it? Your Mr Granowski?'

Janet was holding up a letter in Cyrillic script, which had a photo attached – the memo confirmed the name of Josef Granowski.

'Bloody hell, what's it say?'

' "He was a member of the Polish Partisan Brigade. In March 1945 his group accepted the surrender of a company of retreating and defeated German troops. After disarming them, Granowski made them form a line, and proceeded to shoot each one in the back of the head. There were eighty-six bodies, looted and left unburied, when the Red Army took over the area. Local witnesses testified that this was a trademark of Granowski." He was one too, Frank! Another butchering bastard!'

Brennan reached out for the papers and read them again and again to confirm the précis that Janet had delivered. He recognised the eyes and the jawline of the little old man in the Bath chair at the seaside. The old man who'd told him he'd killed many people in battle.

'Sounds like he did this sort of thing for fun, as well as for his country,' Brennan said quietly.

'Does it affect your story badly?'

Brennan shrugged.

'I was never going to paint him a hero. But there would have been an element of understanding as to why he'd killed the Dentons.'

'Now he's just another psychopath in a uniform?'

'But one our country chose to welcome . . . C'mon, let's get this done with!'

Brennan poured coffee for both of them, went upstairs to fetch his cigar, rolled a sheet of paper into the typewriter and began to work. He kept up a constant dialogue with Janet, shooting out questions, absorbing her replies and suggestions. They'd never worked this closely before. In the old days, the researchers withdrew a safe distance from the Great Writer, awaiting a summons to his office for fact checking. But now Janet was as much a part of Brennan's writing as his own eyes and fingers.

They managed to get close to three a.m., before Brennan signalled a halt to the session. He had the bare bones of the story down, the main players and the list of unanswered questions which would be set in bold type in the paper, and which would keep the issues boiling for several days. What he did *not* do was make any reference to Mark Fraser-Williams or to Home Office leaks. This was one story where the sources could stay in the wings. To introduce any connection to Mark's death would invite an instant ruling of *sub judice* from the courts.

Despite the late hour, Brennan insisted on collecting up all his papers from the table, including the Home Office file. He took them up to bed with him and kept them within arm's length for the rest of the night.

He and Janet were woken by a bewildered Lester, who wanted to know who was the mad woman in the kitchen. For a second Brennan thought it might have been an intrusion from the 'Referee', the woman who'd supervised his surveillance at the theatre. But then he realised it was Sandra's day to clean. He went downstairs and introduced Lester to her, explaining that because of his work, she'd just have to do the kitchen today.

'You got a big story on, then, Mr B?' she trilled.

'Maybe, Sandra, maybe. Look, Lester here can get his own breakfast, and he'll make you a cup of tea while he's doing it, okay?'

Sandra eyed Lester saucily.

'Be a first for me that will – getting a cup of tea off a bloke in the morning! Normally I has to make it every time!'

Brennan nodded patiently.

'I have to go back to bed for an hour or so if you don't mind . . .'

'Been on the nest, have we?'

'Fat chance. Look, Sandra, don't get alarmed, but I don't want you to open the door to any strange men today.'

'You got some coming for me?'

'It's too much to explain – but they're rivals, shall we say. They don't want me to write my story. So they might try and stop me. So just be careful if anyone starts sniffing around the house, okay?'

'You can rely on me, Mr B.'

Lester gave Brennan a look of quiet amazement as his father retreated upstairs, leaving him alone with Sandra.

'You named after Lester Piggott, I bet, aren't you?' she said, unerringly hitting Lester's one raw nerve first time out.

Brennan and Janet resurfaced at about ten-thirty, took a shower, then brought all the work back down to the kitchen table. Lester, increasingly unimpressed with this new lifestyle, was banished upstairs to the living-room, although the blow was somewhat softened by the fact that there was a one-day cricket international on the television.

Brennan reread the skeleton of his story – the structure seemed fine. It just needed more details, more 'colour', as Gill called it. But he was burdened by Mark's death, not just as a friend, but as a material witness. He would already be liable to charges from the police for deserting the scene of a major crime, assuming they didn't try and pin the crime on him. Brennan looked at the Home Office documents again. The story needed the colour from these to make it live. Certainly the design boys and picture editors would drool over all the death's head stuff, old ID photos, passport stamps – it would give the pages a good lashing of 'lurk'.

'I'm going to get these photocopied, Jan. Gill's going to want them for the story – I just know it.'

'But you'll be up for the same offence all over again!'

'I'd settle for that rather than be fitted up for a murder charge! I'm going to have to go to the police tomorrow and confess my presence at the scene of Mark's death. If I've delivered Gill the story by then – and he likes it – I'll have more chance of getting his backing for an investigation into Mark's death.'

'But you won't be able to do it, will you?'

'I'm the only person who *can* do it!'

Brennan piled up the papers and placed them in an innocuous-looking carrier bag.

'I'll try Robert at the bookshop. He's got a copier in his office. Keep everything locked up. If any police turn up, get them to push their warrant cards through the letter-box and ring their headquarters to confirm their identities.'

'What about you? You're the one going out.'

Brennan crossed the kitchen and took a long Sabatier out of the wooden knife block and dropped it into the carrier bag. This worried Janet even more. But she opened the door for him, and then he was out.

Brennan paused on the path to look both ways. There was nobody in view – the line of gardens seemed quiet and listless. He walked to the left, partly because that was the shortest route into town, partly because there was a hidden path, about half-way along, which led down to the next terrace, Middle Rank. Brennan took it. The stone steps were completely in shadow from overhanging foliage, giving it the feel of a secret tunnel in Sherwood Forest. If the Big Lads were in town and knew about it, however, it would be a great place for an ambush.

Brennan emerged on to Middle Rank, turned right, and took another flight of steep stone steps down to Newtown. Once there, he could make his way down the priory steps and end up smack in the centre of town,

almost without having used a pavement. This enclave was a mini-
Marseilles if it needed to be – Brennan worked out that it would need at
least a dozen people to cover all the paths, steps and alleys down from his
house. Reassured by this, Brennan sauntered across to Robert's bookshop.

There was nobody in apart from Robert, who was sitting back in his
chair reading *The Independent* – for an instant, Brennan envied him.

'What can I do for you, Frank?' Robert asked, languidly laying his
paper to one side.

'I need a bit of photocopying . . .'

'Yeah, okay – leave it with me . . .'

'Actually, if you don't mind, I'd rather do it myself. It's better that you
can say you didn't know what it was, if you understand . . . ?'

Robert smiled at the sudden intrusion of intrigue into his steady
existence.

'Give me a clue then!'

'Something the Home Office would prefer to keep a lid on, rather than
reading about it in these – ' Brennan tapped Robert's paper.

'How exciting!' Robert said with relish.

'With respect, Robert, it's not an adventure. Three people have *died* in
this chain of events . . .'

'Bloody *hell*, Frank! Sorry, I didn't mean to trivialise it!' Robert said,
sitting bolt upright. 'Can I help in any way?'

'No, not really – just keep an eye out for any strange blokes hanging
around on Tory, that's all, They may be after what I've got. If you see
anything – call the police.'

'Right, I will! I'll let Alice know as well.'

'I don't want you to go scaring people, Robert!' Brennan said with a
smile.

'But that sort of thing just doesn't happen here – our crime is petty
theft, nicking plant-pots, mountain bikes.'

'That's selective memory, Robert, there were two armed robberies on
shops here last year, weren't there?'

'On the outskirts, yes.'

'Bradford's a pretty and historic town, but it's still connected to the
real world. I just hope to God I'm not personally responsible for bringing
too much of it with me. Now, can I get started?'

'Sure. Once you've switched it on, give it a few minutes to warm up.'

'We had photocopiers in London, you know,' Brennan said drily as he
made his way up the stairs to Robert's office.

Once he was done, he crossed The Shambles to the post office, bought a large brown envelope and placed the original documents inside it. He sealed the envelope, addressed it to the 'Home Office, Queen Anne's Gate, London SW1', and then bought the precise postage for a first-class delivery. When the police got hold of him, his line would be that he took the envelope without looking, and once he realised what the contents were, returned them immediately to the Home Office like any good citizen.

Brennan crossed Market Street to the phone box outside the Catholic church. He placed a transfer charge call to Stuart Gill's private line at the paper, hoping that no minions, or even the removal men, would answer it. Fortunately, Gill was ensconced and took the call without hesitation.

'What's the panic, Frank?'

'Listen, Stuart, there's no panic. Just a bit of *breugas* . . .'

Gill liked a bit of Yiddish slang round the office – schmuck, schnorrer – so Brennan hoped this would seem less alarming than its Anglo-Saxon equivalents, 'aggro' or 'trouble'.

'Tell me,' Gill said.

'I've got the double-murder story nailed down. And I'll bring it in tomorrow morning so we can go through it . . .'

'Great – I can sense a big "but" coming up though, Frank . . . so, what is it?'

'Right, can you have a look on PA, see if they've got anything down for the death of a civil servant in Hammersmith last night?'

'Hang on a mo' — '

Brennan listened, hearing Gill tapping away at his computer keyboard to access the Press Association's news index. After a few moments, Gill came back on, reading direct from the screen.

'The body of top civil servant Mark Fraser-Williams was found at his home in Hammersmith last night. Police are regarding the death as suspicious and wish to interview a middle-aged man who was seen leaving Mr Fraser-Williams's flat at about seven-thirty . . .'

'That was me, Stuart,' Brennan said matter-of-factly.

'Fucking hell, Frank! What have you got into now?'

'I'll tell you tomorrow. I may need to borrow the paper's lawyer again.'

'You're not on the staff now, Frank, and I don't want your shit on my doorstep again.'

'I'll take the story elsewhere then, shall I?'

'Don't fuck me about, Frank, you know the score. I can still get your stuff in the paper, but if anything goes boss-eyed you're on your own. There's no access to briefs and defence funds and all that shit. You're liable for your own behaviour now, got it?'

'Yes, sir . . . Ten-thirty all right tomorrow?'

'Make it ten . . . and Frank, I don't want to know about the other stuff – just give me the story we talked about. That's the way it is now. I demand, you supply.'

The phone went dead. Brennan left the phone box and tramped back up the hill, feeling lower and more isolated than at any time in prison. Back home, there had been no calls or alarms, but Lester was getting restless. Janet volunteered to take him to Bath for a few hours, while Brennan got on with his writing. Brennan nodded glumly at the prospect of being left alone with his typewriter. But the thought of Stuart Gill's overbearing arrogance spurred him into action – he'd make it the best newspaper story of the year. But if Gill didn't let him follow up on Mark's death, he'd take the whole lot elsewhere – even to one of Murdoch's.

Brennan battered away at the typewriter until his fingertips hurt. By four o'clock, he'd managed to condense the story into five thousand words – which was about twice as much as Gill would tolerate. The second coming of Christ would be pushed to get more than a front-page pic and one paragraph of editorial comment from Gill.

Brennan broke off for a coffee, his head and heart were pounding, the adrenalin of writing being matched only by the sublime relief of not writing. He went upstairs to the stereo and put on his Vienna Philharmonic version of Mozart's Requiem. The piece would now be associated for ever with the death of Mark Fraser-Williams. Brennan's mind was already leaping ahead to the next story, and in reflex, to his own defence against the inevitable police charges.

He tried to imagine what the Big Lads had done to Mark – there'd been no bruises visible in that one horrific glance at the body. Maybe they'd chloroformed him? But would that show up in a post-mortem? Brennan made a note of this question as it occurred, before resuming his mental reconstruction of the previous day's events. It seemed unlikely that they'd have gone into Mark's home without some intention of recovering, or indeed planting, evidence of his treachery to the State – but why hadn't they just arrested him?

Brennan listened to the music intently, imagining Mark's last moments as it played – a grotesque joke from the master of droll understatement. Maybe the idea was just to dress him up in the négligé then haul him off to the police so they could do their worst with him? What if Mark had called their bluff and drowned *himself* as a last 'fuck you' to his employer? The playing of the *Confutatis* seemed more than a coincidence. Brennan checked the translation inside the compact disc's sleeve:

When the wicked are confounded,
Doomed to flames of woe unbounded,
Call me with Thy saints surrounded!
Low I kneel, with heart submission!
See like ashes my contrition!
Help me in my last condition!

Mark wasn't one to give up life meekly – not with dreams of serene retirement painting the glories of the Suffolk coastline. Brennan could see it suddenly – the ski-masked terrorists laughingly dangling the négligé in front of him; Mark obliging, no doubt with a joke; and then a last request for some music, the killers' suspicions neutralised by the help this noise would give them in their final task; and then they do him, a needle or a spray, and dump his body in the bath; the child porn is produced and scattered around, as if in a gesture of distress and self-disgust by a man too shamed to live any more.

Brennan let out a yell of rage and frustration – the late-fucking-running train, the gob-shite stroppy taxi-driver, the shitty little gas leak which closed the bridge! They'd all stopped Brennan getting to Mark in time to save his life! Brennan turned up the volume on the stereo to its full level. The sweeping chords and vocal swoops of *Dies Irae* thundered out, rattling the windows in the room. Brennan wished it could purge his soul of the guilt which overwhelmed him, for deep inside, in a dark, hidden corner, he knew that, despite the sanctimony of accepting the gaol sentence, he'd always been prepared to sacrifice Mark in order to get his stories out.

Sandra was just on to her second bottle of Diamond White in the Mason's Arms when she saw the red Sierra pull up outside with two blokes inside. They both had leather jackets, and the fair-haired one was quite tasty looking. They were probably not locals, because no sooner had they parked than they did a three-point turn in the car in order to leave it pointing out of town.

She watched as they came into the pub and ordered themselves Scotches, taking them over to the far corner to drink. They were chatting quietly until one of them produced a street map of Wiltshire towns and began to study it. *Definitely* not local, Sandra concluded. And then the long-broken light bulb in the centre of her head suddenly flickered into life after too many years without power. What had Mr Brennan said that very morning? Something about strangers?

* * *

About half an hour later, Moira Backhouse saw two men with leather jackets taking a walk along Tory while she was watering her geraniums.

'Good evening!' she'd said, as she did to everybody who passed, known or otherwise.

But these rude blokes just gave her the curtest of nods and kept on walking, right along the length of Tory and off towards the Church of St Mary. They obviously didn't know who Moira was!

Alice was tidying her aromatic oils away for the day when she caught sight of two men she hadn't seen before coming away from St Mary. They didn't have cameras or guidebooks or anything, which was unusual for the people who ventured this far up. Nor did they seem to react to the view spread out to one side of them. They simply rejoined the main footpath and turned back down towards the stretch that would take them down to the old brewery on Newtown. She wondered if she ought to mention it to Robert, after what he'd told her when he'd come in from the bookshop after work.

Brennan packed up the manuscript inside an envelope, together with the photocopies of the Home Office papers, Janet's photographs and Cathy Aldridge's sworn affidavit. Janet had phoned to check he was getting on all right, and to let him know that she and Lester were planning to bring back an Indian take-away from the little shop in Silver Street on their way up from the station. It was nearly half-past seven. The cloud cover which had marred the day had finally been pierced by a huge, strawberry-coloured evening sun, which seemed to colour every atom of air.

Brennan felt he deserved a drink, at least for his labours, if not for his methods, so he pulled a cold Becks from the fridge. But then his mental efforts had by now had to be switched to the question of what he would say to the police when he turned himself in. He could fall back on the trauma of the moment and the fear for his own life, which had both certainly been present. But it was more the sort of line a judge would fall for. The hard-nosed gorillas of Special Branch who would probably come to interrogate him would laugh it off in an instant – 'You're supposed to be the journalist with the hardest bollocks in town, Brennan!' That's what they'd say. He would need an alternative strategy to deal with them – but at the moment all he could come up with was the truth.

Janet and Lester arrived back just before eight. Brennan had stuck three dinner plates in the oven to warm, and taken out all the jars of chutneys and lime pickle he could find in the overhead cupboards. Janet unloaded the large brown paper bag of its foil containers and laid them in formation along the centre of the table, before pointing at each one.

'One chicken tikka, one prawn bhuna, one lamb pasanda, a saag aloo, a mushroom bhaji, two pilau rice, two nan and three poppadoms!'

'Yes, but what are you two going to have?' Lester joked.

'Just get 'em open and tuck in!' said Brennan, his mood lifting as the exotic smells filled his nostrils and set his gastric juices flowing.

Janet distributed the food across the three plates and they all sat around the table to eat.

'How did you get on then, Frank?' Janet asked. 'I expected to come back and find the table still covered with papers.'

'I'm all done. Going to try and get the seven fifty-seven from Bath tomorrow morning, then see Stuart at ten. Then . . .'

Lester pricked up his ears.

'What? Then what?'

'I don't know, Lester. It was "Then – question mark", meaning "who knows?".'

Brennan caught Janet's eye with a look which clearly said 'change the subject'. Janet understood.

'Tell your dad where we went in Bath, Les—'

'Oh, right – they've got a Gap Kids shop in—'

'The Roman baths, Lester! Clothes shops are ten-a-penny! Roman antiquities are not.'

Lester gave Brennan a wink before he said, 'It was all right, if you like that sort of thing.'

Brennan laughed at the wind-up, but the humour died in a second as he glimpsed 'Leather Jacket' glide past the front window of the house. Janet saw the instant change of mood.

'What's the matter, Frank?'

Brennan fanned his mouth.

'Just bit into a cardamom pod,' he said, before taking a swig of beer.

Janet knew he was lying, but with Lester there, she couldn't press the point. They ate on in silence, though it was obvious that Brennan's appetite had gone.

When they finally got Lester off to bed, Brennan did a tour of the house with Janet, checking all the window locks were fastened. They held a whispered conversation as they moved.

'You sure it was the same guy?' Janet asked breathlessly.

'You don't forget when they're after you . . .'

'What do they *want*?'

'I don't know – at best, it'll be putting on the frighteners. At worst . . .'

'Look, Frank, if these are the same guys who did for Mark – and you think they are – they know you were there. They probably think you have evidence against them.'

'But I don't really . . .'

'That doesn't matter – they can only have two objectives, to fit you up, or to shut you up.'

Brennan moved downstairs and headed across the kitchen towards the wall phone.

'Frank, you can't call the police—'

'I know that!' he snapped. 'I'm calling up some muscle.' Brennan flicked through his contact book for the number Tommy Preston had given him. He lifted the phone and held it to his ear, and then let it drop, dangling from its cord.

'They've cut the line . . .'

'Christ, this is over the top, Frank! We can't bloody move. There's no roads outside, no passers-by. We can't even pop next door . . .'

'All right, all right, don't panic – one thing I promise to do in future is to get a mobile!'

'What future?'

'Look, let's stay calm. We can't get out, but then they can't get in.'

'They don't need to get in, Frank. They'll probably try to torch the place! I mean, they can step right up to the fucking window if they want to shoot you!'

Brennan crossed the room to draw the curtains.

'C'mon – away from this window and the door.'

Brennan ushered Janet up to the first-floor living-room, where he quickly drew the curtains too.

'I'd better check Lester,' Janet said, disappearing up to the next floor.

'Make sure that skylight's closed and locked!'

Brennan paced the room, twitching. Then he remembered he'd left his package for Stuart Gill downstairs. He put the lights out in the hall as he came down the stairs. The flap on the letter-box suddenly lifted and Brennan rolled to the floor, fearing a gunshot.

'Frank! Frank!' said a voice. 'It's Robert!'

Brennan reached up to open the door and then eased it ajar. He pulled Robert in by the front of his shirt.

'Jesus, you frightened me!' Brennan said.

'I'm not exactly serene either – there's been two blokes wandering up and down Tory for an hour or so!'

'You've seen them?' Brennan asked, superfluously.

'Are they after you?' Robert asked.

'At a rough guess, yes. Is your phone working?'

'No – just tried to call the police, but it's dead.'

'They must have cut off the whole bloody terrace!'

'Who are they, Frank?' Robert asked.

'Probably freelances working for MI5 . . .'

'Secret service?'

'Whatever you want to call it.'

'Then we've found their weakness.'

'Look, Robert. No disrespect, but I need Zen philosophy like I need a tax demand.'

'But don't you see – we can fight back now. Listen to what we're going to do . . .'

Brennan sighed and leant against the wall.

Robert emerged from Brennan's house about fifteen minutes later and made his way down to Moira's. There he rang the bell, aware that he was probably being watched, and conducted a brief conversation with Moira through the small gap in the door which the security chain allowed. He wandered back along Tory towards his own house. At the junction where the path forked up to the Church of St Mary and down towards the old brewery, he could see the two men standing smoking cigarettes, their faces turned away from the street lamp that illuminated that particular spot.

Robert said nothing as he passed within five yards of them, preferring to whistle casually as he walked. The more relaxed he was, the more vulnerable they became. Robert reached his front door and went in. Along the terrace, nobody moved. Most of the downstairs lights in the houses were out now, and the night was warm and still.

The two men in leather jackets stubbed out their cigarettes and began a slow walk back down towards Brennan's house. Then from behind them Robert appeared.

'Excuse me, chaps.'

They both whirled round to be met by the dazzling flash of Robert's camera.

'You fucker!' yelled one of them.

From the other side, Janet ran towards them, also with a camera, and reeled off three shots with the flash-gun exploding into light each time.

Alice came along as they spun back towards the junction, holding their arms above their faces, and let off two shots of her camera. The two men reeled away, cursing, breaking into a run. Behind them Robert had picked up two dustbin lids which he began to bang together to create a crashing noise. The lights in all the adjoining houses began to come on. The men broke into a sprint, only to be blinded again as Moira fired off her camera from her doorway. Alice, Robert and Janet followed, banging the dustbin lids and firing the flash-guns incessantly. Front doors began to open at the commotion, and more and more faces began to look out at the two running men as they beat a retreat out on to Conigre Hill and slithered down towards the road on Newtown. The pack following them grew as it moved, firing off flashes and creating noises, either with their voices – Alice was ululating like an Apache bride – or with whatever they could pick up and bang together. It was the Neighbourhood Watch version of *son et lumière*.

Once they confirmed that the two men had left the area, Robert led Alice and Janet back up the path, apologising for the noise and thanking neighbours for joining in the chase. They checked that Moira was okay, and then they all went into Brennan's house. Brennan was dressed and ready to go, his parcel under his arm.

'Right – Alice and I will stay here tonight. Off you go, Frank. Quickly!'

Brennan smiled and thanked them all

'God knows how you managed that, you mad bastards!'

'It's only the same as your work, Frank – what secrecy fears most is the light of exposure!'

Brennan kissed Janet, and after a look along the terrace, jogged off, taking the path up behind the houses to the Winsley road. He phoned for a taxi from the box by the sub-post office, and the little red cab arrived about two minutes later.

'Where to, sir?'

'I don't suppose you could manage London, could you?'

'Bit strong for me, sir. But I know a bloke who can. Hop in!'

Brennan dived into the seat alongside the driver. He spun the car round and left the town on the Chippenham road. He picked up his radio handset and called control to see if Roger could be booked for a London run from Chippenham station. About a minute later the controller's voice came back on to say that Roger would be ready and waiting.

Roger had a big, new Volvo Estate, with leather seats and air-conditioning. He was used to doing long-distance runs, either to airports or ferry terminals, so going to London at night presented no problem to him as Frank transferred to his car on the forecourt of Chippenham station.

'You can recline the back of your seat if you want a kip, sir,' Roger said, as they set off.

'That sounds good . . .'

Brennan lifted the lever and the back of the seat fell away under his weight. He cushioned his head on the rest and stretched out his legs. On the car radio, Paul Simon was singing:

Everybody loves the sound of a train in the distance . . .

Brennan lay back in the seat and looked up through the Volvo's sun-roof to see a night sky filled with stars. It would be the nicest trip to prison he'd taken so far.

CHAPTER SIXTEEN

Stuart Gill pulled on a cigar as he read. Brennan sat across the table from him, in this eyrie of an editor's office with views across the City of London. Docklands wouldn't feel like a fair swap. Brennan watched Gill impassively, seeing his lips purse occasionally, and the pencil descend on to the page for a reflex act of sub-editing.

'This Cathy Aldridge bird is the one you think we should protect?' Gill asked without looking up.

'It's up to you. Her affidavit is the best account of what happened from the point of view of the cover-up. She's the natural follow-up – the rest of 'em should be in a police cell as soon as the paper hits the streets.'

Gill leant across to his intercom, pushed a button and barked into it.

'Stacey, get the Hit Squad organised. With five grand in readies, and a road map of Dorset.'

'Yes, Mr Gill.'

Brennan smiled and shook his head.

'You had breakfast?' Gill suddenly asked.

'Me? Well, let me see now – I had two Armagnacs at the Atlantic bar just before three a.m. I had a hot chocolate with an old mate of mine who's the night porter at the Waldorf. And I had the full works over at the Fox and Anchor in Smithfield at about seven o'clock.'

'You should have given me a bell, I'd have joined you!'

'At what stage?'

Gill refused to answer and returned to the copy.

'They give every patient drugs to knock 'em out?'

Brennan nodded.

'Bastards,' Gill muttered, circling that section of the story with a yellow highlighter. It was no doubt destined to be printed in bold type in the paper with an appropriately attention-grabbing strap-line above it.

Brennan rose and crossed the room to where Gill's editorial coffee machine was burbling to the end of its production cycle. Brennan poured himself a black coffee.

'You want one?'

Gill shook his head. Brennan was quietly delighted – he was engrossed in the story.

'Does executing German soldiers really count as a war crime?'

'It does if they've surrendered.'

Gill sat back in his seat.

'Story of the fuckin' year this, Frank! That spell in jug has sharpened you up no end! I'll get our news team to go over it pronto.'

'All the contact numbers are in the file. When do you think you'll run it?'

'Day after tomorrow if it all stands up.'

'It will. About the fee?'

'Frank! You know I'll see you all right.'

'That's not an acceptable agreement now I'm freelance. I need figures.'

'Five grand?'

'You'll get a week's worth of follow-up out of this! Make it ten.'

'Seven and a half?'

Brennan offered a hand. Gill spat on his fingers and slapped them on to Brennan's hand.

'You got a contact number for today, if we've got any queries?'

'Sure – Hammersmith police station.'

'You're not serious about this Home Office geezer, are you?'

'Like I told you, I was there. It was a toss-up between being a good citizen and getting my story in.'

Gill grinned at the cynicism, he liked that.

'My man at the Yard tells me old Fraser what's-his-face was into little boys.'

'Not true – just the Big Lads making sure he didn't die a martyr. I suppose I can tell you now that Mark was my source on the repatriation story.'

'There you are then – you spent six months in the nick to save his job, and the ungrateful cunt goes and drops you in it again! You owe him nothing, Frank!'

'I'd still like to do the story. I've got pole position after all.'

'And the gist is?'

'That he was topped by the security services. If he'd gone to trial he could have become another Ponting—'

'Who?'

Brennan sighed.

'A hero figure to the dissident classes.'

Gill shook his head slowly.

'It's not what you'd call sexy though, is it?'

'But it *is* important.'

Gill sucked on the end of his pencil, which couldn't have been a pleasant experience because it had a rubber inset.

'Let me know how you get on, eh?'

'I expect you'll hear on the news . . .'

Brennan stood. He'd had a few lines of praise, agreed a fee and enjoyed half a cup of stewed coffee. It was almost a result.

'You got a brief organised?'

'I've earned so little over the past four months I probably qualify for legal aid.'

Gill leant into his intercom again.

'Stacey, get one of our legal boys down to my lift immediately, will you. Tell him to go with Mr Brennan. They can use my car, okay.'

'Thanks, Stuart . . .'

'Don't let it get around that I'm going soft in my old age. Bell me later, eh?'

'I will.'

Brennan left the room, leaving Gill to read on.

On the way over to Hammersmith, Brennan used Gill's car phone to call home. The line had been restored. Janet was ecstatic with relief to hear from him. Brennan had to let her know that he was in a car with two other men. So she settled for telling him she and Lester were both fine. Robert and Alice had stayed with them all night, and Moira Backhouse had ensured that a squad of Wiltshire police had searched the Tory this morning for clues about the mystery intruders.

'Look, I'll call you later – I want to know how those photos turned out.'

The driver shot Brennan a look as he hung up the phone.

'Holiday snaps,' said Brennan with a smile.

There was a knock on the front door as Janet put the phone down on Brennan. The young police constable, whom Moira had insisted stand guard on the house, had Sandra standing behind him.

'This lady wants to see you, Mrs Brennan . . .'

'Sandra! Come in – what's the matter?'

The constable pushed the door open for Sandra to go in, then pulled it shut after her.

'Do you want a cup of anything?' Janet asked Sandra, who seemed distinctly ill at ease.

'Look, I don't want to sound stupid or anything, but that young copper said you had a couple of head-bangers up here last night.'

'That's right – but we managed to chase them off.'

'Only – when I was in the Mason's last night, I saw these two prannets, and I didn't like the look of 'em at all.'

'We took some photographs of them. The police are going to look at them when they're developed.'

'I may be able to do better 'an that, Mrs Brennan!'

Sandra opened her bag and very slowly produced a small parcel wrapped in tissue. Sandra unravelled the tissue carefully to reveal a whisky glass.

'I got he after they left the pub. An' there's the other one here as well. They weren't drinking with gloves on, Mrs Brennan . . .'

'You're in deep shit this time, Brennan,' Detective Inspector Boyle snarled.

Timpson, the young legal adviser assigned to nursemaid Brennan through this preliminary interview, sat forward in his chair.

'Forgive me, Detective Inspector Boyle, but my client is here to assist you with your enquiries, not to be threatened. And I'd prefer it if you refrained from profanity – it might constitute harassment.'

Boyle looked as though he would explode all over the room.

'You can tell your fucking client he'll be up for obstructing police enquiries, perverting the course of justice and possibly murdering Mr Fraser-Williams if he's not careful,' Boyle spluttered.

'Are they formal charges?' demanded Timpson.

Brennan intervened – a referee in his own dogfight.

'Look, I've made a complete statement of my movements and observations on Sunday night. I've apologised for the delay in coming forward . . . now if you want me to help any further, I suggest you calm down and ask me politely.'

Boyle stopped pacing. He looked at Brennan with a blowtorch of a glare.

'Did you kill him?'

Brennan smiled patiently – there was no harm in them trying Route One. It probably got enough results in a year to justify its usage.

'No,' he said emphatically. 'Mr Fraser-Williams was already dead when I found him.'

'The pathologist has put T.o.D. at between six o'clock and seven-thirty – when did you say you arrived at the flat?'

'About ten to seven. There's a stroppy arse of a cab-driver whose number I took – he'll remember me if you need confirmation of the time. Paddington to Hammersmith Bridge.'

'You admit you were there during the estimated time of death?'

'Yes, I've said that! But I'm helping you narrow it down. If I got there at about ten to seven, he was already dead by then! What's the cause, by the way?'

'I beg your pardon?' Boyle exclaimed.

'What was the result of the post-mortem?' Brennan repeated.

'You must be off your fuc— flipping trolley if you think I'm going to tell you that!'

'It would have to be disclosed if you're going to charge my client,' Timpson intervened.

'Technically, it was drowning,' Boyle conceded reluctantly.

'Technically, he swallowed too much water,' Brennan corrected sarkily. 'The question is, was he drugged or doped before they dumped him in the bath?'

'You're a prick, Brennan, do you know that? You think you're a copper, don't you?'

'Only in my worst nightmares . . . so was he? Drugged?'

Boyle shrugged.

'You tell me – you were there.'

Boyle resumed his prowling of the interview room.

'Did you find any note or anything, Brennan? Hide it away – protect your friend's integrity?'

'What are you getting at now – *suicide*?' Brennan asked, incredulous.

'You really must make up your mind, Detective Inspector,' Timpson chided.

'He knows!' Brennan exclaimed. 'He knows! It was a murder that was meant to look like a suicide. But my turning up gave them the chance to make it a murder again! What did they say when they phoned in, Inspector? What time was that call logged? Somewhere between five and ten past seven, I bet. Who did he claim to be? I'd love to hear the voice-recording! Or might you even have tracked down the number of the mobile phone that was used yet?'

Boyle's eyes conceded little defeats, but he said nothing to confirm them.

'You were there to commit a crime, Brennan, admit it!'

'I was there to see a friend for a drink!'

'Come off it – you're not a woofter. You weren't there for fun. He was supplying you with highly confidential information, wasn't he?'

'Some of my best friends are gay policemen, Inspector. Be careful.'

Timpson looked at his watch.

'Mr Brennan's given enough of his time now, Inspector. I think we should be going.'

'Wait a minute. I want to read through this statement again.'

Brennan sighed with exhaustion. He'd almost be willing to sign a confession now in exchange for an hour's sleep.

And then a detective sergeant came in, and beckoned Boyle over for a whispered conversation.

Timpson retaliated by talking into Brennan's ear.

'If this is something new, let me handle it.'

Moments later, Boyle came over.

'Your wife's been on the phone, Mr Brennan. It seems like she wants to join you in prison for obstructing justice.'

'How's that?'

'Claims she has photographs and fingerprints of the two men you think were responsible for Fraser-Williams's death! She's as barking mad as you by the sound of it! Setting up your own little firm, are you?'

'I think you'll find she's telling the truth, actually. Why don't you drive me home and find out?'

Brennan's look challenged Boyle unswervingly. And Boyle was the first to blink.

Josef Granowski's story appeared in the paper two days later, with a lead on the front page and a two-page spread in the middle. Gill had timed it nicely for the weekend market to react to it, making the original story all the more potent. Gill's companion Sunday paper, for instance, was able to run Cathy Aldridge's 'nightmare story'.

Brennan had sat buck-naked on the photocopier in Robert's office above the bookshop, and then faxed an image of his hairy arse direct to Mike Watkiss's office in Bridport on the morning the story broke. It was Brennan's only gesture of triumphalism.

The feeding frenzy he had unleashed consumed the careers of Dr Simmons and his wife, Liz Jobson, while Furnival's body was found washed up on Chesil Beach the morning after the story – a man of military honour to the last. Green/Granowski was taken into custody, while the police and the Home Office decided what they should do with him, as much for his past crimes as those in the present. Chestnut Grange was taken over by the local social services, so that the patients should suffer no further disruption to their lives. And Cathy Aldridge soon turned up on GMTV, with an astonishing make-over, to relive her private horror. Stephen Green, the policeman son of Josef, wrote Janet a hostile letter, which was understandable in the circumstances. But he managed to sell his story of his killer father to the *Sun*, who easily outbid Stuart Gill. And Brennan got a postcard from Laurie at The George, thanking him for quadrupling the pub's takings, even though all the profit came from what she termed 'media arseholes'.

Despite the evidence which Janet, Brennan and the others on Tory submitted, Inspector Boyle's team made little progress with the enquiry into Mark Fraser-Williams's death. The coroner ruled that the death was 'accidental', with the implication that the chemicals found in Fraser-Williams's body, allied to the wearing of the négligé, had been a misguided attempt at a sexual high. No forensic evidence was found to link the two men in the blurred, flashlit photos on Tory to the scene of crime at Mark's flat. Nor were their fingerprints matched to any on file in the Criminal Record Office.

And as summer turned to autumn, Brennan gave up the pursuit of a result in the case, and settled for writing an elegant appreciation of Mark's life and bitter accusations about his death, for the *New Statesman*. There was always the chance that somewhere, even in the dark heart of the security machine, someone might be moved to make a sympathetic leak.

Lester started at St Laurence Comprehensive in Bradford-on-Avon at the beginning of September, having decided, without undue pressure, that he could come to enjoy small-town life as much as his parents seemed to do. He was, as he had secretly suspected, something of a celebrity at the school in the early weeks. Firstly because of his London connections, and secondly because his dad had been dubbed a 'Nazi-hunter' in one of the tabloids, putting him on a par with Indiana Jones.

More resonant was the steady stream of letters which now arrived for Brennan, inviting him to look into other neglected crimes, bizarre ecological happenings, a ring of Satanic computer-disc suppliers, and the whereabouts of Lord Lucan.

Janet helped him sift through the letters – those half-way serious, but not too demanding, were forwarded to Stuart Gill, who in the light of Brennan's success had set up a weekly 'Case-book' feature, staffed by graduate trainee hacks. Those which looked promising in terms of their depth, and their importance, were replied to by Janet, requesting further information, a screening process that they decided was necessary after what Josef Granowski had subjected them to.

Brennan had never really figured out why Granowski had risked exposure of his past by boasting about his killing of the Dantowiczes. He could have stayed silent about it, and enjoyed the cover which the home misguidedly provided for him.

But then one brilliant, blue-skyed Sunday in November, as Brennan and Lester walked down into town to collect the papers from the Roundabout Shop, they stumbled upon a remembrance ceremony taking place on the little green by the river. The town's churchmen, the boys' brigade, scouts and girl guides, and assorted dignitaries and old soldiers, stood alongside them with multicoloured banners as prayers were said and wreaths of poppies laid at the foot of the town's war memorial.

Brennan had never noticed the memorial before, perhaps because, as today, it was swamped by the beauty of the backdrop behind it, with the golden stone of the houses reflecting the low winter sun. But as the ceremony progressed he could see that the plaques on three sides of the obelisk listed the best part of a hundred names of war dead. The two horrific wars had been bludgeoned into the consciousness on such a huge scale that such miniatures of information seemed impossible to process at first.

And yet it was in small towns and villages across Europe that the losses came home in all-too-human scale. The deaths of these Wiltshire lads, taken from their fields and their factories, and never to return, were no less painful than the secret slaughter of villagers in a Polish forest. Brennan began to understand that Granowski's killing of the Dantowiczes was, in its own way, an act of remembrance too. And not just for those who died on that day he'd heard the gunfire through the trees, but for their unborn sons and daughters too.

Brennan held Lester close to him as the last post was played by a solitary bugler, the final notes echoing around the hills of this small town which they now both called home.